T0033457

HARVEST DREAMS

Visit us at www.boldstrokesbooks.com

HARVEST DREAMS

by

Jacqueline Fein-Zachary

2023

HARVEST DREAMS

© 2023 BY JACQUELINE FEIN-ZACHARY. ALL RIGHTS RESERVED.

ISBN 13: 978-1-63679-380-1

THIS TRADE PAPERBACK ORIGINAL IS PUBLISHED BY
BOLD STROKES BOOKS, INC.
P.O. BOX 249
VALLEY FALLS, NY 12185

FIRST EDITION: APRIL 2023

THIS IS A WORK OF FICTION. NAMES, CHARACTERS, PLACES, AND INCIDENTS ARE THE PRODUCT OF THE AUTHOR'S IMAGINATION OR ARE USED FICTITIOUSLY. ANY RESEMBLANCE TO ACTUAL PERSONS, LIVING OR DEAD, BUSINESS ESTABLISHMENTS, EVENTS, OR LOCALES IS ENTIRELY COINCIDENTAL.

THIS BOOK, OR PARTS THEREOF, MAY NOT BE REPRODUCED IN ANY FORM WITHOUT PERMISSION.

CREDITS
EDITOR: JENNY HARMON
PRODUCTION DESIGN: STACIA SEAMAN
COVER DESIGN BY TAMMY SEIDICK

Acknowledgments

It's been an awesome journey working on this novel for more than a decade. I would like to thank my teachers, especially Julia Glass at the Fine Arts Work Center in Provincetown and Sophie Powell at GrubStreet in Boston. I'm indebted to my writing coaches who guided me through my early years: Lisa Tener, Elizabeth Ridley, Donna Montalbano, Elisabeth Kauffman, and Trisha Blanchett.

Many wonderful friends read and commented on my drafts: Diane DiCarlo, Julie Rich, Deb Morin, Gillian Mueller, Lisa Curnan-LaCava, Margaret Frank, Jessica Kidd, Wanda Shelton, Kris Clerkin, Lynn Schweikart, and Ann Whittaker. Thank you. Your positive feedback kept me writing.

A fun part of writing is the research. I had invaluable help from local winemakers Mathias Vogel and Milan Vujnic of Truro Vineyards on Cape Cod, where I worked for several years. I enjoyed working with Mathias in the winery and out in the vineyard. Milan read the wine sections of the manuscript for accuracy, but any technical mistakes are mine. I would like to recognize Alice Wise from the Cornell Cooperative Extension for her help about Long Island vineyards. I so appreciate Louisa Hargrave, who opened her home to me to share planting records, photographs, and her memories of creating the first vineyard on Long Island—Hargrave Vineyards.

Other friends and family also gave me information that made a difference in the story: Sandy Williams, Jean Weisshaar, Nancy Macht, Anne Taylor, Brenda Gailhouse, Beth Bye, and Jeanne Leszczynski. Special thanks to JC Garner and Chessy Busalacchi for continually asking about the book; to my brother, Don Zachary, for his sage legal advice; and to Tracey Wilson for reminding me why I began writing in the first place.

When Radclyffe, Bold Strokes Books publisher, called to say she was interested in publishing my novel, I was ecstatic. It has been a great honor and experience to work with the entire Bold Strokes team.

Mega thanks to senior editor Sandy Lowe, who answered all my many questions, and to Jenny Harmon, editor extraordinaire, whose final edits allowed me to cross the *finished* line.

Most of all, I am grateful to and thank my amazing wife, Valerie, who has shown me every day of our life together what love and support is. She has been my champion and editor from the very beginning. We can—at last—share the office.

To Valerie

Of course, to Valerie.
Always Valerie. Only Valerie.

CHAPTER ONE

September 1982, San Francisco, CA

Sydney was only at the red light for a second, maybe two, when she spotted a young woman sitting in the window seat of a nearby restaurant. Her head was tilted back and the sun poured onto her face. She seemed quite oblivious to the noise and movement around her. Staring at the stranger, Sydney didn't notice the light turn green. The driver behind her blasted his horn, shocking Sydney into full attention. She drove on, immediately longing to return to the look of pure contentment on that woman's face. Sydney had left campus less than an hour ago in such a rage. She'd felt trapped, suffocated. After a year of freedom in Paris, she was back to rules and demands. She needed to get out of there, blow off a little steam. She was hoping that at the bar later that evening, she'd find an enticing woman who'd like a little company—hers. And then, there it was, the solution to her first problem. The 450 Sutter Garage was only a block ahead. Sydney pulled up front, grabbed a twenty dollar bill from her emergency stash, and jumped out of the car. "Valet!" she called to the uniformed attendant. When he approached, Sydney gave him her keys and the money and told him she'd be back. "Take care of the car," she implored. She had to get back to that restaurant.

Entering through the front door, Sydney spotted the hostess talking to a customer, her pile of menus held firmly in her arm. Sydney slipped by the long line of patrons waiting to be seated, hoping not to be noticed. She was within three feet of her goal when she heard the hostess's harsh voice.

"Excuse me, miss!"

Sydney stopped. The hostess, a plump frizzy-haired woman, looked like she would unapologetically kick Sydney out. Sydney tried to look innocent. "I'm sitting with her," she said, pointing to the woman in the window seat, who stared at her with brown eyes—expressive brown eyes, Sydney couldn't help but notice. She approached the table and lowered her voice.

"Would you mind terribly if I sat with you? The line is huge and I'm really hungry."

"Miss!" the hostess repeated in her grating voice.

"I understand this is bizarre," Sydney continued, ignoring the hostess, "but I won't bother you." She tried an appeal to the woman's sense of equality. "This table is big enough for two, don't you think?"

The woman looked at Sydney quizzically, then down at all the books and magazines she'd spread around the table. "I was working," she answered.

"You have to wait for a table like everyone else," the hostess insisted, standing within a breath of Sydney, one hand on her hip, the other gripping the menus.

Sydney had but a second. She leaned toward the woman and whispered, "I'm not a weirdo, I promise."

The brunette let out a short laugh and looked up at the hostess. "It's fine. She can stay," she said, gathering up her heap and putting it into two orderly piles. She sat back against the booth and looked curiously at Sydney.

The hostess dropped another menu on the table and huffed off.

"Thank you," Sydney told her tablemate, who was pushing her thick brown hair behind her ears. "I'm Sydney."

"Kate Bauer," she replied, her brow furrowed. "I *was* kind of stuck." She glanced again at the books and sighed.

Sydney followed her gaze and noticed a brochure on top. *Best of the Best San Francisco Attractions.* "Not to worry. If there's anything you need to know about this city, I can help you."

Kate smiled shyly, fidgeting a bit in her seat. She had an earthiness Sydney couldn't put her finger on. She wore a plain navy T-shirt that showed off broad shoulders and a lovely hint of breasts. Athlete? Model? Her face, flushed at the moment, looked perfectly sculpted.

Deeply tanned, she obviously spent a lot of time outdoors. Sydney was intrigued.

The waiter appeared. "Would you two like to order?" He was in his mid-twenties, with a full mullet. "Or I could come back?" He raised one eyebrow at Sydney. He must have seen her whole maneuver to get seated. Sydney knew a gay brother when she saw one. She winked at him, and the waiter smiled back.

"I would," Kate answered and grabbed the menu. "Give me one minute." She perused the selections quickly, suddenly serious.

Sydney took her cue, snatching up her own menu.

"The Californian," Kate told the waiter. "And fries, not the salad."

Hearty choice. It seemed half her class ordered salads and only salads, day in, day out. Sydney stalled, trying to decide between what she really wanted—the rack of pork ribs—and the safer fish tacos with chipotle-lime dressing. Dare she risk spilling red sauce all over her dressed-to-impress blouse? "I'll have the fish tacos." Sydney had lined up two museums, some shopping, and a snack before heading over to the bar, not lunch. But to hell with those plans. "So, Kate, where are you from? First time here?"

Kate's face reddened. "I actually go to school nearby. I've never, uh, taken the time to come into the city."

"Not ever? Where do you go to school?"

"UC Davis."

"You've got to be kidding. That's right up the road. Any chance you're a farmer? Isn't Davis a big agricultural school?"

"Well, yeah, but there are other programs. Engineering, law, business—"

"Sure, but you?"

Kate put both her hands on the table and looked directly at Sydney. "I *am* a farmer. There is nothing I like better than working with plants. Officially, I'm studying agronomy. I just don't like stereotypes, that's all."

Jesus. The woman was gorgeous and feisty. Not to mention sexy. Sydney had a quick desire to put her hands around those strong shoulders that she knew pulled out crops from the soil. Very earthy indeed.

"And what do you do?" Kate asked.

"I'm a senior at Berkeley. Business. Marketing, mostly."

Kate coughed, almost choking. "Business?" she squeaked out. "Really?"

Had she been insulted? "I'll bite. What did you think I studied?"

"Something to do with art or film? You're all dressed up, like a model or something."

"Is this coming from the same person who doesn't like stereotypes?"

Kate looked sheepish. "Got me."

"Sorry. I couldn't resist," Sydney told her, immediately regretting the negativity. "But, hey, thanks for noticing. I do have other plans later this evening."

The waiter returned with their order, saving Sydney from further comment. Kate dug into her sandwich with gusto. They ate in companionable silence, Sydney looking at Kate as surreptitiously as possible. When Kate took a second huge bite, catching an edge of avocado with her tongue and sliding it back into her mouth, Sydney had to keep herself from swooning.

They continued eating. Sydney noticed Kate was also sneaking peeks across the table. After a couple of minutes, Kate put down her sandwich. Lots of veggies and no meat as far as Sydney could tell. *Vegetarian?*

"My turn to ask a question," Kate said.

"Sure. Fire away."

"My uncle just arrived and I volunteered to give him a tour of the city." Again, a lovely blush. "Yeah, me. What would you suggest we do?"

"What does your uncle like to do?" Sydney asked. "Would he want a walking tour or does he like museums?"

"I have no idea."

"Where are you meeting him?"

"Across the street at the Sir Francis Hotel." Kate looked at her watch. "Oh my God. I have to go. I totally lost track of the time." She wiped her mouth with her napkin. "I'm usually prepared, organized. And never late." She pulled a worn cloth book bag from the floor and shoved all her reading material into it.

"Kate, wait. I can help you."

"What? How?" She had edged forward but stopped.

"I've been coming into the city almost every weekend since I started at Berkeley. I can tell you all the museums, every attraction. You name it, I've been there." God, she sounded desperate, but more than anything, she didn't want Kate to walk away. She looked Kate squarely in the face to keep her focused. She could feel her heart pounding and a sudden wrench in her stomach. Another woman she desired walking away? She'd worked so hard for this never to happen again.

"Well, maybe. But let's see what my uncle wants to do."

Sydney let out a breath, then turned to search for the waiter. "Let me get the check." Sydney caught the waiter's eye and signaled for the check. "Lunch is on me. Squatter's payback. Got your library?" Sydney pointed over to the pile of books, her pulse finally calming down.

Sydney left several bills on the table with the check. Standing at the same time as Kate, she was flabbergasted to see they were the exact same height. Sydney was used to being the tallest, certainly among her women friends, at almost five eleven. "Wow, tall," was all Sydney could manage.

"Yeah, you, too," Kate replied, hiking her book bag over her shoulder but not looking away.

Out on the sidewalk, Sydney hurried to keep up with Kate's powerful stride. "Oh, there he is, out front." Kate rushed ahead. In seconds she was grabbed into a bear hug by a tall, broad-shouldered man with wavy dark hair who spun her around, set her down, and hugged her again.

When Sydney approached, they pulled apart. Up close, Sydney noticed the tufts of gray at his temples. He was perhaps a little older than her own father.

"Uncle Louie, Sydney's offered to be our guide today."

Sydney stepped closer. "Sydney Barrett." She held out her hand, which he shook with a quick once-over.

"Kate's never mentioned you."

"We just met."

"Oh?" He turned to look at his niece.

"She knows the city well, Uncle Louie. You know I don't get off campus much."

He pulled Kate in closer and gave her a quick kiss on top of her head. He was barely an inch or two taller. He turned to Sydney. "So you're a professional tour guide?"

Sydney laughed. "Hardly. I'm a college student like Kate." She could feel herself sweating. "Kate and I just had lunch."

"Is that so?" He crossed his arms, but Sydney noticed the charming dimple when he turned and smiled at his niece. Their fondness for each other was obvious.

"First things first," Sydney continued. "Have you been here before?"

"No." He chuckled. "Once I settled in Cutchogue, I don't think I traveled more than twenty miles east or west."

"Cutchogue is on Long Island," Kate explained.

"Ah, well, then, let's decide. There's always the cable car." One rumbled past as they talked. Sydney shuffled closer so she could be heard. "Or I can take you around the city and show you the historical sites. We've got great architecture. And there's a ton of art museums. Are you guys thinking indoors or out?"

"Out," Kate and her uncle said at the same time.

The three of them laughed. Sydney relaxed. Chinatown? Alcatraz? "Maybe you're a sports fan, Mr. Bauer, we could—"

"First of all, young lady, please don't make me feel old. Call me Lou, Louie, or even Uncle Louie." He bumped his niece. "I only have one niece and she's very precious to me, but perhaps she'll share."

"Whatever you two want to do." She stood back motioning for them to discuss.

Another cable car rumbled to a stop. People started to get off.

"I say we take the cable car. They're famous." He glanced from Sydney to Kate. "What do you say, sweetheart?"

Kate quickly looked at Sydney, who motioned for them to hop on.

"Hooray!" Uncle Louie took Kate's hand and started for the car. Sydney walked back to the conductor to pay. She made her way forward and grabbed a pole about three people away. Kate turned to find her. "I'll pay you back," she mouthed.

As if that mattered. Sydney watched them enjoy the sights, delighted to be in their company.

❖

After the cable car ride, they walked through Ghirardelli Square and the Fisherman's Wharf area, a typical first-day visit. Both seemed very content to be together. From questions Sydney inserted into the conversation, she found out Lou was a potato farmer and Kate's father grew corn. She asked him if he was a first- or second-generation farmer.

"Oh, Zeke and I are newbies, relatively speaking. Zeke, short for Ezekiel, is Kate's father. I was back home in Brooklyn—this was way back in my twenties, you understand—when I met Marvin, the friend I'm traveling with, at a market in the city. He was the one who introduced me to the famous Long Island potatoes."

"New York City?"

"Yep. I don't remember what made me go into the city that day. Anyway, his family's been farming for generations. But it turns out, Marvin wasn't the farming type, not like Kate's dad and I became." He pulled her closer for another hug.

Sydney envied their affection. Her own father hugged her only on special occasions. Her mother never. "So," Sydney asked, "what happened?" Sydney couldn't believe that a few hours earlier she'd been desperate to get off campus, and lonely as hell. Here she was witnessing what a loving family could be like. This was definitely not the relationship she had with her parents.

"I fell in love with potatoes. Kate's dad came out to visit the following summer, and he, too, fell in love with the soil and, as it turned out, the farmer's daughter next door. The two of them got hitched the day after graduation. They had a beautiful daughter." He pointed to Kate. "The years quickly flew by and here we are." He beamed, and Kate and Sydney laughed. "But Marvin likes to travel, that's how he visited San Francisco. Me, not so much." His whole expression suddenly changed. He stopped talking. Sydney noticed him swallow and take in a breath. A single guy traveling to San Francisco with a male friend? Sydney's gaydar started flashing.

Lou continued. "Know what I'd really like to do?" He stepped back and looked at the two of them. "I'd like to go over that bridge." He pointed to the Golden Gate. "Kate says you have a car here. Could we?" He gave them another of his adorable grins.

"You're kidding? That's what you'd like to do? You're in luck. I love to drive and my car's parked not far from here. Shall we go back and get it?"

When the valet brought Sydney's red BMW around, Kate whistled. "Most kids at Davis own bicycles, not fancy cars like this."

"My father bought it for me." Sydney knew how lucky she was. Her father was a banker. Kate's family were farmers. There had been huge protests on campus against Reagan's international farming policies. It seemed that farmers had been overinvesting in land and equipment for years. Finances for farmers were really bad these days. Prices going down the tubes and farms across the US going under. Were the Bauers among them?

"And red?" Lou teased.

"Well, let's just say"—Sydney pointed to the car and then to her hair—"red's my signature color." She grinned. She liked this upfront guy.

Kate hopped in back and gave her uncle the front seat.

"Top up or down?" Sydney asked.

Lou leaned around and looked at his niece. "Your call, Katie, but I say we enjoy this fully."

"I like your enthusiasm, Lou." Sydney turned to Kate. "What do you say?"

"Why not?"

"Good answer," Sydney confirmed.

She stopped for the view at Vista Point, right over the bridge, and got out. The panorama always enthralled her. They could see the entire San Francisco skyline, Alcatraz, San Francisco Bay, and even back to the Golden Gate Bridge itself. "This is for you two. The next stop is one of my favorites. Shall we?" She pointed toward the car.

"Have you ever been up to Napa?" Kate asked from the back seat. They'd only been back on the highway a few minutes. "It's farther north." In the rearview mirror, Sydney could see the gleam in her eyes.

"Oh, dear, I forgot I was with a plant person. No, I haven't." She'd spent her junior year in Paris and had visited a lot of vineyards all over France—and had acquired a discerning palate, she'd been told—but had never even been curious about the California grapes. She looked back at Kate. Her disappointment was easy to read. "Bet you'd like to see all those grapes. Hold that thought. Here we go!" Sydney gunned it up the hill, thrilling—or possibly scaring—her passengers. She stopped ten minutes later for a dazzling view of the Pacific Ocean. This time they stayed in the car. No one said anything for several minutes. Finally, Uncle Louie broke the silence.

"Thanks for bringing us up here. Perfect choice. For a moment I forgot all about…" He turned to look out his side of the car. When he turned back, Sydney sensed a deep sadness had engulfed him.

"Uncle Louie?" Kate leaned forward and put her hand on his shoulder. "You okay?"

"Of course. Shall we head back? I promised Marvin we'd be back by six."

"On it!" Sydney put the car into gear and headed back to the city.

❖

"You sure you can't join us for dinner?" Lou asked. They had arrived back on the sidewalk, in front of the hotel.

"Sorry. I have plans this evening. It was a pleasure meeting you." She held out her hand, but Lou pulled her into a hug.

"Any friend of Kate's…" Again, he didn't finish his sentence. "I'll meet you inside, Katie." He left the two of them standing by the car.

They shuffled by the curb for a second until Kate spoke up. "Sydney, the afternoon was perfect. I can't thank you enough."

"It worked out for all of us." She looked at Kate, who nodded. Sydney was all fidgety and noticed Kate seemed to be squirming as well.

"I have an idea," Kate blurted out. "Why don't we check out a couple of those vineyards up in Napa? You said you like to drive. I'd pay for all the gas, even throw in breakfast or lunch. What do you say?" Her face turned red.

Sydney blinked, wondering if Kate was asking her out, like on a date, or simply expressing her gratitude? Or maybe she thought she'd found a sucker to drive her up to the vineyards? She looked at Kate, hands in her back pockets, bouncing nervously up and down. No, Kate was the real deal.

"I lived in France last year and went to loads of vineyards, but have never been to a single one here. I'd love to go. Know anything about wine?"

"Me? Not a thing."

Sydney fingered her keys. "Bet you could teach me a little something about growing grapes, being a farmer and all." She smiled to show Kate she was teasing.

"Not this farmer, not about fruit, anyway."

"You grow and plant things, right?"

"Of course."

"That'll do. We can do wine tastings up there. Give me your phone number and I'll call you."

Sydney shook hands with Kate and drove off. At the stoplight, she untucked her blouse from her slacks and settled into the soft leather seat. She no longer had an appetite for the anonymity of the bar scene. How refreshing to do a good deed and be acknowledged. And that bond between Kate and her uncle!

When the light turned green, Sydney gunned the engine and headed back to campus. Tonight she wanted the comfort of sitting around with pizza and friends. She'd forgotten how important good friends were. She imagined at least one or two of them might be interested in hearing about the captivating farmer she'd met today.

CHAPTER TWO

"Knock, knock!"

Kate jumped at the sound of the voice, dropping the shirt she'd been holding up to her chest. Sydney? She swerved around to face her friend Abby. Remembering what a sophisticated dresser Sydney was, Kate had recruited Abby to help pick out an outfit.

"She's here," Kate said as calmly as her emotions would allow. It had only been a week since Sydney had given her uncle the tour, but as the week went on, Kate got more and more excited—and nervous—about their upcoming adventure. Her week revolved around her classes, the library, and her field experiments, with occasional movie breaks in town. Today it would be just Sydney and she alone. Kate hurried to open the door to her dorm room.

"Ready to see some vineyards?" Sydney asked, standing in the hallway, a big grin on her face.

Kate knew she should say something but found herself suddenly tongue-tied. She didn't feel this way around Abby or any of her other female friends. Nor did she feel this way about any of the guys she'd gone out with. Maybe it was Sydney's energy or her striking confidence.

"I'm not early, am I? I'm pretty sure you're Kate Bauer. Did you forget I was coming?"

"Of course not. I expected to meet you downstairs, that's all."

"Sorry. Someone was entering the building, so I—" Sydney stopped talking when Abby opened the door wider. "Oh, you have a roommate."

"Hi, I'm Abby," she said with a wave. "I hear you're off to Napa today."

"Abby's my lab partner and friend," Kate said. "She helped me pick out something to wear."

"Aren't we simply walking through vineyards and tasting wine?" Sydney asked, then turned toward Abby. "Hi, I'm Sydney." She held out her hand to Abby, who shook it, but by the look on Abby's face, she was surprised at the formal gesture.

"Come inside," Kate said. Sydney entered, stopping a few strides inside the doorway. Kate noticed Sydney—wearing slacks, not jeans, and a casual blouse—take a peek around the room: two desks, two bureaus, and two single beds. Kate doubted Sydney lived in a dorm. She probably had her own apartment. Kate couldn't even afford her own phone line.

"Should I have cleaned out my back seat for another passenger?" Sydney asked Kate.

"Oh, no," Abby answered. "Even if I'd been invited, I would have refused. I've tons of stuff to do today."

"Okay, then," Sydney said. "Nice to meet you, Abby. Kate, shall we go?"

"I'm ready." Kate turned to Abby. "You'll leave whenever you want?"

"Of course," Abby answered.

Kate grabbed a jacket from her bed and, as an afterthought, the textbook from her desk. She led the way down the staircase to the lobby, awkwardly leaving Abby in her room.

"Need any help carrying that book?" Sydney asked. "It looks heavier than my spare tire."

At least Kate understood Sydney was teasing. She held up the text, *Microorganisms in the Soil*, and smiled. "Nah, I got it, thanks. A little light reading," she joked back.

They headed out to the parking lot which, at eight on a Saturday morning, was three-quarters full. Kate immediately spotted Sydney's BMW, taking up two spaces.

"Sorry for the mess." Sydney indicated the back seat, which was filled with posters and placards. "We had a lobby day in Sacramento yesterday. Yikes, and for this." Sydney reached inside to take out a disposable coffee cup on the passenger side. "Needed a little caffeine this morning."

"Hey, didn't I promise you breakfast?"

"You did say something about that."

"There's a great diner off the highway at Dixon," Kate suggested.

"You passed Dixon—"

"Before the Davis exit. I remember. Food any good?"

"They have homemade muffins, doughnuts, and scones."

Sydney nodded and pulled out of the parking lot. "You see a lot of Abby?" she asked, not a minute later.

"Pretty much." Abby had been keen on socializing since freshman year. "What makes you ask?"

"No reason. Just wondering."

Sydney didn't expand on her statement, but something told Kate not to engage further on the topic. Unless she was mistaken, there was something uncomfortable about Sydney, Abby, and herself all being in the same room. But unable to understand what she was sensing, she decided to let it go. "Are you excited about seeing the vineyards?"

"Me? I'm only interested in the end product. What the grapes taste like. You?"

"Yes, very. I did some research about growing grapes." Kate had spent hours studying the species, *Vitis vinifera*, assuming all the grapevines they'd see today were from European varieties. She knew nothing about the growth and production of grapes, and she had no idea how one vineyard differed from another. She'd looked at photos and tried to memorize the contours of different grape varieties in hopes of at least recognizing a few on the vine.

"You did research?"

"Of course. Doesn't everyone before doing something new?"

Sydney merely chuckled.

When they reached Dino's Diner, the parking lot was almost full. It was a shiny aluminum throwback to the days when diners were actual railroad cars. Kate slid out of the car.

"Wait for me." Sydney caught up and they headed inside. "This diner looks amazing. What's your favorite here?"

"The blueberry muffins."

"How's the coffee?"

"Almost like home."

"We'll get along famously," Sydney stated, grinning.

Kate could only hope.

❖

When they stopped for gas along Route 29 in the Napa Valley, Sydney asked if it'd be okay to put the top down. Kate said sure, remembering the wonderful ride with her uncle, who had said later, not once but twice, that he really liked Sydney. All Kate knew was that she felt like a country bumpkin around Sydney. How the heck did she manage to be so poised all the time?

"So what brought you all the way out to California to study?" Sydney asked, surprising her. "You're a long way from home."

"A better scholarship," Kate answered. "I only applied to two schools and Davis made the better offer."

"And the other school?"

"Cornell."

"You're really all about farming, aren't you? Ever want to do anything else?"

"Never." Kate's first memories were digging her hands in the soil, trying to imitate her father. She'd planted her first garden at six. In middle school she'd loved 4-H, and in high school had worked with her father after school and on weekends. "What about you? Where are you from?"

"The other coast as well." Sydney pointed her thumb toward the east. "Massachusetts."

"But a business major? Why not Harvard, Princeton, Yale?"

"I needed to get as far away from home as possible."

"Ah." That could mean any number of things. "Tough home life?" Kate tried.

"Let's just say my mother is not the warm and fuzzy supportive type. So, tell me about the soil. I assume it makes a difference to the plants. And not textbook talk. The plainer, the better."

"Got it." Kate tossed the heavy book onto the back seat. "Okay, for one thing, soil is part sand, clay, air, water, and organic matter. People think it's just one thing. It's not." This was fun. Kate actually loved the whole symbiotic relationship that went on beneath the surface, but she was not about to talk about that. She didn't want Sydney to think she was strange.

Sydney glanced quickly at her then back to the road. "Wait. I get sand, water, and air, but organic matter? Is that the leaves and cow manure?"

"Very good, city girl."

Sydney laughed. "Go on."

"Well, that combo gets decomposed by microorganisms into a form we call humus. The soil gets its nutrients from this humus. No matter the crop, whether that be grain, fruit, vegetable, or grapes," Kate said, "the most important thing is a healthy soil." Which meant not using commercial pesticides or even herbicides, a subject she and her father hotly contested. She thought pesticides contaminated a healthy soil. He said they enhanced it.

"You know your stuff, Farmer Kate."

Kate perked up. "Thanks. And no doubt you understand how important water is for crops."

"Of course."

"Well, this organic matter acts like a sponge. It absorbs the water and releases most of it to the plants."

"I wish you'd been my biology teacher."

Kate's turn to grin. Sydney should have said botany teacher, but she wasn't about to correct her. Either way it was a compliment.

❖

As they drove past the rolling hills, Kate admired one vineyard after another. She asked Sydney about marketing but found herself unable to pay attention to her comments *and* look at the vineyards.

"Over there!" she exclaimed, not being able to hold it in any longer. "There are vineyards on every hill."

"We've come at the perfect time," Sydney told her. "My sources tell me they're harvesting."

Kate looked at Sydney. "You have sources?"

"I did a little homework, too." She looked over at Kate and smiled. "I say we go directly to Mondavi. They supposedly make the best wine."

"Okay with me."

Sydney shifted into a lower gear as she slowed to look for the entrance to the winery and brushed against Kate's knee.

Kate jumped.

"Oh, sorry," Sydney said.

"No problem," Kate said, her heart fluttering at the unexpected contact. She could feel the perspiration on her top lip. Kate was used to the ample front seat of a truck. This car was so damn small. It had been one thing sitting in the back seat with her uncle up front but today, only inches and a gearshift separated them. Kate had been having difficulty keeping her mind on the conversation, noticing Sydney's long legs, how she'd kept one hand casually on her lap, the other on the steering wheel. She'd noticed the rings on both her forefingers. Her fingers were long, sensual. No soil under those nails.

❖

They were barely through the expansive arch at Mondavi when Kate overheard that they were crushing the grapes. She seized Sydney's forearm. "We've got to see this. We can taste wine later. You coming?" She rushed off, bumping into an older man and almost knocking over the woman with him. "Sorry."

"Well, take a look at that," Sydney said, once they'd found the crush pad. She, too, seemed amazed. "They're crushing them whole." She pointed to a huge pile of spindly stems that shot out of one end and formed an enormous mound on the ground.

Kate smiled. They watched as several more bins were emptied into the machine. "Is this machine called a crusher?" Kate asked the worker. She wanted to be sure.

"A crusher-destemmer," the man said. "This is the first thing you do with the grapes to make wine, after the harvest."

A few minutes later, Sydney tapped Kate on the arm. "What do you say we try the wine? My taste buds are drying up."

Kate laughed. "Ten minutes?" She had so many more questions.

"Not a minute more."

❖

"The first thing you do is hold your wine up to the light to check for clarity," the wine attendant instructed. Sydney had staked claim to two seats at the end of an L-shaped bar. The server gave them each a pour of last year's zinfandel.

"Always hold your glass by the stem," the young woman insisted, lifting her glass and tilting it, "and then swirl."

Kate tried to concentrate but her mind was running amok.

"You want to look carefully at the color," the server said.

"This is cool," Sydney whispered. Since they were sitting next to one another on bar stools, each time Sydney rotated toward Kate, she touched Kate with her knee. And each time Kate felt an electric tingling, unrelated to the wine or the way she was holding the glass. That wasn't helping her brain function.

"You can tell a lot about the wine simply by looking at it," Sydney said, facing Kate. "This wine is better than I ever imagined."

Kate was more fascinated by the color of Sydney's eyes. She'd never seen an iris so green. She wanted to look closer at them but didn't dare. What was happening to her? Kate swallowed and almost dropped her glass.

"Are you paying attention?" Sydney asked.

"What? Of course."

"Let me see you swirl."

Kate almost spilled the wine in Sydney's lap.

"Oops, I should have added, gently, and in one direction." Sydney put her hand around Kate's fingers and rotated the glass in one direction. "*Comme ça.*"

Good Lord.

Kate looked hopelessly back at the woman behind the bar. Please continue, she begged silently.

"Check its aroma," she was saying. "See if it smells earthy or fruity, floral or vegetal."

Kate wanted Sydney to put her hand on hers again.

"And finally, we taste. Let the wine fold around your tongue."

Kate took a sip, seriously doubting her ability to *fold the wine*. But she bet Sydney could.

"What do you taste?" Sydney asked.

"Oh no, a quiz?" Kate asked lightheartedly. She hoped her voice didn't betray her. Had Sydney noticed her staring?

"Very funny. Do you taste any sweetness? If it's not sweet, it's considered a dry wine. There are ranges of sweet and dry. What about any puckering in your mouth?"

Kate looked at Sydney's mouth. If ever God—or genes, as she knew better—had created perfection in lips, there they were. The perfect size and contour. Kate swallowed quickly.

"Well, what do you taste?" Sydney asked again.

"You can't be serious? You want me to explain, in words?"

"Yep. Go on, try."

For the first time Kate noticed a tiny dimple in Sydney's cheek. Could anyone be more beautiful? But Sydney was waiting for an answer.

"Actually, I find it quite velvety," Kate said. "Did you get that hint of clove on the finish?"

"Good job," Sydney said. "You get an A."

Kate took another sip, her heart jumping. For God's sake, did she have a crush on Sydney? She needed fresh air and some distance. "I need a break. Keep drinking. Meet you outside." Kate was off her stool and heading toward the door before Sydney could answer.

What was going on? She felt dizzy. *Focus on the grapes.* She walked down several rows of vines, allowing Sydney's presence to fade. She wasn't sure if she was allowed to be wandering around out here, but she wasn't ready to go back in.

She walked up and down several more rows, letting herself relax, comforted by a familiar plant environment. Kate forced herself to forget what happened at the tasting. Staring at the individual clusters, she was captivated by the lushness and abundance of the grapes, amazed even by the variety and shape of the trunks. She put her hand on the fruiting wire and wondered how they'd decided on this particular trellis system. She suddenly wanted to learn the grapes' entire life cycle, when and why they turned from green to red or to blue or black, whether there was one soil better than another. How did the farmers manage the pests? Which grapes worked in which soils? What kind of machines did they use, what work was done by hand? Even asking the questions excited her. Exhilarated, she caught herself smiling. As she looked up, there was Sydney staring at her.

"You okay? You tore out of the tasting room."

"I wanted to see the grapes. They're beauties, aren't they?" she said, pointing to the nearest cluster. "Each one is unique but similar to the one next to it." She picked up a cluster. "Feel it."

She heard Sydney chuckle. Goosebumps traveled up and down Kate's spine and she felt her face warm. "Very funny," she muttered. "Listen, I want to wander a bit more. I'll meet up with you in another row or two. Okay?" Fortunately, Sydney said sure, so Kate walked on alone as nonchalantly as possible. Stay focused on the grapes, she commanded her brain.

By the time she met up again with Sydney, her fascination with this plentiful crop, as she'd been trained at Davis to call it, had fully returned.

"This particular fruit, these vines. It's much more than I ever imagined," Kate tried to explain. "You know my father grows corn. I grew up helping him plant, watching the stalks grow. But in comparison to grapes, those ears seem ordinary, almost boring." Was that disloyal? Since she could remember, she'd helped her father in the field, following him around, glued to his side. He was the one who'd taught her to love farming. Kate took a few steps down the row as Sydney followed behind. It was her uncle Louie who had taught her how to dig in the warm earth for potatoes. He was always proud of his spuds. Potatoes, too, were a wonderful crop.

"When I was on my junior year abroad," Sydney responded, equally as serious, "I met a woman whose father was a wine *négociant*, that's a French term for someone—usually a man—who buys grapes and sells them as wine. She and I went on trips with her father to taste wine from different regions. She thought it funny that an American would be so interested in wine. I was fascinated by all the varieties of grapes and wondered, for example, what made some cabernet sauvignon grapes turn into a fabulous vintage and others into an ordinary table wine. I wanted to know everything about making wine. I get your amazement."

They stood there, looking out over the vast estate.

Sydney broke the silence. "I say we drive to one more vineyard before heading back. You game?"

"Definitely."

❖

Rutherford Hills couldn't have been more beautiful, located on top of a big hill overlooking the Napa Valley. In the car, Kate asked Sydney, "Why Rutherford?"

Sydney quickly answered, "Merlot. The climate and soil condition supposedly resemble those of Pomerol, that small but distinctive merlot-growing region of Bordeaux."

Kate had no idea what or where Pomerol was, but she loved Sydney's excitement and was impressed with her wine virtuosity.

"Tell me how you learned to taste wine," Kate said, simply enjoying the sound of Sydney's voice, and trying to pay attention to what Sydney was saying.

❖

It hit her as she was tasting the merlot. The inky blue color reminded her of blueberries. And Lily. Lily Carmichael, who'd moved into town with her family during Kate's junior year of high school. Lily's parents bought the farm next door and turned it into an impressive equestrian center, boarding horses and giving lessons to both kids and adults. She and Lily met at a county fair. Kate had been sitting at the table, guarding her vegetable entry, when Lily appeared—in her riding outfit, complete with crop—and asked her why she was sitting around waiting for the judge when they were giving out free homemade blueberry pies at the main pavilion.

Kate's eyes welled up. She put her fist to her mouth, unable to stop her tears. The memories flooded back: She was once again waking up and rushing to catch the bus. Lily was the next stop. They had twenty minutes, side by side, on their way to school. Lily was always laughing and egging Kate on. Kate rushed through her chores to be in Lily's barn, mucking the stalls, getting lessons on how to brush down a horse, speaking freely—about anything and everything—because she knew Lily was listening and Lily cared. Kate closed her eyes, swiping away the tears. These feelings she was having for Sydney, she'd had them all before. She recognized now that Sydney reminded her of Lily's vivacious personality. Kate stared straight ahead, not daring to look at Sydney. Fortunately, Sydney was talking with a woman on her left.

For heaven's sake, she'd had a huge crush on Lily. She was sure of it. She remembered coming up with every strategy possible to spend time with Lily and her family. She and Lily had planned to go to college together. But Lily had died—leukemia—and that had ended every dream. Sydney glanced over at Kate and smiled, continuing her conversation.

Why, Kate wondered, had she not felt anything for anyone since? Ah, because everyone had put her feelings down. *You're lucky to have had a good friend.* As if that was all Lily had been to Kate. *You'll get over her.* And so Kate had shoved all her feelings into a box. She didn't know how to deal with them and had no one to talk to about them. Kate took a full chug of the wine and studied the bottles on the shelf. But now she knew better. She had been heartbroken. And had never wanted to feel that pain again.

"This merlot's fabulous, don't you think?"

Kate jumped. "Yes." She attempted a smile.

"This was the last glass. Ready to head back? It's late."

Kate nodded, turning away from Sydney to hop off the stool, not ready yet to face her.

Several miles down the highway, Sydney suggested one more stop. "Hey, I'm starving, aren't you? Let's get something to eat. I have in mind just the place. My sources have been spot-on up till now."

Kate reluctantly agreed. She was eager to get home to think more, but she knew she needed to eat something.

"Hang on. It's near here. We passed it on the way up." Several minutes later, Sydney pulled off the highway and into the parking lot of a small restaurant. She went inside and came back out with a baguette and several chunks of cheese on a paper plate.

Sydney got back into the car and handed the plate to Kate. "I thought cheese would go well after all our wine." She started up the engine. "Hope it's okay to eat while we drive. Would you do the honors?"

Kate looked at the plate, then over to Sydney. Did she want to be fed? No way. She broke off a hunk of cheese and handed it to Sydney. After she ate it, Kate gave her a piece of the bread.

"Hey, this is good." Sydney said.

Kate munched on a chunk of bread and then some cheese. She passed more cheese to Sydney. On the third round, Sydney said her hands were getting sticky.

"Just pop it in there." Sydney opened her mouth.

Kate complied, finding the setup most unsanitary. And extremely sexy.

"We're messing up your car," Kate said. "The crumbs are everywhere."

"As if I care."

❖

"Thanks for doing all that driving," Kate told Sydney. They were back at the door to her building. Kate put her hand on the doorknob to go inside. Was she supposed to ask Sydney up? Talking the last hour of the trip about the differences in the wineries they'd visited had helped calm her nerves. Sydney seemed obsessed with the idea of making wine. It was not like Sydney had any feelings for her. Besides, this was a thank-you trip, her rational mind assured her. She'd learned she was capable of falling for another woman. No small thing, but never mind that for the moment. Time to say goodbye.

"Listen," Sydney said, interrupting her thoughts. "I bet what we saw today was only a fraction of what's up there. I say we go back. Sonoma or some other area? There's more I want to learn. You?"

Kate let go of the doorknob. She turned toward Sydney, her heart thundering. "Yes," Kate responded, before she could change her mind.

"Good. Next Saturday? We have to take advantage of the harvest."

"Of course."

They stood there, inches from each other, neither budging. "I'll call you," Sydney said then turned to leave.

"Wait," Kate called out. Sydney stopped and turned around.

"You're not too tired to drive?"

"I'll stop at our diner for coffee. Where we stopped this morning."

Dino's Diner was *their* diner? Kate wanted to laugh. She watched Sydney walk through the parking lot, open her car door and slide inside. Kate had no idea what she was supposed to do with her newfound veneration for grapes, much less the whole emotional avalanche from the day. But they had a diner. That was something.

Chapter Three

Leaving Kate at the entrance to her dorm, Sydney drove off. A mile outside the Davis city limits, she started fantasizing about becoming a winemaker. She had no idea what she needed to do first or what she needed to learn, but she would find out. All she could imagine was people drinking wines that she had created. Other than sailing, nothing in her entire life had ever excited her as much. Could it be that she had finally figured out what she wanted to do with her life? Sydney turned on the radio and blasted the music, tapping the steering wheel to the count of the beat.

Two songs in, her mind took her back down that row of grapes looking for Kate. She had instantly missed her presence at the wine tasting when she took off. There was so much about Kate that was alluring. And not just the fact that she was also excited about grapes, albeit for a different reason. Maybe Kate could grow the grapes that she—well, *they* would make into wine. Wasn't that a wonderful fantasy. Sydney continued driving, imagining the two of them standing next to their own crusher-destemmer, when suddenly she remembered her own survival rules. Her stomach clenched. Kate and she could not establish a vineyard together unless those rules were strictly in place.

Yes, she was attracted to Kate. She'd have to be blind and a fool not to be. But she wanted to be a winemaker more. Which meant that she could not sleep with Kate, assuming Kate was a lesbian and interested. But details aside, she had established years ago—back in high school to be exact—that she would never get involved with anyone like that again. Never. Besides, deciding to become a winemaker was *huge*. She already knew the resistance she'd get from her parents.

❖

"May I speak with Kate Bauer, please?"

"Is this Sydney?"

"Have we met?" Sydney hadn't spoken to anyone at the dorm except Abby.

"I took your message earlier and taped it on Kate's door. She's never around till the library closes."

"Thanks." Sydney hung up. Great. She had a reputation at Davis for being an obsessive caller. Lesson learned. Sydney returned to the couch and picked up the pages of notes she'd taken at the library about viticulture and enology. As much as she hated to, she'd decided to call Kate to cancel their Saturday vineyard trip. It would be easier to stop any further affiliation with her now. She could become a winemaker on her own.

At half past midnight, she called Kate back. Sydney had paced the last ten minutes. Kate picked up after one ring. At least Sydney hoped it was Kate.

"Ever think about getting your own phone?" The decision she'd made plus the waiting had put her in an especially bad mood.

"Can't afford it. Don't know if they're even allowed. Hi, Sydney."

"Sorry, hello. Get a lot done at the library?" Sydney let out a breath and sat down.

"Yeah, Abby and I were among the last to leave, as usual."

Again, Abby. Did she have to hear her name every time she called? What was the deal with the two of them anyway? Was Kate a lesbian or not? It would certainly be easier for her if Kate wasn't. Then there would be no temptation, no conflict about the two of them exploring grape growing or making wine together. Maybe she should hold off on canceling until she found out. "Still up for more vineyard adventures this weekend?"

"You bet. Have another list of wineries for us?"

"I will by Saturday morning." Sydney heard the phone booth door squeak. Sydney settled back into her oversized chair, the grip on her bad mood loosening. She looked around her apartment, where the décor ran contrary to her mother's refined tastes. On the walls, Sydney had hung a portrait gallery of her personal heroes and heroines, hand-sketched and then painted over in acrylic. As a kid Sydney was forever creating sketches of people. Her brother Rusty must have noticed because for Christmas one year, he gave her a sketch pad and a giant box of colored pencils. It wasn't until her college friends pushed her to draw political posters for them that she finally recognized and accepted her talent. She'd taken extra care with the drawings of John Lennon and Harvey Milk, as well as her own favorite activists, Del Martin and Phyllis Lyon. Ronald Reagan had been drawn with a big slash across his caricature. When he'd run for governor, he'd promised to "clean up the mess at Berkeley." As far as Berkeley students were concerned, President Reagan was the mess.

"I recollect you like wandering among the grapes, Kate. What about the wine part? Tasting it, that is?" Kate had looked so cute sitting on that bar stool, swirling her glass of wine.

"I'm not very good at it. And I still have no idea how wine is made. Isn't all wine just vinified grape juice?"

"Ouch. Just? There are all types of wines, certainly more than the ones we tasted last weekend. Making the wine is the most interesting part. At least for me."

"I am aware that the quantity of grapes grown to make wine has increased year after year."

Sydney sat up. "There are so many big and subtle differences. For the past three years, all my economics professors seemed to talk about were processes: marketing, research, promotion, sales, distribution. Until recently I found it all quite boring. But as it turns out, it's literally the process of making the wine that excites me, that of going from grape to bottle. I want to learn everything I can about how to make wine."

Kate laughed and the sound tickled Sydney's ear. "At my school they call that science."

"Maybe, but I think there's more to it than that." She'd studied all the art books in her parents' home and walked through the MFA in Boston and several of the art museums in both Oakland and San Francisco. "The nuanced differences in color, texture and taste, for example. It feels more like art to me." She thought immediately of Monet, Renoir, Van Gogh. They each took the outside world and interpreted it in their own fashion.

"Well, I know zip about that sort of thing."

"Then it's good we're going back," Sydney said. "You get to see more grapes and I get to taste more wine. Saturday morning, bright and early?"

"I'll be in the lobby."

Sydney put the phone back in the cradle and hopped up. It wasn't too late to make her last two semesters at school interesting, if not useful. Surely she could design some projects around the wine industry. And maybe, just maybe, she could get Kate interested in growing grapes instead of corn.

❖

As before, they picked up their breakfast from Dino's. This time Sydney discovered the diner's exceptional homemade French crullers with nooks and crannies to hold the light honey glaze. She couldn't resist ordering two. Kate had both a blueberry scone and a muffin. Both had sugar highs, so the driving time flew by. They talked about their respective families and what it was like to grow up in a small town where everyone knew their parents.

At the first vineyard, Kate once again practically jumped out of the car before Sydney had the hand brake on. Sydney tagged along behind Kate as her eyes devoured the landscape. She pointed out to Sydney the trellising—the wires on which the grapes hung—and told her there were many different kinds, depending on the site, cost, and especially how the grapes would be harvested. "And this is the cane, Sydney," Kate said, caressing the main branch. "It's been pruned to grow horizontally. Each spring, the leaves and future fruit pop out from tiny buds on the cane and grow vertically. That's what you mostly notice in a vineyard."

"I see you did more homework," Sydney teased.

"Oh, yeah." Kate bent over to rub a little soil over her fingers. "Do you think they'd let me take a sample to analyze back at school?"

Farmer Kate seemed completely hooked.

❖

At their third stop, a small winery way up in Sonoma County, Sydney was all business. They were part of a small group of tourists.

Kate was listening intently to the guide, so Sydney wandered ahead to explore on her own. She headed first to a row of huge stainless-steel tanks and stood in front of one, close enough to feel the condensation. How much did this thing hold and what wine was in it and at what stage? Several smaller tanks had hoses connecting them to a larger one. Sydney was down on her knees poking at a hose to see if it was wine-filled, when she looked up to see Kate staring at her with a smile on her face.

"This is so cool," Sydney admitted, motioning all around her.

Kate nodded. "We're going on to see the barrels. Want to come?"

Oak barrels! That meant red wine. Sydney jumped to her feet. She caught a glimpse of a wall of tools as she turned the corner. Clamps, fasteners, shiny metal parts—a profusion of hardware she knew nothing about but instinctively wanted to collect. Talk about being hooked.

"But when and how do you stop the fermentation?" Sydney asked the guide. He had no idea. He admitted that he usually only worked in the vineyards and was subbing for the regular guide who was out sick. Too bad. Sydney had a dozen more questions. She was going to have to do her own research.

"What about that malolactic fermentation you mentioned? What does that do?" Sydney hoped he at least knew that much.

The man threw up his hands. "Miss, you ought to go to enology school."

Perhaps she should.

"Why don't we let the group go on?" Kate suggested. "I have another idea." They waited until the tour left. "What do you think she's doing?" Kate pointed to a worker who was in a back room where there were at least eight large rectangular bins, each about four feet deep. The woman stood near the top of a ladder placed alongside one of the wooden bins. She was facing the open bin and looked like she was pushing some sort of metal tool up and down. Sydney knew her from somewhere. Her tattoos were hard to forget.

"I bet there are grapes in that bin," Sydney said. "Let's find out." They walked quickly into the back room and looked into the first bin. It was lined in rubber and was packed within inches of the rim with hundreds, maybe thousands, of crushed grapes. Grapes, skin, seeds, pulp, all mashed together.

"That's amazing," Sydney exclaimed.

"Open vat fermentation," said the woman up on the ladder. "Best way to integrate the cap." She tapped on the top of the grapes with her metal tool. "You have to push all this down to get to the juice below. Can't let it dry out. It's not quite wine yet but it's getting there." She winked at Sydney. It looked like she remembered her, too. From where?

Sydney stared at the woman and especially at the flower tattoos all around her neck and up and down both arms. Ah, Maud's. Everyone went to that bar. Butch, femme, leftover hippies. Lately it was the lipstick lesbians. To everyone it was *home*. Sydney remembered those particular arms at Maud's wrapped around another woman's body on the dance floor. Sydney glanced over at Kate, who was staring into a bin.

"Like the job?" Sydney asked her.

"It pays."

Sydney couldn't resist. "Listen, I don't want to get you into trouble, but any chance I could climb up and take a crack at using that thing?"

The woman took a gander at the door then back to her visitors.

"Why not?" She grabbed the handle tightly and slowly pulled up the long, metal shaft, holding the dripping juice over the bin. "This is a paddle," she said, looking directly at Sydney. She held it in the air. At the end of it was a round, flat plate with a series of holes in it. "We call what I'm doing punching down the grapes. Come on up quickly. I shouldn't allow you to do this but, hey, what the heck." She came down the ladder and handed the tool to Sydney. "Bet you want to show off for your—"

"Thanks a lot," Sydney interrupted. "I'll be careful."

Sydney climbed up. The tool looked like a giant potato masher. She spread her feet evenly on the ladder rung for balance. So far, so good. She pushed down through the thick concentration of grapes.

"Whoa, this is...hard to...push through." And Sydney was strong. Slowly the metal plate slipped through the grape cap as the holes in the plate let the juice through.

"Yup. We do this a minimum of twice a day, until it's all liquid. Push it all the way down to the bottom," she told Sydney, "and pull it back up again." She turned to Kate. "This is how we release all the tannins and other compounds from the skin. And how the wine gets its color and taste."

Sydney pushed through the grapes, trying not to fall into the bin.

She liked the feel of her muscles pushing against the grapes. She pulled on the handle and plunged it back in again to another spot next to where she'd pulled it out.

"What's the chemical process?" Kate asked.

"The fancy terms, I can't tell you," the woman told Kate, walking up next to her. "It's about kick-starting the fermentation and getting oxygen to the yeast cells that are eating all the sugar, changing this lovely mass into alcohol. My name's Sam, by the way. Samantha, but I prefer Sam."

Sydney looked down. Suddenly her interest in punching down the grapes stopped. Sam was standing way too close to Kate.

"Coming down!" Sydney chimed, carefully holding the paddle over the bin. "Want to grab this, Sam?"

Sam was forced to take her eyes off Kate.

Kate backed up to give them both room.

"Listen," Sam said, looking from one to the other, "if you two want to come back after work, I'll, uh, have time for lots of questions."

Sydney restrained herself. "We'll pass on that lovely offer, Sam, but thanks for letting me get up there." She walked toward the front room, praying Kate would follow. She did.

"Well, she certainly was an interesting character," Kate said, as soon as they were outside. "I wonder what she had in mind for later."

Sydney looked at Kate, noticing her cheeks reddening once again. Well, well. Kate might indeed be interested in women. She had forgotten how protectively Abby stood by Kate's side back in her dorm room. Were they a couple? Grape-punching Sam sure seemed interested in Kate.

"Beats me," Sydney fibbed, wanting to change the subject, "but I can tell you it felt amazing to push through those grapes. I'd love to work here."

"You would?" Kate asked. "With her?"

Damn. Sydney had to change the subject. Kate was strong, sexy, smart, and very observant. Just her type. And just the type who would break her heart. If ever she were to contemplate the two of them working together—still a fantasy—there could be no cozying up. "I'm not interested in Sam, Kate. I want to learn anything and everything I can about making wine. Sam would be a means to an end, that's all."

Sydney closed her eyes for a second, forcing herself to think about the equipment hanging on the wall, the hoses neatly coiled in the corner. The intoxicating smell of yeast in the bins of fermenting grapes. Anything to turn her own thoughts back to the vineyard at hand. The winery walls were screaming at her, begging her to pay attention. Equally screaming was her rule not to get involved—not with Sam or Kate, or anyone. Not romantically.

"But you would go out with a woman?"

"Oh, for heaven's sake." Sydney took a few seconds to think. She might as well find out if this was going to be a problem. "I'm a lesbian, Kate. Does that matter?"

Kate took a step back. As Sydney expected, her face turned a bright pink. "No, not at all. I—"

"What about you? Do you date women? Abby, for example?"

"Abby? Oh, no. She's just a friend."

Kate stood there fidgeting so much, Sydney decided to let her off the hook. Perhaps Kate had yet to come out or was beginning to think about it. "Shall we talk about this later? I say one more winery before we head back?"

Kate looked decidedly relieved.

❖

The sun had gone down by the time they were seated on the deck of the restaurant recommended at their last stop. The evening was cool as usual, the sky full of stars. Even food seemed unappealing to Sydney at the moment. She felt itchy, unsettled. She wanted to talk to Kate about someday making wine together. The waiter handed them two menus and left.

"What a view," Sydney said, trying to act casual. She and Kate both put their napkins on their laps.

"Look, if you don't let me pay for dinner, I can't eat," Kate burst out. "You paid for the gas. I want to pay my share." She sat back and crossed her arms.

Kate wanted to talk about the check? Money was the least of her issues, though Kate wouldn't know that. Her father paid her credit card bills, paid her rent, and gave her gas money. Sydney looked at the intense brown eyes staring at her. She had not intended for Kate to feel uncomfortable. She was only trying to be her usual gallant self. "The check's all yours. I understand. Shall we order?" Sydney picked up the menu. They'd barely eaten all day and Kate had refused any wine at the last tasting. Maybe this was Kate being cranky. After all, Sydney hardly knew her.

From the rather ordinary menu, Sydney ordered a steak. Kate followed with an order of the penne pasta.

"Not a meat and potatoes woman like the mighty farmers of yore?" Sydney asked. She wanted to insert some levity into the conversation.

"I'm a vegetarian. I don't believe in killing sentient beings, even for food." Kate sat upright, poker-faced.

"Oh, wow. I had no idea. Good for you."

"Since we're asking questions," she said, "I have one for you. What's it like to be gay? Or should I say lesbian?"

"Whoa, that's quite a question. Didn't expect that." Sydney couldn't help but feel disappointed. She wanted to talk about making wine, not lesbian stuff. "May I ask why you're wondering?"

"Oh, perhaps we shouldn't talk about this. You tell me."

Sydney leaned closer to Kate, who seemed barely able to sit without squirming. "Kate, look at me, it's okay to talk about this." A wealth of tenderness slowly flowed down Sydney's body as she noticed the vulnerability of this otherwise indomitable woman.

"I guess it was the way you interacted with Sam. Your ease with her, I…I've been wondering about myself." Kate looked down, clearly uncomfortable.

"You've had feelings for another woman?"

Kate's mouth opened, but she only stared at Sydney. Seconds passed. "Maybe," Kate whispered. "Back in high school."

Sydney wanted to jump to the other side of the table, to hold Kate's hands. This was huge. She remembered when she came out. She couldn't wait to talk to her best friend, MJ, about it.

Before either could say anything else, their waiter dropped off a basket of rolls and then, to Sydney's horror, pulled out a steak knife from the pocket of his apron.

"Is that really for me?" she asked. "Perhaps you could bring me a fresh one?"

"I just pulled this from the cutlery bin."

Sydney shook her head. Was she really scandalized about the knife or horrified she was imitating what her mother would have done?

Kate started laughing, softly.

Sydney looked at her. "Was that funny?" she asked, curious.

"No, not really." Kate began laughing for real. "Sorry," she managed to say after a couple seconds. "But the look on your face. Guess you're used to fancier places. Again, my apologies, but that was a good conversation break. My question was way too serious after such a wonderful day."

"Your question was a good one. I may not be the best person to talk to, that's all. Sex, yes, relationships, no."

Unbidden, Sydney pictured Blaye, her first girlfriend, waving goodbye as she pulled out of the driveway, her car packed full of all her belongings. Sydney had fallen head over heels in love with Blaye her senior year of high school. She was arrogant, sexy, and a powerhouse in and out of the water. Blaye had transferred in from a private school in New York City and joined their swim team. She had broken every record in the state in the butterfly, and the team won the state title that year, due largely to her. Well, to the two of them. Sydney was captain and not a bad swimmer herself. Dating Blaye, Sydney had broken all her family rules—not the least of which was coming in and going out at all hours. She had been so sure the two of them would go off into the sunset together, she'd flouted her relationship all over town, embarrassing her parents, of course. Sydney loved that part. The day after graduation, however, Blaye told Sydney it'd all been fun—*fun*? That's all it had been for her? And then she drove away. Sydney swore she'd never let anyone hurt her like that again.

"I don't understand."

"Lesbians and gay men have been around forever, Kate. If you want to get a little taste of gay politics, come spend a weekend at my school. That's all my friends talk about. Do you know any gay or lesbian couples?"

"No."

"You're a reader, perhaps you can get some books out of the library." Sydney knew this was not being supportive or helpful. But she was hardly the right person to talk to about successful gay relationships. "I kind of blew it with my coming out, but others have no problem. Sometimes it's easy, sometimes not." Sydney smiled, but then to her surprise, Kate's demeanor totally changed. She pulled her napkin from her lap and started twisting it. Was it something she'd said?

"You okay, Kate?" At the very least, she'd need another napkin.

"So there's a lot of homophobia?"

"Homophobia exists, big time, but you learn to cope with it."

The waiter returned with their dinners. Kate sat back, sighed, and put her crumpled napkin back onto her lap.

"I'm glad you didn't fall into the fermentation vat," Kate said, after Sydney had taken a few bites of her steak.

"Yeah, that wouldn't have been funny." Sydney didn't want to talk about that either. Did Kate need to talk more about her new emotions? Sydney fiddled with her mashed potatoes. The moment to make her proposal seemed to have gone.

"Listen," Kate leaned forward, "I'm trying to get us back to talking about wine." Kate put down her fork. "I hope it's not your turn to laugh, but I think these past two trips may have changed the course of my life, work-wise."

"What?" Sydney sat up straight. "How so?"

"I love working outside. I love the whole process of planting, nurturing a crop until it's ready to be harvested. That hasn't changed. But seeing these grapes? Everything I've seen and all that I've been reading at school? Well, I think that's the crop I want to grow."

Sydney swallowed.

"I'll be more sophisticated about farming than my father, for sure. He—"

"Are you serious?" Sydney interrupted. "You really think it's grapes you want to grow?"

"You saw all the different types of grapes. They're strong, resilient, and gorgeous. They're already growing grapes on Long Island. The soil, the climate is perfect for grapes. Several vineyards are already doing well."

"You are serious." Sydney could barely contain herself. She could feel her feet tapping and wanted to jump out of her seat. "I can't believe you're thinking about this, too." She placed her knife and fork on the table. To hell with any former thoughts. She could make this work. "Kate, I've been thinking about this all week." She obviously hadn't worked out the details—like not coming on to Kate—but she couldn't resist. This is what she wanted. "Why don't we start our own winery? You grow the grapes, I'll make the wine."

Kate gasped.

"I'm serious." Sydney leaned even farther toward Kate. "You are up on everything there is about growing grapes—"

"Hardly. Two trips up here, I've read a few books, poked around the library."

"But you will, you could—"

"What are you saying?"

"You're a junior. You have a whole year to learn whatever we need. There must be tons of experts at your school in planting vines, taking care of them. You're at Davis. You have professors who teach these things. I'm a marketing major. I'll start on a business plan, get a job out here working at a vineyard. Figure out the people I need to meet, start learning everything about vineyards and wineries. What do you think?"

Kate looked thunderstruck. She started blinking madly, her mouth trying to form words that weren't coming out. The waiter approached, but Sydney waved him away.

"All I've been learning for three years is how to market and sell. Making wine is my future. I can feel it in my bones. Nothing has ever excited me like this before. I'm good with people, Kate. If we make wine, I can sell it."

Kate sat back, shaking her head. "This is a wild idea, certainly a bit premature, don't you think?"

"Maybe. Maybe not. If you are as possessed about grapes as you say you are, then why not?"

"First of all, I was thinking about introducing grapes on my father's property. And he's as obstinate and old-fashioned as they come, not to mention anti-everything I feel about the environment—"

"Then we'll get our own land," Sydney countered.

"And where would we get this land and how would we pay for it?"

"Good questions. Keep 'em coming. I bet I can answer each one." Sydney was delighted with this turn of events. She might doubt this later, but for the moment, she was deliriously happy. "You finished with that?" Sydney pointed to Kate's plate.

Kate nodded, so Sydney signaled for the waiter. Details aside, she'd never wanted anything so badly in her whole life. The wine would be her masterpiece. She could picture her name on the bottle. Bottles.

"Where would I begin? What would I do first?" Kate asked.

Sydney smiled broadly. "You know that heavy textbook you

brought along last time? Now you have a real reason to ace that course."
Sydney knew that was not what Kate meant, but she had Kate thinking
about the idea. "Still want to pay the check?"

Kate nodded, getting out her wallet.

Fabulous. Kate was undeniably interested in a vineyard. Sydney
relaxed. She had the whole ride back to continue her pitch.

Chapter Four

December 1982, Davis, CA

Kate saw the scrap of paper sticking out from under her door. Expecting it to be a message from Sydney, her pulse quickened as she opened the door and bent over to pick it up. Since their last trip to Sonoma, Sydney had been sending articles from current wine journals, prestigious magazines, and newsletters.

What do you think of this? Check this out! she'd written in a boldly inscribed note. Several times there were plain newspaper clippings about different vineyards and once a review for a used wine press. As befitting a marketing major, Sydney was pushing her idea of the two of them creating their own vineyard. An idea Kate continued to take for a lark.

Call your mother! this message read. Kate rushed down the hall to the phone, hating to reverse the charges, but not wanting to waste time looking for her stash of quarters.

"Hi, Mom, everything okay?" Kate sat down, willing herself to be calm. Her mother never called this late. Rarely called at all, in fact. She liked to write long, newsy letters.

"Your dad and I are fine."

Kate waited. She had to be calling for a reason. Neither of them was very good at idle chatter.

"Listen, honey, in your letter you said you were staying at Abby's for the holiday break. I appreciate you wanting to save money, but I think you should come home. Uncle Louie is not feeling well. He'd love to see you."

"What's wrong with him?" There was silence for several seconds, enough to make Kate stand up in the tiny booth. "Mom?"

"The doctors aren't certain. I'm afraid he's been getting worse."

Kate's whole body tightened. "Why didn't you tell me?" Kate was livid. She adored her uncle and often felt closer to him than to her own father. He'd made his monthly Sunday call in October but in November, he shortened it, saying he had a bad cold.

"I kept hoping he'd get better," her mother said.

"I'll call the airlines."

"Tell us when you'll arrive. Jerome will pick you up at the airport. Can't wait to see you."

Back in her room, Kate poured herself a glass of water and walked over to the window. She had just seen her uncle in September. How could he be this sick? Did it have to do with Marvin being sick? Was Marvin contagious? The story she'd always been told was that, once her uncle decided to stay in Cutchogue and farm, Marvin had rented him a room in his house. Two bachelors, Kate heard her parents call them. She never questioned why her uncle never wanted his own place. For heaven's sake. How naive could she have been? They were a couple! Kate froze. That new disease that she'd heard rumblings about. That was attacking only gay men. Could Marvin have that?

❖

Long Island, NY

When her plane landed on the runway at JFK, Kate was surprised to see snow. She made her way through the massive crowds in the terminal, looking for Jerome's familiar face. Jerome had worked for both her father and uncle for so long, he'd been given the official title of farm manager. He lived with his wife, Annie Mae, on her uncle's property, having converted the old migrants' dormitory into his own home. Kate immediately recognized his hard-earned muscular body and bright smile. He pulled her into a hug and they both held on.

"Look at you. I swear you're getting taller," he said, once he let go. Jerome was no doubt stronger, although Kate did have a couple of inches on him.

Kate noticed specks of gray in his beard, but other than that, he seemed his usual spirited self. "Think so?" she asked. Kate took a step back and beamed. In the early seventies, Jerome had driven up from rural Virginia with a group of friends looking for work. He'd been a young man then. The small group worked their way up the coast and then out to Long Island. Marvin, who owned the potato farm next door to Kate's father, hired him and three others. By the end of the season, Jerome had fixed every piece of equipment on the farm and proven himself indispensable. He alone was asked to stay on permanently.

Jerome grabbed her suitcase. "I parked way down at the end. Hope you're good with walking."

Even with his limp, Kate could barely keep up with him. "I'm glad to see you, but why didn't my dad come?"

He looked at her. "Wait for the truck, okay?"

First her mother wasn't talking, and now Jerome. Kate's stomach flipped. She sat patiently while Jerome exited the parking lot and pulled onto the highway.

"Okay, what's going on at home?" Kate took a deep breath and waited.

"First of all, Marvin died," Jerome told her.

"What? That's not possible! He was in San Francisco in September."

Jerome turned to look at her. She knew that look. He was deadly serious. She took off her coat and tucked it on the seat between them.

"Marvin was really bad off."

"From what?"

"Some type of pneumonia, best they could say."

"But pneumonia is treatable," Kate insisted.

"Not his kind. Plus, he had these purple blotches all over his body." Jerome passed several cars on the highway. He was comfortable with speed. "It gets worse."

Kate was suddenly sweating. She wiped her brow with the back of her hand and cracked open the window. It had to be this new disease.

"How?"

"Your uncle's sick now, too. Might be the same thing."

So Marvin had been contagious. Kate turned toward Jerome, her breathing shallow. "How is he? What are his symptoms? Has he been to the hospital? My mother's not told me a thing."

Jerome sighed. "Kate, your mother's been brokering the truth for years. Trying to protect you, I think. Your father, well, that's a whole other story."

Her father never liked Marvin. He'd made that obvious, but it was only now that Kate understood it was because her father had probably figured out the real relationship between Marvin and his brother.

"I think the world of your uncle. That's old news," Jerome said.

"Of course." She'd heard the tales of how it was her uncle who insisted Jerome stay after that first summer, her uncle who literally saved Jerome's life when a piece of heavy sorting machinery fell on his leg. Uncle Louie had lifted the sorter and pulled him out from under the machine. He'd been left with a huge scar and a permanent limp, but he was alive. "What does that have to do with anything?"

"He's homosexual, Kate. Gay, they call it."

"Yes, I figured that out."

Jerome looked quickly at Kate. "People around here don't like that. Your father especially."

"Oh dear." A chill ran up her back. She remembered how her father reacted when she told him he shouldn't use pesticides. Had he become even more self-righteous? "How so?"

Jerome glanced over at Kate then back to the highway. "Since Louie's been sick, it's gotten worse. You'll see soon enough."

Kate felt queasy. "Never mind my father. How is Uncle Louie doing?"

"He's having trouble breathing and sometimes even standing. He sweats all the time. Then he's cold. He has no appetite. I try to help out as much as I can."

"But he went to the hospital. What did they say?"

"They sent him home. They told your mother they don't know what to do."

"That's not possible. They're doctors. They've got to do something."

Jerome hesitated. "Some of them were mean to him, Kate. I saw it myself. I took him twice. One doctor refused to come inside his room, only talking to him from the door. I was furious." He shot another glance at Kate. "This is how folks treat people they despise. Or fear." He paused. "But at least we can help him at home. That's why I came to pick you up. I wanted to make sure you knew what was going on. It's mostly his breathing. At least he doesn't have those skin things."

"Jerome, I"—Kate scooped up her coat and scooted over, putting her hand solidly on his forearm—"I don't want to lose him."

"I know. But I doubt he can hold on much longer," Jerome said, a faraway look of sadness in his eyes. He laced his warm hand over Kate's. "You're home. That'll help."

The bottom was falling out of Kate's world. She bit her lip to hold back tears. Kate tuned out everything, hearing only the sounds of the passing cars.

❖

It was dark when they reached Cutchogue. Kate had already decided to drop her suitcase and go directly next door. Her father would be in bed, and frankly, she wasn't in the mood to see her mother, either. An irrational, simmering fury at her parents, the medical establishment, even Cutchogue was mounting. She needed to see her uncle.

Kate tiptoed through the back door, but within seconds her mother was standing in front of her. She must have heard Jerome pulling in the driveway. She was wearing a robe over her old flannel nightgown, looking a bit disheveled. Her short-cropped brown hair was mashed on one side.

Kate dropped her suitcase. Her mother threw her arms around her.

"Katie," she whispered onto Kate's shoulder. She held Kate tightly, not letting her move. "I'm so sorry," she said. Her mother stepped back and almost tripped on her own worn slippers.

"I'm going over to see Uncle Louie."

"You don't want to wait until morning?"

"No." She didn't want to get into it with her mother. "I have to go." She turned and walked back out. She crossed the driveway where Jerome had parked, the driveway that separated the two houses. She could walk this path blindfolded. Surely she'd crawled it before she could walk it. More than once as a toddler, one of her parents had snatched her up and carried her back home before she reached her uncle's door.

Kate entered the back door, slipped through the kitchen, and found her uncle asleep in the living room—or what had once been his living room. He was lying on his back in a hospital bed. The covers were pulled up to his chin and one arm dangled off the side. She pulled up a chair and cradled his fist in her hand. His skin was so soft. Kate knew he hadn't planted potatoes last spring, so it'd been a while since he worked outside. But still, someone was rubbing his hands with lotion. A fog of helplessness enveloped her. Her rational mind evaporated, leaving her heart exposed. He could not die. She needed her uncle back. She didn't care how selfish that was. At last, assured of his labored but steady breathing, she allowed herself to look around the room.

In the corner, a cushy armchair had been replaced by a wheelchair. On the opposite wall stood an old-fashioned armoire and a dresser. There was a watch on top of the dresser and a stack of magazines, nothing else. The room seemed very sterile, very unlike her uncle. The metal nightstand next to his chair was on wheels. It, too, looked like it had come from a hospital. On the nightstand, someone had added a little color to the room with a sprig of flowers and sage in a tiny vase. Kate remembered that her uncle had once told her that his bedroom was the best room in the house: in the back, on the second floor, overlooking the potatoes. Kate remembered distinctly that he'd said *my* bedroom and not *ours*. She'd not been allowed to go upstairs. She had no idea she'd been part of a well-orchestrated veil of silence. Kate took in and let out a gigantic breath.

"That's a mighty big sigh." Louie's eyes were open and he was smiling.

"Uncle Louie!" Kate let go of his hand and leaned over and gave him a hug. "I'm so sorry to see you sick."

"Don't you worry. You're home. That's good." He squeezed her hand, but then his eyes drooped. "Medicine. Sorry. Talk in the morning?" Kate gazed down at her uncle, her father's once-idolized big brother. He'd lost a great deal of weight and his ruddy cheeks were now ashen. How had he survived Marvin's funeral? Had there been anyone to comfort him? Had she missed any of her uncle's early symptoms when he was in San Francisco? How could she have been so oblivious?

Kate heard the back door open. Seconds later her mother appeared in the room carrying a big pot.

"Mom?" Kate jumped up. "Here, let me take that."

"I brought you some soup. Your flight got in so late, you have to be hungry. Let's go into the kitchen," she suggested.

Kate made sure her uncle was breathing easily before following her mother.

"I brought enough for you and Louie. His angels can heat it up for him tomorrow. Softer foods are easier for him to eat."

"Wait. You're bringing him food? Jerome said…never mind. Who are his angels?" Kate put the tureen down on the counter, more confused than ever. She stared at her mother, who seemed to be fidgeting.

"Of course I'm bringing him food. But don't tell your father." She looked down.

Kate let that comment pass for the moment. "It seems I missed Uncle Marvin's funeral. What's going on here?"

"Marvin was not your uncle."

"Mom! Technically not, but I have known him my whole life. I recently figured out he and Uncle Louie were more than friends living together. They were partners." Kate paused. "You did know that, didn't you?"

"This is not the time or place, Kate."

"We're not going to talk about this?" Perhaps this wasn't the best time, but at some point Kate needed some answers. "Is Dad behind all this?" She had to find out. This was about Uncle Louie, of course, but how they felt about him would be telltale should she ever want to come out.

Her mother ran her fingers through her hair. She wore a coat over her nightgown but had not put on a hat. "I support your father. He thought it best."

"Best what? Not to tell me anything? Best to treat his own brother this way?"

"People around here talk. It was hard when I first married your father." She shuffled her feet, looking away. "He was not from here. Not a farmer. And Jewish, too. They've only begun to accept him these past few years. Your father asked Lou to, well, keep his private life to himself."

Private life? She meant shameful life. "Thanks for the soup, Mom. I'll come over later. I want to sit with Uncle Louie." And figure out how she was supposed to navigate her time home with a homophobic father and complicit mother.

❖

Her mother had left the Christmas tree lights on for her. Kate turned them off when she walked back to her parents' house a few hours later. Their bedroom door was closed, thank goodness, so Kate headed quietly up to her old bedroom, skipping the steps she knew squeaked the most. She'd had no idea her own uncle was gay, her father virulently antigay, or that her mother kept secrets. No wonder she'd grown up clueless about her own sexuality. Reeling with confusion, Kate tossed her suitcase into the corner and fell onto the bed.

Kate woke to the familiar smell of baked goods wafting under the door but resisted the temptation to go downstairs. In fact, she deliberately waited until her mother left for the farm stand. A few minutes later, her father drove off in his truck. Perhaps he was avoiding talking to her, as well. But wasn't he supposed to be the grown-up?

This was the only week during the winter that her mother kept the farm stand open. Even with space heaters, it had to be freezing out there. But they needed the income. So many people had company between Christmas and New Year's, she sold tons of bread, cakes, and pies. Money used to be their only concern. She assumed hiding her uncle's illness now approached the top of the list.

Kate left a note saying that she was going to pay a visit to the Carmichaels, then spend the day with Uncle Louie. She added that she'd be back for dinner. She'd have to bite the bullet and talk to them.

❖

Rushing from a great visit with Mary and Finn Carmichael, Lily's parents, Kate was almost at her uncle's when a woman wearing a winter coat over a bright orange floral skirt came striding out of her uncle's front door and hopped into her truck. She drove off before Kate could reach her. Was she the angel? Kate went around back, knocked softly, and walked in.

"Uncle Louie, you're sitting up!" Kate was thrilled to see him with a little color in his cheeks.

"Yes, having a good morning. Come sit."

After giving him a hug, Kate pulled over the chair and sat. He smelled fresh and clean and had been expertly shaved.

"Uncle Louie, who was that woman who just left?"

"That was Amber. One of my angels."

"You have more than one?"

"The social worker at the hospital contacted them. Evidently there's a whole group out here helping, well, adorable sick folk like me. I remember you coming in last night. While I'm awake, let's talk." He took a couple of short, quick breaths. "Got my pills in me, I won't last long." He smiled.

Kate took one of his hands in hers. By the light of the day, she could see how his once beautiful brown hair was whitening and very thin. She had to remember to ask him what pills he was taking and what the doctor had said. "I'm sorry I missed Marvin's funeral. I wasn't aware he was that sick, and now you—"

"Tell me what's new at school."

"Can't we talk a little about you? About what's going on? No one's told me anything."

Louie closed his eyes. He took his other hand and put it on top of Kate's. "Maybe that's for the best."

"You, too? Really?" Kate forced herself to calm down. "Has Dad even been over here? Jerome told me how they treated you at the hospital. That's unforgivable."

"Katie, it will all be sorted out in time. Tell me about California, please. I'm hungry for good news."

Kate acquiesced. And immediately thought of Sydney. Before her mother called, she'd been thinking nonstop about that impulsive redhead. If her uncle wanted a break from his present reality, she had a story for him. "So you remember Sydney, the student who took us for our scenic ride?"

"Of course. You later went up to some vineyards with her. You had a great time."

As sick as he was, her uncle wanted to hear, and Kate needed someone to talk to. "We did. And then we went back again to what they called the Russian River area of Sonoma. It was fabulous, Uncle Louie. I think I've found my new crop, not that I don't love your potatoes or Dad's corn. We walked through the most amazing vineyards and tasted lots of wine. Not the wine that was recently pressed. That has to age." She knew she would begin to babble if she didn't watch herself. "I'm not very good at the tasting part, but Sydney is."

"Well, that's good about the trip and Sydney's special skills. Go on, I'm sensing there's more."

He'd done that all her life. Should she? Did she dare? "I think I have a crush on Sydney. No, I take that back. I'm positive I do."

Her uncle smiled. "Good for you."

"Uncle Louie!" Kate felt the warmth of his words sheathe her. She picked up his hand and kissed it.

"I've been waiting for you to tell me this for years. Well, not specifically about Sydney, but someone."

"You have?"

"I remembered you practically giggled every time you told me about one of your adventures with Lily. That was a long time ago."

"I never giggled," Kate protested, but gently squeezed his hand again. He knew.

Uncle Louie started to laugh but that made him cough. "Take it easy on me," he said, his eyes twinkling.

Kate waited. In a few seconds, his cough subsided.

"After Lily died," he continued, "you seemed lifeless. I felt so bad for you. I was glad you got away from here to go to college." He took a breath. "These last couple of years, I kept waiting for you to tell me that you'd met someone. You never did. My heart ached for you because, well, it's really nice to have someone special in your life. Though sometimes people don't make it easy for you when you do." He barely got out the last part.

Like your own brother.

"I'm thrilled for you, really." He smiled broadly but then bent over, coughing violently, sweat pouring from his brow.

Kate jumped up, ran to the kitchen, and brought back a dampened towel. She placed it delicately on his forehead. "Can you lean back and rest?"

He slowly calmed. Kate pulled her chair over and watched him closely.

"Tell me more about Sydney," he whispered.

"You sure you shouldn't rest?"

He shook his head. So, unable to resist, Kate continued. "On the way home from our second vineyard day trip, Sydney proposed we create our own vineyard. Build a winery and make wine. That's ridiculous."

"Well, it's a huge leap from visiting a winery."

"Plus, I have another year of school. And what about Dad's farm? He needs me. It's absurd, really, the whole idea." Kate stood up and walked to the bureau. Should she really be talking about this?

"Go ahead," he gently prodded.

Kate was embarrassed but desperate to figure out what to do. "She's only talking about business, and I, well, I have no idea if she has any feelings for me."

"Ah."

"She's big on saying she's a lesbian," Kate let out, "yet I'm pretty sure she doesn't feel the same way I do about her. Does that not matter?"

"When the time is right, love has a way of outing itself. You'll figure it out." Uncle Louie yawned. "Oh, dear, medicine kicking in."

Kate stood and put her chair back by the wall. She leaned over and kissed her uncle on the cheek. "Shall I bring you dinner?"

"My angels," he said, eyes closed. "One of them stops by every night with a meal. Plus, your mother's been stockpiling casseroles and soups in the fridge. Go on. I'll be fine."

"I'll be back," she whispered, and quietly left him to sleep.

A few minutes later, Kate stood on her uncle's back steps, looking out over his snow-covered potato fields, amazed at the conversation they'd just had, with him so sick. How could her father be so insensitive to his kind and sweet brother? She remembered Lily's brother, Ryan, and how mean he was to her. Kate shoved her hands into her coat pockets, not wanting to remember Ryan's cruelty. Back then she'd been unable to process what Ryan had said and done, so she'd buried it layers deep—like she did with all things she couldn't handle—with ever-increasing amounts of schoolwork. Kate closed her eyes and forced herself to refocus. She looked over toward her parents' house. On the outside, the houses were identical, except the builders had put bigger windows on the second floor of her uncle's house facing his fields. In her parents' house, the bigger windows faced Route 25, the main road through the hamlet of Cutchogue. At one point there had been a fence between the two properties, though it had long ago rotted and been taken down. Kate had no idea how to climb the barrier that now existed between the two houses.

❖

"Is that you, Kate?" her father called from the living room.

Kate stiffened and took a deep breath. "Yes," she answered. She couldn't believe that her father could be so casually calling out to her, sitting in his favorite armchair, no doubt.

"Welcome home, Kate," he said, then joined her in the kitchen, with the newspaper still in his hand. He embraced his daughter, then held her back a foot away. He towered over her. "You look good. Sorry I couldn't meet you at the airport last night. Come sit down." He turned and made his way back into the living room. He clearly expected Kate to follow.

She took a seat on the couch next to his chair, trying to figure out how much courtesy she owed him. Damned if he didn't look like the rugged all-American farmer with the good looks of Rock Hudson. Unusual for a weekday, he wore his favorite blue collared shirt. For her? Other than looking a bit tired, he had not changed. Kate wanted him to look older and guilty in some way. Kate looked around the room. That hadn't changed either, except for her mother's Christmas decorations. Kate breathed in the wonderful scent of the decorated Douglas fir in the corner, then noticed the pile of presents under the bottom boughs. Kate hadn't given a thought to gifts, since she had not planned on coming home. She certainly didn't look forward to the next day's pretense of sharing joy. The TV in the old-fashioned cabinet was the most prominent piece of furniture in the room. Farmers can't do without their weather reports.

"Why didn't you pick me up at the airport, Dad?"

He jerked toward her. "Jerome insisted on going."

"And not because we'd have to talk about Uncle Louie?"

"That's not up for discussion." He turned away. Kate thought he was going to pick up his newspaper.

"You've got to be kidding. How can we not? He's really sick."

The back door opened and shut. They looked at each other.

"You might want to say hello to your mother. She's been waiting all day to see you." This time he did pick up his newspaper.

"Saved by the bell, eh?" Kate said.

❖

Her father sat at his usual place at the head of the table, at the far end of the room. Kate took her regular seat in the middle. Both waited, not saying a word. Her mother waltzed in a moment later. She wore one of her favorite dresses and carried a steaming bowl of succotash, which she set down in front of Kate.

"I doubt you've had as much corn at school as here," she said and smiled. She turned to Kate's father and said, "I'll be back with our roast."

If her father didn't have meat at dinner, he didn't consider it a meal. Normally he would tease her about being a vegetarian, but not tonight.

Bread and butter were already on the table on festive green plates. Her mother loved the holidays, despite all the extra work. "Everything's delicious," Kate told her mother, after they'd taken their first few bites. In another minute her mother would launch into whom she saw at the farm stand and maybe the details of what each person bought. Kate couldn't wait any longer.

"Are we going to talk about Uncle Louie or not?"

"He's being well taken care of," her mother responded.

"What, by strangers? I saw a woman coming out of his house today. Who are these people?" Kate asked.

"They own a little farm, not far from the water. They sell fresh flowers and herbs." Her mother paused. "The social worker at the hospital contacted them when Lou was there. More mashed potatoes, honey?"

Kate ignored her question. "I'm thinking about staying at Uncle Louie's this week so I can help."

"No. You stay here," her father said, looking at her. "We don't know what's wrong with him."

"He's sick, Dad. Do you not care because he's gay?"

"Exactly. He brought this on himself." He put his fork slowly onto his plate. "Who told you?"

"What difference does that make? I worked it out myself. I'm not a child."

"You two, stop," her mother pleaded. "This is not dinner conversation."

"Mom, for heaven's sake, we have to talk about this." Kate put her hands on the table and took a deep breath. "All these years," she said quietly. She looked first at her mother and then over to her father. "You never said anything about Uncle Louie and Marvin."

"It's not something you talk about," her father proclaimed. "I lived with the two of them when I first came out here. I didn't notice anything strange. I thought Marvin was his boss and the two of them went off on weekends to date girls. After your mother and I got married, Louie was back here on Sunday night for dinner, as usual. He never said a word."

"Well, you can see why," Kate pointed out. "Look how you feel."

Her father pushed his chair back from the table, his face getting red. "Two men together is unnatural. I made Louie swear never to say anything to you."

"You made him?"

"I asked him, college girl. Don't get smart with me."

Her mother reached over and put her hand on top of hers. "Like I said, honey, Louie's being well taken care of."

Kate pulled her hand away. She had one more question.

"Are you going over to see your brother?" she asked her father.

"I'll see him at his funeral."

Kate didn't move. She stared at her father. Everyone said she was his spitting image. Same dark, wavy hair, same nose and cheekbones. She saw only the stark differences. "I am very sad to hear that, Dad." Kate stood. "I'll be at Uncle Louie's until I return to school." She turned to her mother. "Thanks for dinner, Mom. Good night."

Neither of her parents said a word. She walked out of the dining room, down the hall and upstairs to her bedroom, absorbing the final shattering of her idyllic family with every step. She managed to make it to her bed, the weight of all they'd never say to each other dragging her down. She'd pushed her father for the truth, his truth, and had gotten it. Now she had to live with his answer. She slowly stood and reached for her empty suitcase.

❖

Her uncle had asked Kate not to help with his physical care, so each morning when Magda or Amber came over to wheel him to the bathroom, to bathe him, and get him dressed, Kate took her coffee and breakfast outside. She wrapped herself in a blanket and waited by the old potato grader, where they measured and bagged the potatoes according to weight. When she returned, she read him the paper and they went through his mail, talked casually about farming or her classes, or some neighborhood news. Anything and everything but his illness. He never once railed against what was happening. Occasionally during that time, Kate would visit with her mother at the farm stand. She didn't ask Kate to come home and Kate didn't ask about her father.

Magda had told Kate that she and Amber were a couple and had been living and working together forever. Their laughter and chatter kept Kate sane and grounded. Amber was the shorter of the two. She always wore something winsome—a scarf, big earrings, or rings. Maybe they were former hippies. Magda was tall and solid, with thick auburn curls. She was always in jeans, casual attire. They were probably in their thirties. "All we can really do is keep him company," Magda whispered to Kate one morning in the kitchen. "His bowels are a mess, his lungs congested. Jerome took him to the doctor a week before you arrived. They said his T cells are extremely low."

"What does that mean?"

"His immune system is basically shot. They have no medicine, nothing they can do. They're giving him pills to calm his bowels, to help him breathe, and to sleep. He has that new disease the men are getting. It's a goddamn mystery." She paused. "It's a shame his own brother is such a selfish prick. Sorry, Kate."

"No apologies needed. Listen, I'm wondering if I should stay here instead of going back to school. I feel so helpless. There must be something I can do. This is breaking my heart."

The two of them looked at each other.

"What?" Kate asked.

"He would hate it if you did that," Magda said. "He adores you. Oh, the stories he's told us. It's made such a difference having you home. But you have to go. He has incredible pride. I'm sure he's only holding on for you."

❖

The last Friday evening of her visit, Kate was sitting with her uncle, holding a textbook she'd brought from school in her lap. She'd read the same page over and over. She'd not seen her father since that dinner and doubted she would before she left.

"Hi, guess I dozed off again," her uncle said, opening his eyes.

"Here, let me help you," Kate said, lifting the pillow higher behind his back. He'd been sleeping fitfully for almost an hour. He'd barely eaten that day, so Kate was hoping she could get him to eat something, anything.

"I'm fine, sweetheart. Let me just catch my breath."

Kate smiled but didn't say anything, wishing as always that there was more she could do. "Shall I read you a bit of today's paper while you settle?"

"No, thanks. Actually, there's something I want to tell you. I've been waiting all week."

Kate looked at him. She could see a small gleam in his eyes.

"I need you to do me a favor."

"Of course. Name it." Kate put her book down immediately.

"Open the top drawer of the dresser over there. You'll see a lock box inside. The key to it is rolled up inside a pair of blue socks in the corner. Open the box and take out the papers, please."

Kate found a sheaf of papers stapled together and took them to her uncle. "Top notch security, eh?"

"You noticed," he said, grinning.

"What is this?"

"Marvin's will. I wanted to talk to you about this before you left. Just listen, okay?" He sat up a little taller. "He signed over the house and the land to me, Kate. I plan to sell both to you for a dollar."

Kate sucked in a breath.

Her uncle held up his hand. "Don't fight this. Yes, this is premature, but I don't have the time to wait. When you leave Sunday, I want you to have options. The decisions are yours alone to make, though I hope you'll only do what makes you happy."

"But Uncle Louie—"

"It's not going to be easy, especially with your father living so close. He's as stubborn as they come, but there's a good heart underneath all that gruffness. You'll see. You must live your own truth, Kate, and your own life. Do whatever you want with this land. It's your choice. That and some savings are my gift to you."

Kate was dumbfounded. "Uncle Louie—"

"Just bring me your dollar tomorrow when Magda and Amber are here. They'll be your witnesses. I'll write up what I need to. A lawyer will do the legal stuff."

"Does Dad know?" Kate managed to get out.

"No. He'll find out in due time. Hey, maybe that redhead will help you."

"Sydney?"

"The very one. But first, you must finish school. You'll be the first in the family to graduate from college. You'll figure out the rest. Now help me off with my robe, will you? I think I'll sleep peacefully tonight."

Kate tucked him in.

"I love you, Uncle Louie."

"And I, you."

Kate was at the door, about to turn out the light and go upstairs, when she paused to wonder yet again if she and Sydney could work together.

"You'll find out soon," her uncle said.

"Find out what, Uncle Louie?"

"Whatever you're worrying about. Good night, my precious."

Kate had to smile. She turned and headed quickly up the stairs before collapsing onto a step, curling into a tight ball. She knew once she went back to school, chances were she'd never see him again. Losing Lily had been devastating. How in the world was she supposed to handle losing Uncle Louie? She tiptoed upstairs, slipped into bed, and pulled the pillow over her head to cover her sobs—something her uncle would not want to hear. *Oh, Uncle Louie. I wish I had half your courage or a quarter of your heart.*

CHAPTER FIVE

March 1983, Berkeley, CA

Sydney was standing in front of her couch rehearsing her class sales pitch—which would count for a third of her grade—when the phone rang. She had placed two pillows on the couch to represent the judges. The goal was to convince Sam Goody stores to carry the new AM/FM Stereo Walkman in all of their outlets. And Sam "Goody" Gutowitz himself was coming to be one of the two judges. Sydney looked at her watch as the phone kept ringing. Who would be calling at four in the afternoon?

"Hello."

"Sydney?"

Sydney's heart stilled as she recognized Kate's voice, no matter how many times she reminded herself that Kate could only be her *business* partner. And not to even think about anything else. "Hey, Kate. How was your spring break?"

Kate didn't answer. Sydney didn't budge, the phone cradled to her ear. "Uncle Louie died," she finally said.

"What? Oh my God. Kate, that's awful." Sydney walked over to the armchair and sat down. Because they talked all the time on the phone, Sydney knew how sick Uncle Louie was. Both had scrambled to find out all they could about AIDS. Even though over a thousand once-healthy men were now dead, Sydney soon realized that the government was loath to get involved, saying it was a local issue. They didn't want to touch anything *gay*. Kate said her uncle seemed to be holding on.

Sydney had hoped Kate would be able to see him once more over her spring break. "What happened?"

"He died the evening before I got home." The last few words came out in a much higher range. Sydney heard the phone booth door squeak open.

"Sorry, needed a little air."

"Oh, Kate. I'm so sorry. How are you holding up?"

"I've only been back an hour. I'm walking around in a daze. I can't seem to get my bearings. Nobody here even knew he existed."

Sydney heard a muffled sound. Kate must have put her hand over the phone.

"Kate, I'm driving up. I'll be there in an hour. Don't move."

Sydney hung up the phone. An hour, give or take a few minutes. It was sixty-two miles from the Berkeley campus to Davis. She grabbed her wallet and keys. Sam Goody could wait.

❖

Kate was waiting in the parking lot when Sydney pulled in. She looked through the open window at Sydney. "You didn't have to drive all the way over here," she said.

Sydney opened the door slowly and Kate backed up. She looked exhausted. Her hair was disheveled, she had on a sweatshirt even though the day was hardly cool.

"You've been traveling all day." Sydney wanted more than anything to hug Kate, but resisted. She settled for words. "I still can't imagine how someone could seem so healthy in September and—"

"Dead six months later? Yep, that's the horrific part." Kate viciously brushed tears from her eyes. "Sorry. I'm a mess."

"Kate, please. I'm amazed you're even standing. Is there someplace we can go to talk?" She put her arm around Kate's shoulder and was relieved when Kate leaned in toward her.

"The Arboretum," Kate said, and let Sydney lead her to the passenger side.

❖

After they had walked through the Arboretum, they found a place in the shade of the Redwood Grove. Once settled, Kate told Sydney how her father had to be talked into attending the funeral, and that he seemed unmoved by the kind words of the rabbi, or by the service itself. "I don't get him at all," she concluded.

Talking seemed to be helping. Kate had finally stretched out her legs.

"I assume the Carmichaels were there, and Magda and Amber, and Jerome. All the people you've been talking about."

"Oh, sure. The room was packed. I was surprised to see a lot of farmers and townspeople. I was sure this disease would have, I don't know, scared them off."

"How so?"

"Fear of catching it? Embarrassment to be around a gay man's family?"

"You really believe that?"

"Yes. But mostly I was so angry, so upset, so mystified by my father's behavior, all I felt was anger. I didn't speak to him, not at the funeral, not all week. That was easier than feeling the pain of losing Uncle Louie."

"Very insightful, Kate."

"Ironically my father also did me a favor." Kate sat up, crossing her legs.

"Really?"

"I'm going ahead with the vineyard idea."

Sydney looked at her wide-eyed, not believing what she'd just heard. A shiver went up her back. Kate had told her that her uncle sold her the house and land, but she assumed she'd do something with it—maybe with her father—way in the future. Once again, she feared she was being left behind.

"My father will not stop me from going ahead with my life. I don't care what he thinks. I decided I care more about honoring Uncle Louie. *He* wanted me to do what was best for me. What would make me happy. So," Kate said, with a grin, "I'm going to plant grapevines this summer. Want to help?"

Sydney put her hands on her knees, willing herself to be calm. "You're going to plant grapevines," she repeated, in a state of shock.

"I started already, sort of. I had to do something. It's not like we were sitting shiva or anything. It was my mother who suggested we get a rabbi for the service. After all these years, neither my father nor uncle talked about their parents or Judaism. The whole thing was weird and sad. After the funeral, I plowed the fields during the day, and I cried my eyes out at night."

"What did your father do, or say about you wanting to plant grapes?"

"He went ballistic, as expected, but after I showed him the papers, he backed off."

"What papers?"

"The legal deeds Uncle Louie had drawn up. We were not talking, so I hadn't told him about Uncle Louie's gift to me. Oh, I also had the soil tested. They're sending me the results."

"You really are going through with it. Planting a vineyard."

"I'd rather have my uncle back."

"Of course."

"So, do you want to help?" she repeated. Kate sat up and leaned toward Sydney.

Sydney's head was spinning. Surely after Kate's graduation, her father expected her to help farm his corn fields. But a vineyard? And was Kate seriously asking her to team up with her? She looked over at Kate, who sat waiting for some answer. "Of course. I thought before and I think now, you're the one to grow grapes. If you need a winemaker, I'm very interested in the job."

Kate beamed. "Good. I'll need all the help I can get. I'm hoping grapes are basically like other crops. I'll read everything I can get my hands on between now and then and, like you said, there are plenty of people here I can talk to."

Sydney wanted to know what grapes Kate planned to put in but decided this was not the time to ask. Besides, she had dozens of other questions, specifically how Kate expected to pay for everything. A few weeks ago, Kate was worrying about paying for the plane ticket home. "Have you thought about how to pay for everything?" From all her classes, she knew how expensive it was to start up a business.

"I thought maybe you could help me with a budget, being the business major and all." She put her hands up in an adorable praying position. "I'm going by gut instinct at the moment. I don't have to buy land or a house. That's huge, right? Uncle Louie also left me some money. I plan to use that to buy the grapevines. I'll get a job, of course. I'm not sure how I'll pay for the equipment. Take out loans like every other farmer." Kate paused, looked off into the grove of trees, then back at Sydney. "The truth is, I'm scared shitless."

"Don't worry. We'll figure this out together." Sydney doubted her father's generosity would go so far as to float her a buy-in. Wait, what was she thinking? What about the other issue? "We're still talking business partners, right?"

"You've made that perfectly clear. Yes." Kate stood. "You don't do relationships, I know. I am asking if you want to help with this *business*. I thought about it, believe me. You better have a damn good business plan to sell all that wine you're going to make." Her eyes, from Sydney's vantage point, were sparkling.

Sydney let her finish speaking, then stood. "Fabulous," she said, staring into eyes she'd once fantasized about another way. But this was for the best. "Kate, the women I've dated, the Sams of the world, they've been inconsequential relationships. We're much more than that. What we're doing is important. This is the way I can be there for you."

Kate looked at her, her expression flat. "I'm suddenly exhausted. Shall we go?"

"Yeah, sure." Something she'd said was wrong, but what? Did Kate need more of a commitment? Then it dawned on her. Maybe there was a way she could show her how serious she was. And start to get her parents' approval.

"I have an idea," she said, as they walked back to the parking lot. "Come to my graduation in May. It's only an hour's drive. It's a big fucking deal at Berkeley. So fancy that my parents are flying out for it. Let me introduce you and tell them about the vineyard idea. This will be the perfect time." Sydney could tell by looking over at Kate that she was listening. "You always knew you wanted to farm. My parents have tried to mold me toward a career they think best for me. Since grade school, they've tried to control every aspect of my life—my friends, my activities, even my clothes."

"Sounds like they just care about you."

"I wish. They care about their image and what *they* think would be best for me."

"You want me to run interference with your parents?"

Once again, Kate didn't miss a trick. "No, not at all. I had planned to tell them that I was going to look for a job out here, and that I wanted to learn how to make wine. They've always backed me financially, but with unspoken stipulations. Now is the time for me to stand up for what I want to do. Just like you did."

Kate raised an eyebrow but that was about all. Sydney waited until they were back in her car to continue. "One of my brothers, Rusty, is going to be there. He's usually the peacemaker in the family. Oh, and my best friend, MJ, is coming. In high school we promised we'd be at each other's college graduation." Sydney's heart was pumping like mad. "This is not totally irrational, is it?"

"I don't know—"

"But you'll think about it?"

"I guess. You graduate in May, you said? I have a month or so."

Perfect. She was going to think about it. She hadn't said no. Leaving the car in the lot, Sydney walked Kate back to the dorm, promising to call in a few days.

After negotiating Kate's offer, dealing with the Walkman sales pitch would be a piece of cake. Convincing her parents that she wanted to make wine? That was a whole different matter.

Chapter Six

May 1983, Berkeley, CA

Sydney and her father were seated on the fancy red cushions her mother brought to pad the cold steps of the amphitheater, where family and guests sat to watch the graduation. Sydney was trying her best not to fidget, wanting to savor the time alone with her father. He looked around the immense stone amphitheater, then back at her. "We're so proud of you," he said, putting his hand on top of hers. "And how wonderful that the business majors get to graduate in the William Randolph Hearst Greek Theater," he continued, pronouncing each word of the name slowly and distinctly.

"Randolph knew where to donate his money," Sydney told her father, having learned from him that the biggest donors get the biggest buildings named in their honor. Her father was genuinely proud of her degree, and she wanted to talk to him about this, or anything, but her mind was elsewhere. Had it been smart of her to give Kate's phone number to MJ? MJ had arranged to give Kate a ride, so where were they?

"Wait until you hear what we're giving you for graduation," he said, a gleam in his eye. "Oh, sorry. Just remembered, I promised your mother I wouldn't tell you." He smiled affectionately.

"Dad, four years of college was my gift." She did know how fortunate she was.

"Your mother insisted—"

"Mom, always Mom." Sydney took a deep breath. "Sorry, I'm a little nervous." Sydney reminded herself to be patient, and that her parents would be heading home right after the luncheon. "Where is she, anyway? I have to get in line."

Sydney turned around and looked over the growing crowd. Her mother had insisted they be the first ones in that morning. She, no doubt, was out front having a cigarette and had dragged Rusty to escort her. Her mother was rarely without some man nearby to admire her or do her bidding. As soon as the crowd was at its maximum, she would make her grand entrance.

"Dad, do you mind if I go look for everyone?" Sydney asked, rising. She pulled her arms out from her gown and leaned down to hug her father. He had always tried to be supportive. His number one priority, however, was and always would be first his work, and then his wife. The kids got the leftovers.

"Go on. I'll see you after the ceremony." He picked up the program and waved it.

Sydney scooted down the aisle and out front where the crowds were gathering. Standing on her tiptoes, she scanned the press of folks entering to look for MJ and Kate. Everything was in place. She had Kate's permission to help her plant the first grapevines. In fact, on Monday of the second week in April, Kate had called to ask Sydney if she wanted to help her pick out the vines. That was another turning point in their relationship. They subsequently began to talk for hours on the phone, late into the night, about the pros and cons of each of the varietals, how many to plant, what the market would bear, what type of wine each would produce. Sydney reveled in these discussions. After they planted the vineyard, Sydney would have to get a job. They would have enormous expenses their first few years, but they were forging ahead with their shared dream. She continued to push through the crowd.

Rusty tapped her on the shoulder. "Looking for me?"

Sydney burst into an instant smile, recognizing her favorite brother who always found a way to be at all her special occasions, even when they were kids. Her oldest brother, John Thomas Jr.—affectionately called JT—was working in London. Seven years older, a workaholic, like their father, he'd sent his regrets and a check.

"Of course I am." Sydney gave him a hug. "You and those two friends of mine who should be here by now."

"Would one of them be the tall, brown-haired beauty you keep babbling about on the phone?"

"Rusty! I don't babble. I merely mentioned—"

"Every time we talked."

"She and I have wine in common."

"Yeah, yeah."

Sydney gently shoved her brother. His red hair made him easy to pick out in a crowd. Rusty was big and broad shouldered, just an inch or two taller than Sydney. He was in his third year of a veterinary residency. With the weight he'd put on, it looked like he might be a bit overwhelmed with all his animal care studies. Rusty once prided himself on keeping fit. Now he could barely button his favorite blue suit.

"Where's Mom? Any chance you ditched her?" Sydney asked.

Rusty laughed. "She cornered the chancellor and gave him tips about the entrance to the Campanile."

"The most iconic structure on the whole campus? She's giving *him* advice about it, her first time on campus?"

Rusty shrugged his shoulders.

Sydney glanced over and noticed Kate and MJ walking down the ramp. Kate was wearing a beautiful, tailored navy suit and pearls. The jewelry was a nice touch. Her mother would be impressed. But just then Kate walked out of one heel and tripped. MJ caught her, putting her arm quickly around her waist. Damn, Sydney wished she'd been there.

"Sydney, go," Rusty told her.

"What?" She looked up at her brother.

"I thought you'd want to be the one walking her down the aisle."

"Very funny. That's a ramp and she can walk on her own." They both stood and waited while they approached. When MJ noticed Rusty, she hurried her pace.

"Rusty!" she called and the two of them embraced. MJ, as Sydney's best friend growing up, had spent an enormous amount of time in Rusty's company. They had always been fond of each other. "Long time no see."

Which left Sydney a few seconds alone with Kate.

"You look nice," Sydney managed, wanting to freeze this moment and simply stare at Kate. She had really come. And she looked gorgeous.

Had she done all this to make a good first impression on her family? That's what Sydney would have done.

"Hi, you must be Kate," her brother interrupted. "I'm Rusty. Nice to meet you." He turned to Sydney and held up his watch.

"Oh my God," Sydney exclaimed. "I have to run. See you all at the reception." She took in the sight of the three of them standing together for another second, and then rushed to leave. She would have to miss the dramatic introduction of Kate to her parents. A lot was going to ride on Rusty's diplomacy. Sydney had started telling them at breakfast about their vineyard visits, and even at that, her mother rolled her eyes. Her mother never really cared for MJ, either, so the possibilities for drama were plentiful. Hopefully the ceremony and speakers would be their common bond.

❖

"Slow down, Sydney!" her mother ordered. "Are you trying to get us killed?" Because Rusty had gallantly offered the front seat to his mother, Sydney could literally breathe in her displeasure. They were on their way to the private luncheon her mother had arranged by phone from Massachusetts.

"Yes, Mother." Sydney gritted her teeth and released the gas pedal. Maybe she could just push her out the door? Her mother was driving her nuts with her negative chatter. At least she had the satisfaction of seeing that her impeccably dressed mother was having her outfit rumpled, squished into the tiny seat next to her. She checked the rearview mirror for the tenth time to make sure she could see MJ's rental.

"The speeches were nice, but this new friend of yours? She barely said a word."

Sydney glanced at her mother. "What kind of judgmental, insensitive questions were you grilling her with?" she asked, regretting her words as soon as they were out of her mouth. She knew better than to be pulled into her mother's vortex. Neither sarcasm nor anger ever helped and only fueled whatever conversation they were in. Alas, she knew no other way to react to her mother. They'd been at each other like this for as long as she could remember.

"She was sitting right next to me. I asked her about her family, that's all. She said her father grew corn."

Sydney could feel Rusty's eyes on her. She knew he would tell her not to provoke their mother. As the middle child, he excelled in his job as family mediator.

"And now she's studying agriculture, for God's sakes," her mother continued. "Agronomy, or something. Is she going to raise pigs?"

"Not pigs, Mother. She's going to grow grapes. Kate has land and is going to create a vineyard. Agronomy, by the way, is the science and economics of crop production. In fact I want to help her. I—"

"Crops," her mother said disdainfully, cutting her off. "After four years of this very expensive business education, surely you're not considering digging your hands in the dirt and planting *crops*?"

Sydney held her tongue on that subject. "MJ was there, too, Mom. How was your visit with her?" Her mother was such a snob. MJ's mother, a single parent, had worked in the school system as a psychologist. If she had her own practice, leather chairs and a secretary, that would have been acceptable. But to work every day in the same building with the kids? No way.

"Actually, I was quite impressed with Marguerite. She likes to be called by her full name now. She says she wants to run her own hotel one day. She's been studying hospitality or some such nonsense. But at least her profession makes sense to me."

"The hotel business is an honorable one, dear," her father finally chimed in.

"And look, there's the San Francisco skyline," Rusty said, as they drove onto the Bay Bridge. Everyone looked out the window. In the silence several seconds later, Rusty continued. "By the way, Mom, how did you manage to pick a restaurant way out here from three thousand miles away?"

Sydney knew her brother was using the oldest trick in their sibling arsenal: divert their mother's attention from what was going on and get her to talk about something impressive that she alone had accomplished.

"Well, let me tell you I had a lot of choices," she told them. "But I think I made a very good decision, as you'll soon see."

❖

Twenty minutes later they parked near the restaurant in the Jackson Square neighborhood, not too far from where Kate and Sydney had first met. Rusty and her parents made a beeline for the entrance. Sydney told them she'd wait outside for Kate and MJ. Hopefully, that would give her mother just time enough to order and imbibe her first cocktail. She'd be in a much better mood after that.

Two minutes later, MJ drove up in her rental. Sydney rushed over and stood patiently on the sidewalk, waiting for them to jump out of the car.

MJ popped right out and rushed over to greet Sydney. Kate, for her part, pushed the door open and waved, but then leaned down to grab something from the floorboard.

"Heels," she said, holding up the pumps. "They might as well be stilettos." She put the matching navy shoes on the ground and stepped into them. "Ouch. How and why do women wear these?"

"Thanks for making such an effort, Kate." Sydney put out a hand to steady her, her own emotions frolicking between admiration and gratitude. "I really appreciate you both coming," she quickly added, looking from one to the other.

"You have no idea how hard you will be working in less than a month. Enjoy standing up straight." Kate smiled at her.

"So, is it true you're really going to help plant grapes?" MJ asked.

"I'm going to tell everyone at lunch," Sydney said. She felt a little freaked out. "Shall we?" She pointed to the restaurant door. "First one in gets to sit next to Rusty."

They rushed the door.

❖

Her mother had impeccable taste and had ordered a fabulous meal. "Befitting the wonderful occasion of my daughter's graduation," she told them all. Thanks to her cocktails and the flowing champagne, there was no notable drama and everyone chatted amicably.

Sydney stood, raised her glass, and thanked them all for coming. She made a point of smiling at her mother, telling her how much she appreciated the exceptional luncheon. "I have some exciting news to share with you. It was only recently that I realized what I wanted to do with my fancy degree." She looked around the table, ending with Kate. Then back to the others, she concluded, "Kate and I have decided to create a vineyard and make wine. I'm driving to Long Island in June. We'll plant our first vines then," she said proudly.

"John, did you want to butt in here?" her mother said, looking over at her father.

Her father nodded. Disappointed that she didn't get to say more, Sydney slowly sat back down as her father confidently stood. "Well, it is a father's prerogative to speak at his daughter's graduation. I believe we have a surprise that will change your mind."

Change her mind? Sydney looked at her father, sporting horn-rimmed glasses and an Armani suit. He looked ever the successful businessman. But surely he wasn't about to crush his daughter's dream. Her stomach tightened. Two waiters entered at that moment, bearing trays. Her father held up his hand, motioning them to hold on for a minute. "Your mother and I have a gift for you." He looked at Sydney, all smiles. He walked over and stood next to his wife. Sydney looked over at Rusty. He shrugged.

"You hadn't mentioned what you wanted to do after you graduated, so I lined up a job for you in our Paris office. It's very light work, mostly socializing, and you'll have the run of Paris."

Sydney put her hands on the table, unable to believe this unsolicited, unwanted, and as far as she was concerned, frivolous offer. "You what?" she blurted out.

"Hold on, there's more," he said. He seemed to have misunderstood her tone. "Your mother has gone ahead and rented you a furnished apartment. You'll lack for nothing." He beamed, thinking he had presented the best news ever.

Sydney stood. "But I don't want this. You didn't even consult me."

"But you love Paris," he said. He looked confused.

Her parents had to have been working on this for a long time. "Did you not hear me? I have my own plans," Sydney said. She didn't dare look over at Kate. "But thank you. It was a lovely thought." She dropped down into her seat, her hands shaking.

Her mother blew out smoke and waved her hand in the air. "Don't be ridiculous, how could you possibly give up a job in Paris?"

Sydney looked at her mother, noticing she needed to reapply her lipstick. She hated that both she and Rusty got their red hair from her. Her mother had been told her whole life that she resembled Maureen

O'Hara. She liked that, and she went by the name Mikki, as a nod to the famous Irish American actress. Her mother sold fancy real estate along Boston's former Gold Coast, but what she longed for, Sydney had heard her confess many times, was a mansion in Paris and a summer home in Saint-Tropez. She had presumed her daughter would want the same.

"Well, what do you say?" Her father's deep voice commanded her attention. "This is better, right?"

"You should have talked to me first," Sydney spat, staring at her mother.

"Why?" her mother asked, picking up her drink and holding it in mid-air. "How could anyone pass up this opportunity? It's all arranged."

Sydney heard a chair scrape. Her parents were sitting at either end of the table. Kate sat directly across from her, MJ next to her. Kate stood but then leaned over to whisper something to MJ. MJ placed keys in her hand.

"Excuse me," Kate said vaguely in the direction of her mother, then walked toward the door, as fast as she could manage.

"I'll be right back," Sydney announced and rushed after her.

"That girl's trouble!" her mother's voice rang out.

Sydney kept going.

At the door, Kate took off her heels and sprinted toward the parking lot.

"Kate, wait!"

Sydney caught up with her at the car. Refusing to turn around, Kate opened the side door, reached in for her sneakers and put them on.

"Look, I'm embarrassed to be leaving like this, but I can't stay," she said, standing next to Sydney. "You were right to invite me. I have a better idea who your parents are. I doubt you'll be able to refuse their gift." Kate pivoted away from Sydney, carefully taking off the necklace. "MJ lent me these," she said, handing Sydney the pearls. "Please return them. I've had it with everyone's borrowed clothes. Do you have any idea how hard it was for me to find someone both tall and fashionable? I even bought pantyhose." Kate took a prolonged breath. "MJ will need these." Kate handed Sydney the car keys.

"Kate, please. I had no idea they were going to do this."

Kate slumped. "Does it matter?"

"I want to plant our vines," Sydney persisted, wanting frightfully to take hold of Kate's arms so she'd look her in the eyes. "You've got to believe me. I'll be there in June."

Kate finally looked at her. "Go enjoy your party. Congratulations on your graduation. Say goodbye to your family and tell MJ something came up." She did an about-face and rushed off.

Sydney stood there, dazed. She watched as Kate strode down the street, presumably heading toward public transportation to return to Davis. When she was well out of sight, Sydney looked at the restaurant, sighed, and headed back inside. She knew her mother was behind the job offer. How was it that she had never been able to stand up to her mother? Worse, her mother always made her feel that *she* was wrong. What a mess. What a stupid, needless, goddamn mess.

Chapter Seven

June 1983, Cutchogue, Long Island

Kate obsessed the whole flight home over whether or not Sydney would be there to help her plant. After the graduation disaster, Sydney left two messages at her dorm asking her to call. Kate didn't return either. She wanted to have more faith in Sydney—who'd always done what she said she would do up until now—but after meeting her parents, she doubted Sydney could stand up to their will. Who could? Kate tried to calm her mind by reading, but nothing was sticking. Finally she realized this was not just about Sydney coming to help plant the vines, this was about losing Sydney. She'd lost Lily before they'd had a chance at a life together, or to even realize what their feelings meant. Losing Sydney, even as a business partner and friend, would be devastating.

❖

Jerome met her at the airport, truck keys in hand. "Might as well give them to you now," he said, holding out the keys. "I know you want to drive."

Kate chuckled, grabbing the keys. "You bet. Thanks."

"Let's get on home. The highway's packed already."

The fact that Jerome was her ride told her that her father was still angry and upset that she'd accepted his brother's gift. She had the additional audacity to go ahead and till the land next to his—to grow grapes instead of more corn or potatoes. Would they not speak the entire summer? As soon as she turned onto the expressway and headed east toward Cutchogue, Jerome told her that a gigantic load of posts had been delivered the day before and stacked in front of her uncle's house.

"Did Dad see them make the delivery?" Kate asked.

"Oh, yeah. Couldn't miss those flatbeds rolling up the driveway."

"How are you doing? He's talking to you, I hope."

"Me? Of course. I did a lot of work for him this spring. Every machine's humming and the corn's all planted. Without Louie's fields to work I, uh, had a lot more time."

"But you also have less income. I have no money to pay you for helping me this summer. You'll continue to live rent free, of course. Since my uncle's property is mine, that goes without saying."

"Thanks. After we get the vines planted, I can get another job if I want to. Listen, Kate, I have an early graduation gift for you. Your mom and I worked out the details. Your dad grunted his approval."

"What is it?" Kate asked. She was eager for fun news.

"That old outbuilding where we kept the tractors? I've been doing a little remodeling. I started on it the day you first left for college. When your uncle got sick, I sped up the work. I thought you'd want to get out of your parents' house."

"I do, but how did you know?" Silly question. Jerome probably knew she was not ready to move into Uncle Louie's house.

"Katie, I know what your uncle meant to you. I'd have to have been blind or deaf not to see how your father treated him after he got sick. I'll leave it at that."

Kate didn't know what to say, so she opted for gratitude. "Jerome Morse, if I weren't driving, I'd give you the biggest hug. That's the best news ever!" It was all she could do to keep her eyes on the road.

"Good thing you are driving. You nearly knocked me over with your airport hello."

"Oops." Kate grinned.

"I also have to tell you another kind of car was parked in the driveway this morning. I was leaving to pick you up when I saw it. A red BMW."

Kate tried to swallow, her mouth suddenly dry as a bone.

"Since I knew neither of your parents were home, I pulled in to see who it was."

Kate's heart pole vaulted. It could only be one person. "Does the driver have red hair?"

"Yes. Said she was there to help you plant grapevines."

"Oh, God."

"Oh, God good or oh, God bad?"

"Not sure." Kate gripped the wheel. She'd find out soon enough.

❖

Kate saw Sydney jump up when the truck pulled in. She dusted off her slacks from where she'd been sitting on the ground and gathered up a thermos and something in a shiny wrap.

"You going to get out of the truck or what?" Jerome asked.

Kate didn't answer. When Jerome opened his door and headed toward Sydney, Kate sighed and followed.

"Hi, I'm Sydney. You must be Jerome. We weren't properly introduced before." Sydney held out her hand to Jerome and he grabbed it. Then she turned to Kate. "Here I am. Put me to work." Her face was one big smile.

They were interrupted by the sound of an approaching tractor. The three of them turned and watched it draw near.

"Kate, you behave now," Jerome told her.

The tractor came to a halt and her father jumped down. Seeing the car and then the stranger, he seemed to hesitate. "I heard the truck pull in, but I didn't expect a whole gathering. Kate, Jerome." He nodded to both of them. They waited for him to continue. "Kate, your mother would like you to come over to the stand. There, you see, we're talking." He looked like he was going to say more, but then he looked again at Sydney, and turned to go.

"Wait, Dad, this is my friend, Sydney. She's here to help me plant the new vines."

He paused, took a deep breath and then turned around. "Just what we need, more females around here. Where's she staying?" he asked. Kate had not expected such overt rudeness. Was he thinking about Louie's angels, Magda and Amber, or strangers in general?

"At Uncle Louie's," Kate answered, without stopping to think or decide.

"Well, then, I guess both of you should come to dinner."

Kate might have been more upset had he not looked so pitifully uncomfortable. She almost felt sorry for him.

"We'll be there, Dad. Thanks for the message." And then she rushed over and embraced him before he could back up or protest. "I'm glad we're talking."

"Ha," he muttered, then hopped back on the tractor without another word.

Kate, Sydney, and Jerome all looked at each other. Kate shrugged.

"Let me give you a quick tour of your new abode, Kate," Jerome said, "then I'm going home."

"I'll wait for you here," Sydney told her.

Kate walked with Jerome down the path between the two farmhouses. She remembered the old tractor and tool shed, once shared by her father and uncle—and luckily on her uncle's property. It was a 400-square-foot outbuilding, nothing remarkable. But as Jerome stood back, and let Kate open the door, Kate's mouth dropped. Jerome had put in a new floor, replastered the walls, added a sink, fridge, and stove, and put in a small bathroom.

"Good heavens. Is this really for me?"

"We got you a bed, but we still need to find a table and chair. I'll have any finishing touches done by next year."

This time Kate's hug almost toppled him for sure. "Thank you."

"Come on now, your friend's waiting." He was out the door before Kate could continue. Kate rushed to catch up to him. At the head of the path, Sydney stood looking out onto the empty fields. "Nice to meet you, Sydney," Jerome told her. "I'll be back first thing tomorrow, Kate."

"Thanks for picking me up," Kate called to Jerome, watching him walk off.

"So, finally it's just us," Sydney said. "I'm so excited to be here. Will you show me around?"

"How did you figure out when I'd arrive?" Kate asked, her heart pounding, despite herself. *Stick to the facts. Facts are your friends. Facts never lie or change their minds.* "Or what day?"

"I can do harder questions than that. Come on, Kate, aren't you a little glad I'm here?"

Kate stood there. That one she didn't dare answer. "I didn't give you my itinerary, so I am curious. Plus my dad is not exactly thrilled you're here."

"So I gathered." Sydney fiddled with her thermos. "As to your questions—I called Davis to find out the last day of class. Then I called the airlines. I figured you'd take the first flight out and calculated your arrival time here from JFK. Kate, you're all tightly wrapped. Can you let go a little? I, for one, am really glad to be here."

"How long are you staying?" Kate asked, trying to keep her tone light.

Sydney seemed startled.

"A week? A month?" Kate pressed.

"Until everything is planted, Kate. I won't leave before then."

"What happened to Paris?"

"Wow, I forgot how direct you can be." Sydney wiped her brow and switched her thermos from one hand to the other. "The trip's been postponed. I made a deal with my parents, okay? I told them over and over about our plans, how I wanted to make wine. They refused to take me or our plans seriously. It wasn't a pretty scene at the restaurant, as you can imagine, and the conversation continued once they got back home." Sydney started fidgeting. "This is the hard part to admit. They told me they'd end all their financial support if I kept on with this vineyard idea. I'll spare you their exact words—but I'm not ready to begin my life, well, destitute."

Kate let out a stifled laugh. "It wouldn't be that bad. I'd feed you peanut butter and jelly sandwiches. And Mom's making us dinner tonight. So you'd start out with one good meal." Sydney had been honest. That was good. "Mind if we go say hello to her? Then we'll get you settled. If you still want to stay, that is."

"Of course I do." Sydney let out her own laugh. "I can't wait to meet your mother." They walked side by side down the driveway, turned right onto Main Road, and walked the short distance to her mother's farm stand.

"Hey, look at your mother's sign," Sydney exclaimed. "Great marketing idea."

Kate smiled, feeling the tension lessen. Her mother had named her stand Cornucopia, a play on her father's produce and her mother's sense of abundance. The horn-shaped container on the sign spilled baked goods of all sorts, instead of produce. Her stand was indeed both successful and renowned in Cutchogue and the surrounding area.

Kate's mother, Rachel, was standing out front talking to a

customer. When she looked up and spotted Kate, she let out a tiny cry and rushed over to hug her daughter.

"Are you Sydney?" she asked, holding her arms out. "Kate said on the phone way back in April that you had distinctive hair and that you might be coming to help. Welcome."

Sydney accepted the affection, then looked around. "Kate's been bragging about your baked goods. I can see why. Everything looks delicious."

"You help yourself to anything you want," Rachel said. Two cars pulled into the tiny parking lot. "Kate will take care of you. Gotta go. Come to dinner!" She turned to greet the customers walking up.

Sydney made a show of looking at every single shelf. Kate waited impatiently. Finally, Sydney picked out an oversized peanut butter cookie. She handed it to Kate. "Miss, how much is this? That nice woman said you'd take care of me."

"Very funny. Shall we go?"

At her car, Sydney pulled out a leather duffel bag from her trunk. Kate waited, looking up at her uncle's house. She couldn't believe he wasn't going to be inside. How was she supposed to go on without him?

"You okay to go back to your uncle's house?" Sydney asked.

"Not really, but thanks for asking." Kate appreciated her sensitivity. It was true she hadn't been back inside Uncle Louie's house since his death. She had hoped to put that off as long as possible. Her mother had promised to take care of his personal things. She knew that Jerome had put the bedroom furniture back upstairs and replaced what little living room furniture remained.

"I didn't think I needed much in the way of clothes," Sydney said, hoisting the bag over her shoulder, and breaking Kate's train of thought.

They were standing in the driveway between the two farmhouses. Kate looked at the small bag, remembering Sydney's penchant for fancy clothes. "You're right about that. You'll be working hard." Not going to bars, not that there were any. Well, none that she knew about. "I didn't ask you if you minded staying here? The house is practically empty."

"I'd be honored."

They walked toward her uncle's house. Kate had to believe her uncle would be thrilled that Sydney was here. And truth be told, she was pretty excited herself. Sydney was walking right next to her, talking enthusiastically. Here for the duration of the planting season. Her most basic wish had come true. She'd take it.

Sydney stopped. "Could you give me a minute to take this all in? I couldn't tell a lot from the expressway but driving out here to the North Fork—that's what it's called, right?"

Kate nodded, with another smile.

"Well, it's gorgeous country." She looked out over the two properties. "It's like the map you drew for me, but even better because this is the real thing." Sydney looked out over the two fields, the rows of corn marking the end of her father's property. "Your parents' house and yours," Sydney said, pointing first to her parents' and then to Uncle Louie's. "And that building over there," she said, pointing to the old potato grader a few hundred feet away, "that's where Marvin and your uncle sorted the potatoes and put them into bags, right?" Without waiting for an answer, she continued. "The building you said we could renovate into our winery."

"That's jumping way ahead."

"And I see our fields have been plowed. How rich the soil looks. This is real farmland. I am so excited."

Kate appreciated her enthusiasm. Most people, if they thought of Long Island at all, thought of it as one of America's first suburbs, where folks commuted from their homes into Manhattan. Or they heard people talk about the Hamptons, the fashionable beach playground on the South Fork. Or worse still, they thought of it as too cold and inhospitable to grow anything. Kate knew that Native American tribes had a long history of successful farming for hundreds of years before the Europeans arrived. Louisa and Alex Hargrave, who created the first vineyard, did their research and found out the North Fork, despite its fickle maritime weather, had sandy loam soils, good drainage, and all the nutrients needed to grow vinifera grapes. The Hargraves were thrilled to find out that Cutchogue, where they planted their first grapes, had the same amount of necessary sun during the growing season as California, and the same amount of rainfall as Bordeaux, whose wines they wanted to emulate.

Kate climbed her uncle's back steps. "Anytime you're ready," she said.

Sydney took one last look around, then joined her on the steps.

Kate pushed the door open, bracing herself. "My mother said there are clean sheets. Do you want me to show you around?"

"I need a bedroom and bathroom. I'll be fine. I'll see you at dinner. Six, right?"

"Exactly." Kate walked back toward the truck to get her bags, stifling a giggle. Dinner at six, eh? As if it were a normal thing to be coming from her own place to meet up with Sydney to have dinner with her parents. Kate would have skipped, had she been sure no one was looking. She settled for a huge grin. Facts be damned. Sydney was here and she was tickled pink.

❖

"So, Sydney, Kate tells me you've graduated. How does that feel?" Her mother served her father and Sydney a generous portion of pasta with meatballs. "Kate will be our first graduate. Zeke, as I affectionately call this big guy, and I decided to farm right out of high school."

"Good question. Let me first try this while it's hot," Sydney said, smiling at Rachel. "This is delicious." She dug back in for a second bite.

Kate knew Sydney was stalling, trying to figure out what to say. Everyone continued to eat in silence, waiting for Sydney to answer.

"To tell you the truth, sometimes I do feel all grown-up, but tonight, on the eve of starting our new venture, I'm feeling a bit anxious. I think working here will be more valuable than my formal education."

"You better believe it," her father said, surprising them. "There is nothing like hands-on experience. That's the way you learn."

"That's why I'm thrilled to be working here, Mr. Bauer, and working with Kate. You two are the real farmers. Hopefully my skills will be handy later." She smiled at Kate's parents.

Good for Sydney to be flattering everyone and trying to get her father to loosen up. Kate gave her a smile. "Well, Dad taught me how to farm. I was riding with him on a tractor in grade school."

"You said it. Farm kids work." Kate's father looked directly at her for the first time since she'd arrived. "Your mother used to tell me to let you play, but you never wanted to."

"Farming was fun, Dad."

"Yeah, was for me, too, until the senseless economy fell apart. Now—"

"Green beans?" Rachel held up the bowl.

After another long silence, Rachel asked Sydney about her family and where she'd grown up. The two of them kept up a conversation that lasted the rest of dinner. Rachel served her homemade strawberry shortcake for dessert.

No one mentioned that shortcake was Uncle Louie's favorite dessert. In fact, his name was not mentioned once the whole evening. It was as if he never existed. Even the special chair where he liked to sit at the table had been taken away. But Kate remembered. She savored the shortcake, every single mouthful.

❖

After dinner Sydney went right into the kitchen to help her mother with the dishes, which left Kate and her father sitting alone. He put his napkin on the table like he intended to leave.

"Dad, wait, we have to talk."

"No, we don't. You're doing what you want to do. I saw all those posts. You'll be of no help to me this summer."

"That's not true. I'll help you as much as I can. You became a farmer against your father's wishes. At least I'm still farming, just a different crop. Can't you be a little happy for me?"

"You've gotta be kidding. Maybe my brother thought he was being generous, but I say it was a stupid thing he did. Giving you all this land and encouraging you to start a new crop at this time. That's plain wrong. Have you looked around? Everyone's going under. If we hadn't been given this house, I wouldn't be able to pay the mortgage."

"Times are bad, Dad, I get that. You taught me to be careful, be practical, and work hard. Maybe it's time to look toward the future. Grapes may be the best thing to happen out here. We're not the first."

Her father pushed his chair back and stood. "You think so? Well, go ahead then, plant something you can't sell. But don't come to me to bail you out. I have work to do in the barn." He took two steps, then stopped and looked back at her. "Look, I'm glad you're home. I mean that. I was going to try to deal with all this grape business, but bringing someone else here?" He looked straight at Kate. "I saw the way she was looking at you. Don't you end up like Louie!"

Good Lord. From out of nowhere. Kate froze and waited for her father to leave the room. He clearly meant gay. Kate backed up against a wall to brace herself. But if being gay was the deal breaker, it was too late. She was pretty sure she was not going to change her feelings for Sydney—or even women in general. Did this mean that their father-daughter relationship no longer mattered? He had cut off his brother. Would he now do the same with her? Was this the price of loving someone? Kate felt utterly worn out, exhausted, and sad. It was going to be a very long summer.

❖

Sydney showed up in pristine jeans and an ABBA T-shirt. She radiated energy. Kate faced both Jerome and Sydney. She wished she could share Sydney's exhilaration. She was a nervous wreck. "Just as a reminder, the rows will be eight feet apart. We want to make sure the vines have access to plenty of sunshine since we're not going to be spraying them with pesticides. Plus, we need to have room to drive a tractor between the rows. See this stake here and the one there and all along this row?" Kate asked, pointing. She'd gotten up at first light that morning and inserted over two dozen. "We'll plant the vines exactly to the right of these poles, five feet between each plant. The measuring has to be exact. We're going to put the posts in first. Jerome's friend will be here any minute with a borrowed post pounder."

"Not to worry, boss. We'll do everything right," Sydney said.

"But I didn't even explain what we had to do yet," Kate countered.

"Yeah, I know, but you've got your worried face on. Just wanted to reassure you."

Jerome nudged her. "Shh. Kate was trying to say that the post pounder is a big metal instrument that pounds the posts into the ground, two feet deep. Even if we could do it ourselves, we need to save our strength to put in the plants. My friend, Hammer, is going to do the post work with us."

"Hammer?"

"You'll see how he got that name," Jerome said. "He's strong as an ox. He's doing the work for free to honor Louie's memory. Louie was kind to a lot of people around here. All Kate had to do was rent the machine."

"That must be Hammer now," Kate said, hearing the rumble of the truck. They watched the flatbed approach the edge of the field. He unloaded the tractor with the post-driver already attached.

"That's impressive," Sydney said. Jerome introduced Hammer to Kate and Sydney.

They brought over the first pole and Hammer positioned it into the holder. Hammer started up the machine and grabbed the handles. The three of them watched and cheered as the machine pounded the first post into the ground. "Jerome will use a smaller machine to dig the mid-posts," Kate explained to Sydney. "I thought you and I would be the post carriers. And we'll need to measure the distances between both the vines and the rows."

"Of course. I'm all yours."

Kate looked at Sydney. If only.

❖

By four, Kate had blisters on both thumbs and was sweating massively. Sydney had not once complained. They were on a quick break, downing water by the gallon. It took an effort to straighten out her spine. Sydney tapped her on the shoulder.

"When did you say they were delivering the vines?"

"Tomorrow."

"Tomorrow? We'll never be done by then."

"Not to worry. They're dormant vines. They need a week in the shade to acclimate. But then we must get them in the ground. We're already at risk for planting too late." Kate shuddered. She knew how lucky they were to have had only warm weather, but not sweltering heat. And no pouring rain. Every farmer knew firsthand that nature was the final arbiter. "Besides, Hammer told me he'd be done by the end of the week."

"Remind me how many acres we're going to plant, Kate?" Sydney asked.

"Seven. Uncle Louie left me sixty-five acres altogether, but

I thought it best to start small, considering start-up costs and future expenses." She was actually terrified about the expenses but now was hardly the time to talk about it, especially considering these two folks were donating their labor.

"Thank goodness," Sydney said. "As it is, I need a new back. Inexperienced city girl here."

Kate laughed.

❖

Four days later, true to Hammer's word, the posts were in.

"My mother invited us to come over to the house for dinner," Kate said.

Sydney smiled. "Thanks, but no. I can't wait to get in the shower. I may just spend the night there, letting the water run over my shoulders and back."

Kate laughed. "Amen to that." And then before Sydney could turn away, Kate realized she'd gotten used to her being there and had been looking forward to spending the evening together. Damn. That wasn't good.

"Tomorrow we're planting our first vines," Kate said.

"I like the sound of that."

"What? The planting or the vines?"

"The *we* and the *our*."

Double damn.

❖

Jerome handed her a shovel. Kate dug into the rich soil. She knew she was lucky on that end. Marvin and her uncle had taken good care of their land. And since it had lain dormant a year, any potato roots were dead. Kate had asked Jerome to till the fields one last time before she arrived. She placed some of the amended topsoil into the hole and gently positioned her first rootstock into the ground, building a little protective mound around it. Were the others not there, she might have kissed it for luck. As it was, she gave it a quick pat.

"And remind me how many vines there are?" Sydney asked.

"Over seven thousand. Seven thousand, six hundred and twenty-three, to be exact."

"Yikes. I shouldn't have asked," Sydney said.

"Hey. I think I see reinforcements!"

Magda and Amber joined them, bringing their own shovels, wearing gloves.

"Are you really here to help?" Kate asked.

"Every afternoon. A little birdie called to say you could use some extra hands."

Bless her mother's heart.

"But how—"

"We have a kid watching the shop," Magda interrupted. "Get us going!"

"Yay, I finally get to meet you two." Sydney walked up and shook both their hands. "We'll talk later when the boss gives us a break."

Kate laughed. "You all talk as much as you want, as long as you keep working." She looked over at Amber and Magda, grateful beyond words.

When it was her time to plant with Sydney, Kate was infinitely grateful for Sydney's sense of humor, not to mention her strength and endurance. Sydney shared stories about life in coastal Manchester. Kate tickled Sydney with her 4-H adventures. They kept the conversation light. They all stopped working each day between seven thirty and eight o'clock, parting at the end of the day to go to their separate abodes to eat and rest. Rachel always left Kate dinner. Kate had no idea what Sydney did for food nor what she did each evening. Kate knew her preoccupation with everything Sydney was not mutual. And probably not productive for their *working* relationship, but she couldn't stop her feelings. Mostly she fell asleep every night out of exhaustion and didn't think about Sydney again until the next morning.

They worked six days a week for five full weeks, until finally they planted the last vine. On the last night, Jerome brought over wine glasses and several bottles of wine.

"Until our grapes produce Long Island wine," Kate toasted. They all raised their glasses. "Thank you, thank you, thank you."

"To us," Jerome echoed, "the mighty planters. May the grapes grow and make us proud." They clinked glasses and cheered.

❖

Kate kept meticulous notes about the work they accomplished each day, who did what, any money that was spent, and the progress made. Accurate recordkeeping was important. But that part was easy. It was words and numbers written in a binder. Nothing could contain her gratitude for the work of her friends and especially Sydney's contribution. She'd promised she would come help plant and she did.

They were standing on Uncle Louie's steps. Kate had brought over muffins from her mother to give to Sydney for the long drive home. It was the first week of August.

"You sure you don't want to stay on a bit? You could go to the beach, maybe sail?"

Sydney had regaled them with sailing adventures while planting the vines. Kate tried to make light of Sydney's imminent departure. Rachel had made Sydney a fabulous farewell meal the evening before. The three of them kept up a lighthearted conversation, ignoring her father, who remained mute and sullen throughout the meal.

"I can't. I'm, uh, off to Paris in a couple of weeks."

"The deal you made with your parents."

"Yes." Sydney shuffled her feet and uncharacteristically looked down for a second. "I still don't want to go, Kate."

Kate certainly didn't want her to go, but begging was not an option. A deal was a deal. "You kept your promise. The vineyard is now planted."

The sun hit the tin box containing the muffins Sydney now held cradled in one arm.

"You'll stop for coffee along the way?" Kate asked. Her old question.

"Of course."

Their California days seemed so long ago. Kate concentrated on gratitude now. "Thank you for coming, for all your hard work." She impulsively stepped toward Sydney and gave her a hug, then jumped down the steps before Sydney could say anything.

They gazed at each other across the short distance. "You'll watch over our plants?" Sydney asked, haltingly.

"Until I go back to school," Kate promised, forcing a smile.

"Magda and Amber said they'd keep an eye on them while I'm away. I'll probably call them every two days."

"I'm coming back, Kate. I don't know when, but I'll be back."

Kate nodded and turned on her heels. She gave a backhanded wave so Sydney wouldn't see her tears.

Chapter Eight

September 1983, Paris, France

Sydney stood on the tiny balcony overlooking her lively Latin Quarter neighborhood, her stomach in knots. Her mother had told her that if she didn't accept the Paris internship, they were cutting off further financial support. Her father had been more diplomatic. He assured her that her job was going to be such a positive experience that, in time, she'd realize she was more at home in an urban world. At the time of their compromise—back home in Manchester after her graduation—she'd cowardly accepted the position, if and only if she could leave after helping Kate plant the grapes. Did that lovely deal entitle her to even a smidgen of integrity?

Once in Paris, it took her only a week to learn all the administrative paperwork she was given to do at the bank. When her boss found out she spoke French and was familiar with each *arrondissement*—the sixteen subdivisions of Paris—the job became more interesting. On the bank's payroll, she entertained wealthy Americans who were in town on business, putting on her shiniest running suit to guide them on early morning runs along the Seine, her black evening dress to take them to the *opéra*, and her casual daywear to drive them to Versailles, Fontainebleau, or wherever they wanted to go. She also became the go-to customer service rep for select French clients who wanted to meet the witty American who spoke French. Sydney kept them in stitches talking about American TV. They loved challenging Sydney to talk about President Reagan, but because of her job, she had to be careful what she said. More often than not, she deflected the comments and had them talk about President Mitterrand. Privately she wondered if the CDC under President Reagan was involved in stopping this new disease that had killed Louie and Marvin, and chided herself for not finding out more before she left. Which made her think about Kate, of course. Then there were all the articles in the newspapers about the high interest rates in the US and the continuing farm crisis, which also made her think of Kate's father and his situation. Even when she tried, she couldn't stop thinking about Kate and their vineyard and wondering what the hell she was doing in Paris.

❖

Barely a month later, on a particularly crisp fall afternoon, Sydney stood looking once again up and down her tiny street, rue Galande. She was feeling, despite the exceptional weather, even more befuddled and lonely. On her run that morning, she'd stopped by the post office to mail her application for a long-stay visa card, buying herself more time to figure out what to do. On the bank's *centime*, she continued to eat at all the best restaurants, but now even eating out seemed ho hum. She had to do something, but what? Sydney went back inside and closed the French doors behind her. Perhaps a visit to the Musée de l'Orangerie. The impressionists always cheered her up.

After changing into evening clothes, Sydney left for the museum. The solid symmetry of the neoclassical style fit her mood perfectly. Sydney bought her ticket and entered the building. She was immediately thrown back into the nineteenth century and walked slowly, soaking in each of the masters one by one. Sydney stopped when she heard the giggle and whispers of a trio of women standing in front of Renoir's *Reclining Nude*. Sydney slid back against the door frame to take in the show. She wondered who they were, oohing and aahing over the beautiful contours of the female body. Were they playing hooky from work or in Paris on vacation? Had they left their husbands and children at home? The three of them were laughing, poking at each other, obviously intimate. Sydney inched closer to get a hint of their conversation. One of them, a medium-tall brunette with a fashionable hairdo and handbag slung over her shoulder, asked who wanted to lie down next to this voluptuous woman? Sydney smiled. At least this one, Sydney assumed, would not be going home to a husband that night.

Sydney had just started to move on when one of the women nudged the brunette. All three of them looked over at Sydney.

Oh, those perceptive French. Sydney decided to enter the fray. The afternoon was suddenly more entertaining than she'd ever expected. She immediately put up her hands in the French manner signaling to them that their fun was fine with her. She now had three engaging French women all staring at her. To hell with Monet, she'd have her own fun today.

"*Bonjour, mesdames*," she said and walked toward them. She asked in French if they'd seen the fabulous Cézannes? Or had they come to see *Les Nymphéas*, Monet's *Water Lilies*? If nothing else, she'd distract them while they pondered who in God's name she was. They looked at each other. Sydney noticed their eyebrows lift, shoulders expand, breath let out. Sydney poured on the charm, asking them what they thought of the art they'd seen so far, engaging them eye-to-eye.

"Who are you?" the brunette asked.

A practical question, but one that allowed any number of answers. "Art interests me," she told them. "Well, I've bothered you enough," she continued, "enjoy yourselves."

"Wait," they said together.

Sydney grinned, slowing her step.

"Are you waiting for someone? Do you want to join us?"

Touché!

The women introduced themselves as Jolie, Nicole, and Cécile. When Sydney found out that Cécile, the brunette, was a chef at a château in Bordeaux, she almost whooped in delight. Sydney couldn't believe her good fortune—to make the acquaintance of a chef firsthand, and one who worked in Bordeaux. She looked again at the chef, who seemed on the young side, maybe only ten years older than Sydney, with an enigmatic smile and engaging hazel eyes. Where had she trained and how did she get such a position so young? Jolie was from Champagne and Nicole was in town visiting her. By dinner, Nicole and Jolie, who rarely took their eyes off each other, confided to Sydney that they were a couple.

"You know about these things, right?" Jolie whispered to Sydney, blushing.

"Oh, yes," Sydney answered.

"Good, because I can't seem to take my hands off Nicole."

Sydney smiled. She knew a lot about that.

Cécile told her that Nicole and Jolie had been surreptitiously dating for months. "They seem to be able to let go around me," she whispered to Sydney.

"And you? Do you enjoy spending time with them?" Sydney asked, wondering if Cécile had been candid about why the three of them were hanging out together.

"Oh, I'm in town for business," Cécile said, not answering the question.

After dinner the four ventured over to Champmeslé, the infamous lesbian bar not far from the Place Vendôme. As Jolie and Nicole never left each other's side, that left Cécile and Sydney plenty of time to talk. Now was the time to find out the real story. Did Cécile fancy women or not? Cécile was exactly the type of woman Sydney was normally attracted to—and had learned to run like hell from. Images of Blaye came back in a flash. She would never again trust a super strong, confident woman not to hurt her. Kate was an ocean away, but totally different. Kate was honest—maybe to a fault—and funny, kind, and caring. She'd never known anyone as willing to be vulnerable, someone for whom she didn't have to put her heart in jeopardy—if she remained vigilant. Sydney was doing fine so far keeping her attraction for Kate under wraps. Maybe Cécile could provide a distraction from her thoughts of Kate. She still planned to go back to Long Island to work with Kate on their vineyard dream.

Sydney looked over at Cécile, who was looking out toward the dance floor. At that moment she looked very un-cheflike in her blue sweater and cords. The sweater revealed voluptuousness in all the right places. Cécile kept brushing her long, unruly brown hair behind her ears. What was this woman thinking about, looking out at the crowd of lesbians? They were all leaving in the morning. Sydney would love an invitation to visit Cécile in Bordeaux, but if Cécile asked, should she accept?

"You really know art, Sydney," Cécile said. "How did you learn so much?"

Sydney almost jumped. *How did she know about art?* Sydney told her how she'd spent hundreds of hours as a kid poring over all the leather-bound collections of French masters her mother owned. And how as a teenager, she started imitating the drawings, one by one in her bedroom at night.

"I think creating good food and wine is also an art," Sydney proposed, hoping to redirect the conversation.

"Food, maybe. My husband makes the wine."

Husband? Sydney sat back, totally shocked. She would have bet her passport Cécile was a lesbian.

"You don't say. Tell me about your husband." Sydney's instincts had never been wrong before.

Cécile explained that her husband, Claude, had inherited the château from his family, but she and Claude were cash poor. They rented the rooms out and invited people to enjoy the grounds for events. Claude was intent on growing the attached vineyard to attract more tourists. At the mention of the vineyard, Sydney forgot all about the chef and her kitchen. Suddenly she had a hundred questions. How big was the vineyard? Did they grow all Bordeaux grapes or specialize? Who was their winemaker? At that moment Jolie and Nicole returned to the table, their faces flushed. Damn. Sydney hadn't been able to ask a single question. Nicole excused their interruption, but explained that she and Jolie wanted to go back to the hotel. Her face reddened even further.

"No problem," Cécile assured them. "I suppose it is time to go."

Sydney looked at her watch. It was nearly one. She had lost the opportunity to find out more, but it had been a great, albeit curious evening. Jolie and Nicole walked out to the curb to hail a cab. There seemed to be as many women entering the bar at that hour as leaving. Cécile touched Sydney on the arm and motioned her to lean closer.

"Listen, Sydney, it's almost harvest time. This time of year is quite special. You've heard about Bordeaux wines?"

"Of course."

"If there's a cancellation, and I'm almost certain there might be one, would you be interested in coming to be a guest at the château?"

Sydney looked at her. Had she heard correctly? Come to Bordeaux for the harvest? Her heart flipped. Surely she could learn something and bring it back to Kate and their vineyard-to-be. That would certainly ease her guilt for leaving. She wanted to grab Cécile and kiss her, but quickly curbed the impulse. "I'd love to." She reached for her wallet and nonchalantly pulled out one of her business cards. She handed it to Cécile.

"If that does happen, call the bank and leave your number. I'll call you back." She had no idea if Cécile was playing with her or if indeed this was a serious invitation. Either way, she was willing to find out. Bordeaux at harvest time? Maybe pick grapes—the very grapes she and Kate wanted to grow—and talk to the winemaker? Sydney was jubilant.

She waved to Jolie and Nicole, and embraced Cécile, a kiss on each cheek.

❖

A week later, Cécile called. It turned out that someone's mother had passed away and a vacancy had opened. Did Sydney want to come, Cécile asked in her half-French, half-English. Sydney paused—for effect—before responding.

"Of course. Has the harvest begun?"

"This weekend."

"I'll take off work Friday and leave on the first morning train. And Cécile, I'd love to participate in the harvest. Do you think I could?"

"Really? That's such hard work. You have no idea."

Sydney did know.

"I could perhaps arrange a private tour for you," Cécile said.

"I want to pick grapes."

"Suit yourself. I will speak to our winemaker before you arrive."

Sydney hung up, overjoyed. Even Kate's father wouldn't begrudge her firsthand experience.

❖

The château car was waiting for her at the Saint-Jean train station in Bordeaux. The good-looking young driver took her one bag and led her to the waiting Mercedes. When he opened the back door, Sydney slid in and easily took her place. Her father's driver had picked her up many times. She knew the routine well.

"*Madame le chef* asks that you come to the kitchen when you get in," the driver told her. He pulled out into the traffic without further explanation.

Sydney looked away and tried to concentrate on the city's historic stone buildings as they headed toward the highway that paralleled the Garonne river. She had no idea the city was so immense nor that it spanned both sides of the river. She knew only about its famous vineyards.

Sydney noticed the sign indicating the bridge, the Pont de pierre, just before they drove onto it. She had two seconds to admire the impressive expanse of stone arches under the bridge before her mind returned to the upcoming harvest—and the woman who had invited her there. Within minutes they'd left the city buildings and were cruising past the famed vineyards, each one loaded down with more grapes than the last. Many already had workers out picking. What was it about grapes that so attracted her? Kate saw lush fruit. Sydney saw endless bottles of wine, purpose, possibility. She couldn't take her eyes off the gorgeous fruit. Minutes later, they pulled into what Sydney assumed was the château's driveway. They drove over crushed stones and up a tree-lined entranceway. Sydney was impressed, but nothing shocked her more than the building at the end of the driveway.

When Cécile had said a château, Sydney hadn't expected a real château, as in turrets and towers, yet there it was. She was more excited than she'd been for a long time. The driver pulled the car up to the front entrance, got out, and opened the door for Sydney.

"Thank you. Sorry, I didn't get your name."

"Dominique."

"Very nice to meet you. Thank you for the ride." She nodded to him, took her bag, and walked up the stone steps to the massive front door. The weekend was looking better and better. She was tempted to knock, but instead, taking a deep breath, she opened the door and walked in.

Sydney expected more stone inside but found the entryway to be warm and inviting. She looked at the polished wood of the ornate desk that served as the hospitality desk. Above it hung a coat of arms in an equally ornate gold frame. To the left, Sydney caught a glance of the entrance to the dining room, but her eye was struck most by the imposing regal stairway to the right. Would she be staying up there?

A tall, good-looking man, dressed in a blue suit and checkered red tie, materialized from behind a door. He walked over and extended his hand.

"You must be Sydney," he said in French.

"I am. And you are?"

"Cécile's husband, Claude."

Sydney probably squeezed his hand too hard. She didn't expect to meet him and certainly not right away. She noticed his dimples when he smiled, and how meticulously he had combed his neatly trimmed black hair. "Céci told me you'd be arriving today and staying for the weekend. I'm glad it worked out that you could be with us. Welcome."

Sydney released her grip. The handshake was unusual for a Frenchman. She assumed he had worked with a lot of Americans.

"Come, let me take you to Céci." He led her through the dining room to the kitchen. Sydney was inside the door, watching the scene unfold before she realized Claude had left. The clattering of knives on cutting boards and four people in white chef jackets avidly caught her attention. Then she saw Cécile coming out of a storage unit at the far end of the room. Their eyes met. Sydney's body crackled with suspense.

"Ah, you are here." Cécile crossed the floor, put her hands around Sydney's shoulders and kissed her on both cheeks. She withdrew, quickly giving some instructions to one of her junior chefs, a young man with a tattoo on his left arm. She was assertive in her talk. There was no doubt who was the boss.

"Come. I will take you up to your suite." Cécile washed and dried her hands.

Sydney stepped into the vast guest room and tried to take everything in. This was indeed old-world elegance. The sitting room had a leather sofa and mahogany coffee table. There were fresh flowers on both the table and the buffet in the corner by the draped windows. She spotted a bottle of wine and two glasses. On one wall were three large windows that opened out to an extraordinary view of the vineyard.

"This is an end unit, so there is no one around to bother you," Cécile said, coming up to stand next to Sydney. She wished Cécile wasn't wearing her official whites. She looked quite formidable.

"It's perfect. Are you going to be able to join me at all this weekend?" Sydney asked.

"We shall see. The château is fully booked. And you came to be part of the *vendange*, the harvest, right? I must go back to the kitchen. The pastry chef hasn't come in yet. Gaston is expecting you at the winery tomorrow morning. Come, let me show you the bedroom before I leave."

Normally Sydney would make a joke about being led to the bedroom. Flirting came easily to her, but the situation with Cécile had yet to be confirmed, husband or no husband. Sydney followed Cécile into the next room where she noticed a four-poster bed with an exquisitely carved headboard and matching bed posts. But in the beveled mirror with the same matching detail, she caught a glance of the two of them together. Cécile was checking her out! Her gut instinct at the bar had been correct. Did this married woman have ulterior motives for inviting her to Bordeaux? No doubt she would find out sometime this weekend.

"I will have a table waiting for you this evening and tomorrow at eight," she said. "Does that hour suit you?"

Eight o'clock was very French. "Perfectly. One quick question, *Madame le chef*, if cooking is your thing, what does Claude do?"

Cécile's head jerked up. "We will talk, *Mademoiselle l'artiste*. For the moment, let me just say that he has his life and I have mine." She ran her hand along Sydney's chin and rested it, just for a split second, on her cheek.

Sydney swallowed. Uh-oh.

❖

That evening, Sydney tried to relax as she was shown to her table in the dining room. A shy server brought her a champagne aperitif and an *amuse-bouche* of a single Atlantic scallop with leek cream and truffle oil. "With the compliments of the chef," he said softly. So be it. She would wait. Right now, she would be a fool not to sit back and enjoy this meal. Next came a delicious soup, then a Canterbury lamb rack au jus, with a parsley mash, and braised shallots. The sommelier came by and poured her a glass of the house merlot. Sydney was in heaven.

The dining room was full. Cécile had obviously reserved her table or she would not have found a seat. Next came the salad course—French style, of course, coming after the meal. The server then brought her a wonderful cheese course, with wafers and an exceptional quince jelly, followed by a perfect *tarte Tatin* with cinnamon and Calvados ice cream. Sydney was extremely impressed with Cécile's culinary skills. The meal rivaled the best she'd had in Paris.

Claude showed up as Sydney was wondering whether she'd receive a bill or whether she should leave and go back to her room.

"The chef is magnificent, don't you think?"

Sydney swiveled, looking up to see his handsome face. She complimented the food immediately, but fumbled the etiquette around the check. He immediately responded by saying that she was a guest of the chef. He escorted her out to the front desk where they continued to chat amicably. He explained that he'd been in charge of the front desk that evening because the young woman normally in charge was out on a maternity leave. They chatted on.

"I'd like to think people come for my grapes," he said, "but I'm sure it's the food."

"Food and wine. The perfect pair."

"I've always thought so." He smiled. "I'll leave you now to get some rest."

"*Merci*, Claude." Sydney shook his hand and padded off toward her room. As heavy as the key to her room was, her mood was definitely lighter now. She doubted she'd see Cécile tonight. Tomorrow she'd pick her first French grapes. Her skin prickled in anticipation.

❖

Gaston was clearly not pleased to have Sydney join the crew. He asked an older woman, Josette, to show her how to harvest the grape clusters. He picked out a pair of pruning shears from a basket and handed them to her.

"Be careful. These are sharp," he said. "Don't hurt the grapes." He hurried off.

Josette smiled and shrugged. "Take no offense. He has a good heart underneath. Follow me, please." They joined the large group of mostly older men and women who were standing around congenially talking. The buzz of expectancy among them was contagious. Sydney was excited about picking her first French grapes, but missed having Kate at her side. She looked down at the sturdy old trunks and thought of their stick-size baby plants.

At Gaston's signal, the group walked to the rows of grapes in front of them. The ground was moist beneath her sneakers, but the morning sun already warmed her back. Josette patiently explained to Sydney how to hold the grapes and how to snip them from the vine. "After you snip the branch, toss it gently into the basket," Josette continued. "Don't go over the top when you fill these. The boys will collect them later."

Sydney looked up at her craggy face and into warm, light-blue eyes. She thought immediately of her grandmother—the fiercely independent, proud, and loving matriarch on her father's side of their family—and a wave of nostalgia settled her. Josette's curly blond hair was short and neatly coiffed. She wore a plaid shirt over cotton overalls. "Okay, I think I've got it."

Compared to the work she'd done in the summer, this was easy. To plant the vines, she'd had to get down on her knees for each plant and then hop up again, over and over. Here she was merely leaning over and snipping the clusters. Tiring yes, but in comparison, not so hard. She soon slipped by Josette and the others. She noticed that workers were bringing down filled baskets. Where were they taking them? What did they use to crush their grapes? Would she be able to see the whole process? This was why she was here.

Three hours later, Sydney was sweating. She caught up with Josette in another row. She was positive all these people were volunteers, part of the French tradition to help pick the local grapes. "I need a break. How do you do it?" Sydney asked. She liked this kind woman, who was doing the same work as she, only at a slower pace. Josette smiled.

"Oh, my husband will take the afternoon shift. I will be a sorter."

"A sorter?"

"We go through the grapes and pick out the bad ones. Using the best grapes makes a difference. Ah, here comes our lunch," she said, pointing toward Cécile, who was standing at the bottom of the incline, wearing her whites, and waving them all down the hill.

They settled around picnic tables lined up in the shade. Sydney ate ravenously, as did the whole lot of them. Bottles of unlabeled wine were passed around and Sydney had another taste of Claude's wine. The chatter had been minimal at first, but soon picked up. It was a joyous group of generous, smiling faces who easily included her in their conversations.

After lunch she asked Gaston if she could help sort with Josette.

He hesitated but finally agreed. Sydney was sure it was the specter of Cécile that made him acquiesce. She had no idea what the evening would bring, but for now, for this fantastic experience, she was glad she had come.

❖

Saturday evening's meal was exceptional, as expected. But dinner was one thing. It was after dinner that she was worried about. She was leaving tomorrow. She had a strong suspicion Cécile would pay her a visit later. The wait in her suite was even more intolerable without any distractions. There was no TV. She had already memorized what was outside her windows. It wasn't until after eleven that she finally heard a knock at the door.

Sydney took a breath and called out, "Come in." Cécile slipped into the room immediately. She had her jacket off. Her hair was matted down from her chef's cap.

Cécile walked over to the sofa and patted the seat next to her. "Come sit?" She looked tired and there was something unreadable in her eyes. Sydney sat.

"That was another extraordinary meal, Cécile. The whole dining-room experience. Very impressive." She was sitting a foot from Cécile, who had her hands in her lap. "Really, the château is beautiful. You and Claude—"

"Are you still thinking about him?"

"Excuse me?"

"Claude. Will he be in every sentence of yours?"

"But—"

"Yes, he is my husband. His family wouldn't give him the château without a chef. But Claude is gay. I knew it before we married. Our marriage was a business proposition." Cécile got up. "Do you mind if I wash my face?"

She returned a few minutes later, looking more relaxed. She'd fluffed her hair and unbuttoned her top button. She sat back down, taking Sydney's hand in hers.

"We were not innocent when we married," she continued, as if uninterrupted. "He knew from the beginning I was not like the other girls. We agreed he would have his life and I would have mine." She looked at Sydney. "This is hard for you Americans to understand, *non*?"

"Not really." Sydney understood. She let go of Cécile's hand, needing to stand with all the adrenaline pulsing through her veins. She walked around to the back of a nearby chair to get some distance between them. "So, you're wooing me?" Sydney asked, just to be sure.

Cécile laughed. "Come here, you." She walked over and brought Sydney back to the sofa. "At least sitting I have a chance to be the same height as you."

"You tower over me in your cooking skills."

"Probably." Her modesty was becoming.

They sat for a second, looking at one another.

"And call me Céci, please?"

Sydney started to speak but Cécile put her hand softly on Sydney's lips. "May I?" she continued. "This is the beginning of a very long season for us here. I only get to Paris every once in a while. I like you. Your French is wonderful and you obviously have good taste in food and art. That matters." Cécile paused. "I have a proposal for you." She kissed Sydney sweetly on the lips and inched closer. "I couldn't be more open in Paris because I had to find out if you could be discreet. You proved to me today you can be. Nothing must hurt our business, you understand, Claude's and mine." She kissed Sydney again, more ardently this time. Sydney pulled away.

"What exactly are you proposing? Where do I fit in?"

Cécile sat back, delighted. "Ah, another pragmatist." She paused then started again. "I do not know how else to do this, to meet people, to keep my kitchen going. Americans always seem to want to see the vineyards."

"Well, you were right about that. But I also want to learn how your wine is made."

Cécile looked at her. "That, too?" she asked.

Sydney nodded.

"But perhaps I could distract you just a little." Cécile leaned in again. "What if you pick grapes again tomorrow before you leave, and then you return?" she asked. Cécile rose and walked to the door, pulling Sydney gently along with her, but stopped before opening it.

"And next time you stay with me." She leaned in and put her hand again on Sydney's cheek. "You and I can get acquainted. If you want to make wine, I will talk to Gaston."

Well, well, well. Madame's negotiating skills were finely tuned. How ironic that Cécile was proposing exactly what she'd always wanted: a relationship with no possible risk of attachment. And she could learn as much about making wine as Gaston would teach her. So why did she feel so miserable? Sydney thought immediately of Kate. The two of them didn't have a romantic relationship. Perhaps a casual fling with Cécile wouldn't endanger the relationship with Kate. She didn't even have to tell Kate. Sydney ignored her pounding heart. Besides, this was the kind of relationship she deserved. Kate could do better.

"We shall see," Sydney told her, imitating Cécile's initial hesitation.

CHAPTER NINE

January 1984, Davis, CA

Kate's eyes slowly opened as her mind registered light coming in through her dorm window's closed blinds. She'd climbed into bed way past four that morning. She yawned, stretched and finally leaned over to grab her watch. Eleven twenty-eight! Kate threw the afghan off and sat up, suddenly feeling a bit bewildered and oppressively hot. Then she remembered all the work she'd caught up on, especially the Viticultural Practices class the professor had allowed her to covertly audit. She couldn't afford to pay for the class, as was the requirement, but when she explained that she was already taking a full load and had started her own vineyard, he had allowed her to quietly sit in the back and listen for free.

Kate did a final stretch and hopped out of bed, thrilled that she'd also read all the notes from a couple of enology students she had befriended before they left for the holiday break. She was quite aware how fortunate she was to be at Davis. There was no shortage of students interested in viticulture and winemaking. But Kate knew the only winemaker she wanted was Sydney. *You'll watch over our plants?* Kate could no more watch over them here in California than Sydney could in France. This all made sense in her head—they were both doing what they felt compelled to do—but that didn't keep her heart from feeling so raw. At a knock at the door, Kate jumped. The building was practically empty, and she'd heard no one roaming about on her floor.

"Who is it?" she asked.

"Abby."

Kate grinned. Abby's parents owned a greenhouse and nursery near Long Beach, south of LA. Abby had grown up planting her own vegetables. They had tons of things in common. After Uncle Louie's death, Abby had been particularly kind and accommodating. She couldn't deny that for whatever reason, she noticed Abby more these days. She rushed to the door.

"Abby!" Kate threw open the door and embraced her friend. "You're back early. Classes don't start until Wednesday. How was your vacation?"

She stepped back and let Abby in.

"You think you're the only one with work to do?" Abby looked around. "Yikes, from the looks of this room, maybe you win. When was the last time you got out? It's a little stuffy in here."

Kate laughed. Abby knew her well. She walked over to the window and opened it. "Perhaps I have been a tad overzealous." She walked quickly to stand in front of the hot plate and all the canned goods she'd bought the day before but hadn't put away. She crossed her arms and tried to look nonchalant.

"What are you hiding?" Abby asked.

"What do you mean?"

Abby looked at her. "Since when do you stand like that? Something's going on."

Kate threw up her hands. "I didn't want you to tease me, that's all. I've taken to home cooking." She stood aside to reveal a stack of Campbell's soups, boxes of Kraft mac-and-cheese, her favorite Rice-A-Roni, and two jars of peanut butter. "It's easier than going out. And much less expensive."

"Oh, Kate. What can I say?" Abby sat down on Kate's desk chair.

Kate smiled. Abby was the most nonjudgmental person she knew. She had no idea how Abby managed to be exceptionally social and such a good student. Like Kate, she had loaded up on classes and had her own field experiments, trying out new kinds of fertilizer and mulch. Abby told her she wanted to specialize in strawberries but would grow every fruit native to their soil. Since September they had often met for lunch between classes, and more often than not, they walked home together after a long evening at the library. It was Abby who had left her a plastic pumpkin full of peanut butter cookies and candy at Halloween. And Abby who happened to be at the post office that day in November when

Kate received the hydrometer from Sydney along with the oversized postcard. The card pictured a lush vineyard scene on the front. On the reverse side Sydney had written in her usual bold hand:

> *I'm working on a vineyard in Bordeaux!*
> *It's not our vineyard but I'll be back with real winemaking skills.*
> *Don't forget me. Sydney*

So Sydney did want to return. Kate's heart had pounded away. This year? Next year? Ten years from now? She'd heard nothing else since, nor had Sydney left a return address.

That day at the post office, Abby patiently waited, pretending to read her own mail, while Kate read the card over and over. She hadn't asked Kate who the card was from, but Kate suspected Abby knew. Kate had told Abby about Sydney's vineyard idea and how she'd helped Kate plant. And when Kate had gone to Abby's for Thanksgiving, she opened up to her about her feelings for Sydney. Abby was a good listener.

"Earth to Bauer. Come in, please."

"Oh, my heavens. Sorry! I must have spaced out. Guess I'm more tired than I thought."

"More like exhausted and in need of a change in venue. How about this?" Abby stood. "Why don't you grab your sweater. I am going to take you out of this room for a few hours. Not to worry, you will come back."

Kate decided to indulge Abby and not say anything about the need for a sweater. She'd often teased Abby about her idea about *cold* winter weather. Sure, it was technically *winter*, but this was California cold. Nothing like Cutchogue in January.

"Let's go for a walk. Then I'm going to take you to my place and make you dinner. You know how I love to cook." Abby smiled.

"No, you don't, Abby. You cook only one degree more than I do. You love watching TV."

"At least I use fresh ingredients," Abby promised. "My folks loaded me up with fresh veggies. Tonight I will make—exclusively for you, my dear friend—my famous vegetable lasagna."

"Abby, it's your only dish."

Abby laughed. "But I make it quite well, don't I?"

"That you do." Kate was a good head taller and several pounds heavier than Abby, but at the moment, Kate felt weightless and springy on her feet. "Let me at least bring a bottle of wine." Kate opened the closet door and grabbed a bottle of wine from the floor. Another of the enology students, old enough to buy wine, had gifted her with several bottles of wine before she left for the holidays. To help her study better, she'd said.

"Great," Abby answered. "That's your department, for sure."

Kate closed her dorm door. They started down the hallway to the stairwell.

Once they exited the building, Kate breathed in the fresh air. A few hours off would be a treat. She hooked her arm innocently through Abby's. "It's great to get outside."

Abby smiled and put her hand gently over Kate's.

Kate would have paused had they not been walking so fast. Acutely aware of Abby's hand on hers, she regretfully took her own back. They were out in public. She knew to be careful about others seeing two women together—even just holding hands. She brushed off a memory of Ryan before it could take hold in her mind. *Think lasagna.* Kate quickened her pace.

It was such a beautiful afternoon, neither could resist staying outside a bit longer. Abby suggested they take a walk along Russell Boulevard, still pretty even though most trees had dropped their leaves. It was after six when they finally arrived at Abby's apartment. Her roommate wasn't due back until late the next evening.

"Make yourself comfortable while I start dinner."

That was easier to say than do. Abby was a stack queen. She had stacks of magazines, workout tapes, books, and notebooks all along the perimeter of the living room and piled atop the TV and VCR. She was a Jane Fonda fanatic and a *Dallas* addict. Since she had the smaller of the bedrooms, she was allowed to stack in the living room.

"Why don't you pour us a glass of wine? In all my shows, someone's sipping on a glass of wine while they cook."

"Is that what they do on *Dynasty*?" Kate asked. She knew Abby thought *Dallas* was infinitely the better show.

"*Dynasty*?" Abby asked. She sounded horrified.

"Just teasing you." Kate handed Abby a glass of red wine. "You and the Ewings go way back. Here you go, chef."

Kate found Abby's TV interest curious. She guessed that was how she chilled out. At the moment Abby seemed particularly busy in the kitchen, with a pot of water on the stove that was beginning to boil. She stood peeling carrots and had a colander of other vegetables waiting. Kate studied Abby. She had a farmer's strong body but seemed delicate-boned somehow. Her hair, a warm gingerbread color, looked soft. Today she wore it pulled back behind her ears, other times in a ponytail. Was the texture as soft as it looked? *Why not find out?*

"Abby, I have the strangest request to ask of you."

Abby stopped and held the peeler up in the air. "Sure, go ahead."

"Would you mind if I take a quick shower? I know it's weird, but I didn't shower this morning. I feel all grubby. It didn't help that you challenged me to run that last stretch up the bike path."

"Told you my workout tapes have been paying off." She dropped her hand holding the peeler but kept it by her side. "But—"

"You have a T-shirt I could put on, right? And maybe sweatpants?" They would be short on her, but what did it matter? Just the thought of walking around without any underwear on made her feel ever so rakish. She flashed back to sitting next to Sydney on the bar stool, staring into her sparkling green eyes. It was Sydney she wanted to be with, but Sydney was thousands of miles away. By her own choice. It was time to stop pining for her.

Abby stared at her open-mouthed.

"Never mind, then."

"No, no, that's fine. You just surprised me." Abby tossed the peeler into the sink and zipped quickly past her. "Here, let me get you a towel." She practically ran down the hallway. "Follow me."

She grabbed a towel from the closet and handed it to Kate. "You can change in my bedroom. I have plenty of extra T-shirts, sweatshirts, whatever you want. Luckily I straightened it up before I left for vacation." She peeked in the door. "Phew, even made my bed."

"I just need a change of clothes, Abby. It's no big deal."

"Of c-course," Abby said. "There's shampoo and soap. Help yourself." She walked briskly back to the kitchen.

Kate smiled and watched her retreat. Had she just made Abby nervous? Was it possible that Abby liked her more than as a good friend? Kate had never considered her that way because she'd been so obsessed with Sydney. Should she act on these new feelings? Sydney was the experienced one with women. Kate had zero experience. Kate felt she could trust Abby to keep things between the two of them, should they, uh, begin another type of relationship. More importantly, Kate really liked Abby. She knew that both men and women came to Abby's Friday night *Dallas* events. There was only one sure way to find out. Kate walked into the bathroom and turned on the shower.

A jolt of recklessness pulsed through her. After undressing, the feeling became stronger. She sat on the edge of the tub and looked at her neatly piled clothes on the sink. She stood up and grabbed them, mushing them all together and tossing them around the room. It felt exhilarating.

She had to give credit to Sydney. It was she who had cracked open her hard, protective shell, allowing her to remember Lily. Being with another woman would honor the love she had for Lily. Not to mention that she was very curious about what she had been missing. Like a plant, once the seed is planted, its nature is to thrive. Besides, she was safe here with Abby. No one else really knew her. No one would know what happened inside these walls. What was she waiting for?

To hell with you, Sydney Barrett. Have your fun in France. Kate stepped into the shower and let the force of the warm water roll down her back. She lifted her head up to let the water beat on her cheeks. She didn't care anymore. She had her own life to lead.

Kate grabbed the soap, lathering her arms. It smelled of lavender, not strawberry, as she'd expected. Good, Abby was surprising her. More importantly, Abby seemed to like her a lot and, at this very moment, was waiting for her. Kate washed her hair, rinsed off, and got out of the shower.

❖

While the lasagna baked, Kate and Abby sat with another glass of wine on the two ends of the couch. After the second glass, Kate relaxed enough to stretch out her legs. She wiggled her toes. She hadn't put her socks or shoes back on.

"Put them up on the couch," Abby suggested. "There's room."

Kate stretched out her legs, touching Abby's hip but then froze. She didn't know what to do or say next. They were both dressed but she felt naked. She automatically reached to pull the T-shirt down. Was her belly showing? "That looks good on you," Abby said.

Kate blushed. Maybe she wasn't ready for this. She slowly pulled her legs back and sat up. "You never told me about your visit home. How are your parents?"

Abby recounted several adventures from her trip home and then asked Kate if she'd heard from Magda and Amber, who Abby knew were keeping watch over her plants. It was a wait-and-see year for the new plants, Kate explained. They would survive or not. There was nothing Kate could do to protect them either at home or here at school. Kate felt the disappointment roll through her. She must have been wrong about Abby having feelings for her. They continued to chat pleasantly until the chime sounded that the lasagna was ready.

They got up to eat. As delicious as the lasagna was, Kate wanted to be back on the couch. They continued talking at the small dining room table until Kate asked for seconds. As Abby reached for the pan, Kate noticed the unsteadiness of her hand. Weren't they a pair? After dinner, Kate offered to help Abby with the dishes, but Abby declined.

"I'll just be a minute."

"Abby, I…" Kate hesitated. She had no idea what to say or do. All she knew is that if she didn't kiss Abby right now, she might shrivel up and die. She wanted to touch Abby's body and knew damn well she wanted Abby's hands on her, too. To hell with words. She pivoted toward Abby and kissed her, pushing her gently back against the sink.

"Wow," Abby managed. She dropped the sponge into the sink and grabbed a towel, wiping her hands. "I've wanted to kiss you for such a long time. And a lot more. Come with me." She led Kate to her bedroom.

They sat down on the bed, Kate twisting so she could face Abby, and finally put her hands gently through her hair. Abby leaned into the touch.

"This is all new for me," Kate got out. She kissed Abby again. She loved the soft, sexy feel of her mouth.

"Me, too," Abby responded. She slowly caressed the side of Kate's cheek, then moved her hand and placed it over Kate's heart. "I've been with a few guys," she confessed, "because I never had the courage to be with a woman. Actually, I don't mean any woman, Kate. I mean you.

You caught my eye freshman year when you came into class with your pile of books. You seemed so forlorn that whole year."

"I didn't think anyone noticed."

"I did." Abby dropped her hand into her lap.

"Not surprising." Kate gently grabbed Abby's hand and brought it to her lips. "I was hurting. Badly. Someone I loved dearly had died the year before. I was still dealing with her loss." In favor of staying in the present, Kate purposely pushed aside her memories of freshman year and her lingering sadness about Lily. She kissed Abby again. "We're here now. Why don't I tell you that story another time."

Abby's smile broadened. "Agreed." She leaned in and kissed Kate. She was very good at the kissing part.

"As we're both novices," Kate said, when she caught her breath, "I say we start with that ponytail of yours." Even though part of her wanted to start unbuttoning Abby's blouse, the other part of her was still a bit timid. "May I?"

Abby laughed. "Of course. I'm dying here." She put both hands around Kate's back and scooted closer, taking advantage of the proximity to kiss up and down Kate's neck and shoulder.

Kate had dreamed of this very moment with Sydney, but forced that thought aside, too. She reached for the ribbon and pulled it loose. Abby's hair tumbled around her shoulders. So many around campus had their hair all puffed up and sprayed. Abby wore hers naturally, pulled back behind her head. Quintessential Abby. Why had they waited so long?

She ran her hands through Abby's hair, kissing her. "How extraordinary you are."

"We are."

Within minutes they'd kissed themselves into a frenzy, sprawled all over the bed. Kate's body was on fire. She finally unbuttoned Abby's blouse. The next moment they were both naked. Kate couldn't move her hands fast enough to touch Abby's breasts.

When Abby's pelvis touched Kate's, Kate moaned, barely able to breathe. She began a sensual exploration of Abby's neck, then collarbone, then kissed her breasts before daring to move lower. With each kiss, Kate's body craved more. She feathered her hand down Abby's thigh before moving slowly back up. As Abby's moan met hers, Kate continued. There was no stopping her now.

❖

When Kate woke the next morning, they were still wrapped in each other's arms. She peeked over at Abby—who was still fast asleep—and gently tucked some loose curls around her ear. She felt comfortable and happy in Abby's arms and was awed by the whole experience. She put her head back down on Abby's shoulder and snuggled tighter.

Chapter Ten

February 1984, Bordeaux, France

"Where did you and Dominique go today?" Cécile asked. They were sitting together on the small fabric sofa in Cécile's cottage, holding bowls of leftover boeuf bourguignon on their laps. Nestled in a tiny grove of trees, the cottage gave them the utmost privacy. It had a small bedroom, bath, living room, and tiny kitchen. Sydney wanted to appreciate the intimacy, but each time she walked down the stone path to the front door—the sides of which, Cécile had told her, would be laden with flowers come spring—she thought of Kate, and the path that led to her cottage on Long Island. The cottage that she'd never been inside of, and now wondered if she ever would.

"We concentrated on the vineyards of Saint-Émilion. I met another winemaker today, Céci. Sometimes I just mention Claude's name—and that I'm working here—and often they'll let me wander around their winery. And the wine!"

"Speaking of which, shall I pour you another glass of our humble wine?" She reached over to grab the bottle from the coffee table.

"Cécile Bouvier, don't start." Sydney put her bowl down. "I love Claude's wine. This is my chance to learn about *terroir* and all the nuances of winemaking from other winemakers." Sydney thought of all the long, animated talks with Kate about all things wine and vineyard related. Kate would understand how much she was learning from these esteemed vintners, as the Americans called them. Just recently she'd talked with winemakers in the hallowed wineries of both Château

Mouton Rothschild and Château Haut-Brion. "Besides, Dom is also fun," she said instead. "He's a serious wine aficionado."

"Perhaps he has other intentions for the two of you?"

"We're friends, that's all. He loves his free lodging at my apartment when he goes to Paris." She'd accepted Cécile's offer to return after the harvest weekend—and yes, to stay with her. But it was time, way past time, for her to move out of the cottage. Sydney had talked to her parents at Christmas and mentioned that she wanted to move out of her apartment in Paris to live closer to the châteaux and vineyards of Bordeaux. She had purposely waited until after the New Year to talk to Cécile about it, so she could concentrate on all the extra holiday demands at the château. Her father had already been informed by the bank that Sydney was being paid per diem, though she was working only very part-time. Although he was fine with that, her mother was furious. Sydney had asked if she'd prefer her working on Long Island at the vineyard with Kate. Her mother quickly said no. Sydney had to stop herself from laughing. Anywhere in Europe was more exotic to her mother than Long Island.

"But speaking of lodging—"

"That subject again?" Cécile sighed and settled back against the sofa arm. Sydney took the bottle from her and poured them another glass of wine. Cécile was exhausted, Sydney realized, so this wasn't the best time to bring up a touchy subject.

"Yes, that talk."

Cécile swung her legs around and put her bare feet on the rug. "And you have a suggestion?"

"Perhaps we could talk to Claude about my staying in that old bungalow out back?"

Cécile looked at her. "*We* should not talk to Claude. *I* will talk to him."

Sydney sat up. Dominique had told her about an outbuilding that had been renovated and furnished after the war but later abandoned. It would only need the plumbing switched back on and a thorough cleaning. Who knew what creatures had taken up residence since the late fifties.

Cécile let her head drop.

"Sorry," Sydney said. She took Cécile's wine glass gently from her hand. "It's late. We can talk another time."

Cécile let out a breath. "Give me a second."

Sydney waited.

"I'm quite fond of you, you know that, right?" Cécile said, taking Sydney's hands. "But you want more. You Americans always want more."

"Céci, I've loved being here with you in our cozy abode, but yes, I do want more." *Someone who wants and needs only me.* She swallowed and tried again. "I need to be free to try." Sydney picked up the sweater Cécile had tossed onto a chair. "You want this?"

"Thanks." Cécile said, wrapping it around herself and letting out a big sigh. "Listen, maybe your timing is good. Claude has a new boyfriend."

"He does?" This was not the conversation she wanted them to have, but nonetheless she found it very interesting. She liked Claude and was happy for him.

"On my way home the last several nights, I've seen the light on in his apartment. That could mean only one thing."

"Which is?"

"He has company." She stood. "So, yes, I think the plan you mentioned might work, though I'd love for you to pay occasional visits here." Cécile winked at Sydney. She wasn't giving up easily. "And don't be surprised if Claude talks to you about a job."

"What?"

"He will soon want more time off."

"You're kidding?"

Cécile gave a look Sydney knew well.

"Guess not." She kissed Cécile soundly, then nudged her gently toward the bed. "You need a good night's sleep. Come on." A château job. That would work. Another good excuse to hang around while she figured out what she really wanted to do.

❖

Two days later Claude asked Sydney to fill in for him at the front desk. He said he had to go away for a couple of days on business. This was Claude's way, Sydney was certain, to see how she did with the guests. He told her about each person's job at the château, the differences in every room, taught her how to take reservations, and reminded her to escort people into dinner. There was nothing difficult about the job. Like at the bank, they needed a steady, affable person to be the face of the château.

A week later, Claude asked Sydney to sit down with him for an aperitif. Cécile had been right. By this time, they'd all seen his friend coming and going.

"We could use your charming skills as a front desk hostess," he said. "You're familiar with all the rooms, the menu, the dining room responsibilities. What do you say?"

"That sounds interesting. Thanks for asking me."

"All you'd have to do is seat those who are staying here and handle all phone reservations. You'll be great, but—" Claude paused. Sydney wondered why he was pausing. He lowered his voice. "We can't pay you directly."

Sydney looked up at the confident man facing her. He was a very good businessman. But she also knew how to negotiate. She only needed to save enough money for a plane ticket back home. "I have my job in Paris. Learning about making wine is worth more than a salary, Claude. We'd have to work out our schedules, you and I, so that I am able to return to Paris when I'm needed at the bank."

Claude nodded. "We can certainly do that. And," he smiled, "I can throw a little cash under the table." Claude liked his American expressions. "Anything more that I can do for you?"

"I want to learn how to market wine."

"So it's not just making wine that interests you. You're even sharper than I thought."

"Wise enough to take advantage of your expertise. It's one thing to make good wine, and quite another to sell it. Will you teach me?"

"When do you want to start?" he asked.

"My new duties or learning my first sales pitch?"

"Both."

"Right away." Sydney extended her hand and Claude shook it.

"I believe that's called a win-win." He smiled.

❖

When Sydney first arrived, Gaston had balked at the idea of Sydney working in the winery, or as they call it in France, the *chai*. He gave her all the menial tasks of washing out empty barrels, sweeping the floor, and toting tools for the real workers. She brought someone the chalk and they marked the barrels. She carried the cases of wine that the crew bottled to the wine *cave*. She coiled the hoses at the end of the day, hung the rakes and brooms back on their hooks, deposited the brushes, bungs, and brackets in their wooden boxes. Mostly she watched Gaston transform that vintage—the very grapes she had helped harvest—into juice, then ferment it, and store it in barrels to age. The wine Gaston created was not the caliber of a Margaux, Pauillac, or Saint-Estèphe, but he was making good wine and she had the phenomenal opportunity to witness the process.

Sydney never found out what changed his mind, but one morning Gaston asked her to bring him a crescent wrench and then showed her how to tighten the valve on the bulkhead fitting of one of their stainless tanks. Sydney's hands shook. She understood the significance of him showing her. From then on, she slowly became part of the team. He kept giving her tasks and she kept learning.

❖

Perhaps it was the unseasonably mild April weather that made her so despondent. She had missed budbreak on the vines that she and Kate had planted and by now, if not soon, they would be flowering. Sydney was sitting at the front desk, waiting for the last guests to leave the dining room. Surely her skills could be better used—say, in a vineyard on Long Island—than being an overeducated, underpaid receptionist. Or perhaps it was her usual thoughts about Kate. Sydney had sent a gift box of essential winemaking apparatus to Kate at Davis—refractometer, wine thermometer, and air locks—with a note saying *we'll need these one day*. But had never heard back from her. This time she'd given her the château address, but Kate still had not responded. And why should she? They had not spoken all this time. She knew why *she* was not talking to Kate—her goddamn guilt about leaving Cutchogue in the first place, not to mention that she'd been living with someone else. She had told Kate she only wanted a business relationship. Why? Because she was too chickenshit to go for a real one. A real one would mean opening up to Kate about her worst fears. Like could she be a successful winemaker—did she have the skills and ability? This fear of failure, this feeling of inadequacy, was so deep-rooted, she didn't know how to shake it. She had loved—and been very good at—swimming and sailing, for example. But her mother had scoffed at all her athletic achievements. Said they weren't worthy of her time. But at least she had been good at them. Could she ever learn enough to make her own wine?

And then there were the Kate questions. Did she think about her at all? Would Kate want her to return? How did her pruning go? Was Kate's father as homophobic as ever? Would he or Rachel go to Kate's graduation? Her mind kept going, on and on. But, always, the question she wondered the most: Had Kate met someone? Kate had told her she'd had feelings for another girl back in high school. Had she finally come out or not? Sydney remembered how the tattooed Samantha had been interested in Kate. Kate would surely have dozens of offers and opportunities to meet someone at Davis. How could she have been so stupid? Sydney hopped off the chair and rushed to the front door to open it, gasping for fresh air. Of course there would be cute future winemakers cozying up to Kate. Sydney could, at the very least, be replaced by someone more available. Sydney looked up at the door through which she'd entered how many months before? Why was she still here?

After an interminable wait, the dining party finally left, having laughed their way through the meal, ordering rounds of cognac to prolong their departure. By the time Sydney checked on the kitchen staff, Cécile had already left, every prep area was cleaned, and all but the last few dessert plates washed and put away.

Sydney grabbed her coat and walked outside. It was after midnight, her new normal end-of-the-day hours. She slowly walked the perimeter of the château, checking to make sure all the doors were closed and secure. She'd taken over not only all the hosting responsibilities but several new ones Claude had tacked on. She was rarely in Paris anymore, and then only on weekends when Claude was back. She had told herself that she'd stay to witness budbreak. Now she wondered, did she really want to wait until the flowers morphed into grapes?

Sydney sighed and walked over to the winery. Whenever she got lonely, the tanks and barrels and the smell of yeast in the winery always cheered her up and lured her to stay longer. She knew the back door by the crush pad was unlocked. She slipped inside and hit the light switch.

She looked around the familiar room. Stashed on a shelf, off-limits to everyone but Gaston, was his precious wine-tasting cup. Sydney picked it up and rolled it over in her hand, staring at the cup's contours, thinking about his phenomenal ability to distinguish levels of sugar, acidity, alcohol, tannins. She bet he hadn't learned his skills hanging around watching someone else taste wine. She shoved the cup back on the shelf, knocking off a box of labels printed with the château logo. Sydney picked up the box and noticed the addressee: Gaston Humbert, winemaker. She stared at the labels, her eyes welling up. She wanted *her name* on a wine label. She brushed the tears aside. That wasn't going to happen standing here envying Gaston. Sydney froze, as a flash of insight assailed her. That was it. Her time in France was done. If she truly wanted to become a winemaker, she needed to leave, and start making her own wine.

Sydney gave the *chai* one last look, walked toward the exit, switched off the lights, and shut the door firmly behind her. Why had she stayed so long, furthering Cécile and Claude's dream, instead of her own? Fear. Yeah, well, she'd had enough of that. Staying here wasn't helping. She needed to go back to Cutchogue. Back to their vineyard, if it was still *their* vineyard. That's where she wanted to make wine.

Why had she been away this whole time? The answer started out simply enough. She'd been afraid of losing her parents' financial support. But then as she learned winemaking skills from Gaston, she felt justified in staying. Kate would be back in Cutchogue after her graduation in June. She would meet her there. It was now or never.

Sydney rushed back to her bungalow. Sitting on the edge of her bed, she began a mental list. She had to give the bank notice and call her parents to make them aware she was leaving France. She would, of course, tell Kate she would be back soon. She wanted to talk to Claude and Cécile individually. Meanwhile she'd push Gaston to continue teaching her all he could about making wine. Sydney collapsed backward onto the bed, her courage and bravado exhausted. She hadn't the foggiest idea what to do once she returned to Cutchogue.

What would she have to do? Beg? Plead? Crawl on her knees? How could she explain to Kate why she should be their winemaker?

Why she'd been gone so long? She had no idea. She'd do whatever it took. And then of all people, her mother popped into her head asking her why she was going to dig in the dirt on Long Island. Because Kate was there. She could learn winemaking anywhere. But Kate was on Long Island.

Chapter Eleven

June 1984, Cutchogue, Long Island

Kate knew he meant well, so she pushed herself to insist. "Jerome, I've got this." She took the crowbar from his hands and waded into the pond. She wasn't sure what was keeping the water from flowing from one pond into the other, but she had to find out. One week ago today, she'd graduated from college. She was on her own now and wanted to at least pretend she knew what she was doing.

"Here I go. I'm walking over," Kate declared, as she waded through the water, holding the crowbar above her head. "At the grill." Kate looked back to make sure Jerome was still out of the water and only watching. "Going under."

Kate pulled the goggles down over her eyes, took a deep breath and sank down into the water. Though the water was murky from her shuffling around, she saw the problem in seconds and stood back up. "It's just a big branch that's stuck in the grill, collecting leaves. It's blocking the flow. I can get it."

Kate took another big breath and ducked back down. Using the crowbar as leverage, it took her only two tries to pry off the branch. She brought it up to the surface and held it up in triumph. "See…"

As she gripped the branch to show Jerome, Kate was startled to see someone standing right next to him. Someone who had not been there a minute before, someone who looked exactly like Sydney Barrett. She lowered the branch immediately, her heart suddenly pounding. She looked at Jerome for a reality check. He shrugged. Kate looked at Sydney. The damn woman was smiling.

Kate waded over, hesitated for a moment, then grabbed Sydney's extended hand when Sydney leaned over to help pull her up and out of the pond. At home in Cutchogue after graduating, her mother had given her a third gift box from Sydney, sent from her hometown in Massachusetts. It had contained the message: *Back in the US. See you soon!* But with Sydney, of course, she hadn't known when *soon* would be. Now, standing eye to eye with Sydney and totally self-conscious of her soaking wet and clinging clothes, her mind rushed to say something, however idiotic. "You're here!"

"As promised."

Jerome patted Sydney on the arm. "Hey, I thought you were in Paris. Welcome back!"

"I was," Sydney answered, but nothing more.

"You two get reacquainted," Kate said, leaving them by the pond. "I need to change." She needed a few minutes to gather her wits.

"I'm going to say hello to Rachel. See you in a bit," Sydney called.

Her mother. Kate had forgotten how tight Sydney was with her mother. And how much Jerome adored Sydney. She snuck a peak and sure enough, Sydney had her arm around Jerome's shoulder. She was here, standing mere feet away.

Kate rushed to her cottage to shower and change. Toweling off, she made it to the edge of the bed and plunked down, her head in her hands. Oh my God. Now what? More than anything else, she knew this was what she wanted, what she'd always wanted—for Sydney to return, and work with her on the vineyard. But what was she supposed to do? Kate threw on some clothes, but then slung herself down into her one chair, only to hop up again seconds later. She walked to the window over the sink and looked out. She could see the grader and, looking straight out, the rows and rows of fragile vines steadily growing up their stakes. How was she supposed to act with Sydney? Kate grabbed hold of the sink and tried to calm down.

She'd always wanted Sydney to be their winemaker, but she also knew damn well, she had wanted a lot more. And now since Abby, she knew exactly what *more* could be.

❖

When she walked outside, Sydney was standing by her car, holding up a brown paper bag. "Doughnuts! This is a new item at the farm stand. Could I tempt you with one? Or maybe we could sit a minute and talk? The vines look amazing, by the way."

"I'm on my way to weed. If you saw the vines, you probably noticed all the weeds." Kate was so flummoxed, she was sure she'd be tongue-tied if they sat down to talk.

"Not really." Sydney let the bag drop to her side, her eyes crinkled. "Say, your mother invited me to dinner. You're coming, right? We have lots to catch up on."

"I don't eat with them anymore." Yikes, that was abrupt. Kate took a breath. "You remember I have my own place, right? So I only eat with them on special occasions. My mother will be thrilled to have you to talk to. My father and I still aren't talking."

Sydney was staring at her.

"What?" Kate asked.

"It's going to be a bit awkward without you there." Sydney shifted her weight, standing there looking as gorgeous as ever in her dress blouse and slacks. "We have a lot to talk about, don't you think?"

"Right now I only have questions."

"Like?"

"What made you return? How long are you planning to stay?"

"Ever direct."

"Unlike you who just shows up——"

"Hey, this time I did give you hints of my return. And even waited a week after your graduation to let you settle in."

"So, you're here to work?" Kate retorted.

"Of course."

"Then you'll need a place to stay."

"Well, yes——"

"Your room at Uncle Louie's is still available," Kate said.

"Good. Still calling it that, I see."

"What? Uncle Louie's?"

Sydney nodded.

"Yes, well, technically it is mine, but it's still difficult for me to go in there with Louie gone."

"I'll take good care of the house, Kate. I'll be ready to get started tomorrow morning. Bright and early, right? Is there anything else I should know about where things stand?"

"We have to put in the irrigation system and fruiting wires this summer," Kate said, backing up.

"I meant personally. Like between you and me."

"Oh, that kind of stuff. Well, I have a girlfriend."

Sydney drew in a breath. "You do? Good for you. Have I met her?"

"As a matter of fact. Abby."

"Well, well, well. I didn't think it would take you long. Good for you."

Kate looked at her watch, pretending to care about the time. If she didn't start weeding, she'd babble. "Work and talk in the morning?" She stepped away. A few feet down the driveway, she stopped and swung around. Sydney hadn't budged. "Hope my father behaves."

Sydney nodded. "I'll get my bags."

Kate weeded vigorously, trying as hard as she could to keep her mind on the plants. They'd survived their first winter and looked strong. She couldn't believe that they would soon start bearing their first grapes. This summer they'd have to discard all the immature clusters that emerged. Developing grapes so soon took energy away from the growing plant. Kate bent down and caressed the green leaves of a vine and cupped one of the embryonic grape clusters. Bless Magda and Amber, who had taken her weekly calls to report on the weather and the precious vines as they continued to grow and put out tiny leaves. The weather had held. Torrential rains or bad winds could destroy a vineyard's entire crop before it ever got started. Nature was never, ever, to be taken for granted.

Calmer now, she walked back toward her cottage. One foot inside the door, however, her emotions unraveled once again. She looked out the window and up at Uncle Louie's second floor. Had Sydney unpacked? How had the dinner gone? Had Sydney met someone in France? Why was she really here?

❖

Kate tossed and turned half the night, unable to relax. Finally, at first light, she got out of bed, dressed, and walked the path that led from her cottage out to the fields. She walked and waited for the sun to rise. She'd only gone in about three rows when she spotted something shiny on a leaf. Thinking it was a piece of metal that had caught the light, she dropped to the ground and pulled the vine toward her. A beetle! Strangely beautiful, but slow-moving, with a shiny metallic green body and copper-colored wing covers. Kate's stomach tightened. She inhaled deeply and stood, making her way slowly down the row. She saw another, two plants over. Her stomach convulsed this time. Sweat broke out on her brow. She'd had the soil tested and it was in great condition, needing only lime to up the pH. The land had lain dormant a year before they planted the vines. Her uncle had sown a cover crop of alfalfa and clover the winter before she planted. Kate was pleased the soil had a rich and healthy ecosystem, sustainable without chemical inputs. Yet, even with all that, here were her first pests.

Her second day back in Cutchogue, Kate had driven to the Cornell Cooperative Extension in Riverhead to make sure she wasn't missing anything, soil-wise. She planned to use natural deterrents, like aphids or aromatic herbs that would deter predators. Kate leaned over and took a beetle in her hand, trying not to panic. She needed to find a solution for the problem. She stared at the beetle another several seconds, then tore down the hill, back to her cottage.

She dug out her Integrated Pest Management manual given to her as a graduation present by her mentor, Professor Ziegler. He was the one professor advocating nonchemical means of pest control. She looked up the beetle—under the class Insecta—and there it was. Order Coleoptera. Species *Popillia japonica*. Japanese beetles were known vineyard pests and they had to be removed, one by one, if necessary.

She grabbed a paper bag, ran back to the vineyard, pulled off several beetles, bagged them and raced back to the truck. Sitting outside on her uncle's back step was Sydney, coffee cup in hand.

"What's happening? You're all flushed," she called out, stepping toward Kate.

It was so strange to see Sydney on the property. "Beetles," she said. She kept going toward the truck, and Sydney followed. Kate opened the door and jumped onto the seat. "I'm going to verify what I need to do. Don't go away." If Sydney was here to work, her timing was perfect. Kate started the engine and sped off, sending dust, no doubt, right into Sydney's face. *Oops.*

Kate drove directly to Magda and Amber's house. As natural herb farmers, they not only would have encountered these pests but would have the experience to deal with them. Growing herbs since the late sixties, they used neither pesticides nor herbicides. Kate had no idea where they got their information or how they made their concoctions, but they swore that they worked. And people bought them.

Kate rapped soundly on their door. Several seconds later, Magda—obviously awakened from sleep—opened the door.

"Kate?"

"Beetles." She held up the bag.

Magda laughed, hugged Kate, and asked her in. Fifteen minutes later, Kate was on her way back to the farm with a promise that Magda and Amber would come help. With Sydney, they'd be an army of four. Picking hundreds—hopefully not thousands—of beetles off the vines was not going to be fun.

Sydney was sitting in the shade of a tree waiting for her.

"So?" Sydney said, reaching Kate as she hopped down from the truck. "What did they say?"

"Japanese beetles, which is what I thought."

"I don't think it's so bad," Sydney said. "I took a quick run over to the vines while I was waiting. They're not on every plant. And I talked to your father about them."

"You talked to my father?" Kate asked, shocked.

"Evidently you blazing out of here in the truck first thing in the morning is a big deal."

"Never mind that. What did he say?" she asked, her curiosity overruling her reluctance to involve her father.

"He said to spray the hell out of them. Which you should have done from the beginning. Not that you should have planted grapes at all." Sydney put up her hands in apology for his words. Kate was about to comment, when she saw another early riser approaching.

"What's going on?" Jerome asked, looking from Kate to Sydney. "Good to see you're still here this morning," he said to Sydney. "Kate?"

"I found Japanese beetles on some of the vines. I want to get rid of them while they're feeding so they don't lay eggs. If they get into the ground, we've got a bigger problem. They're a little sluggish first thing in the morning. This is the best time to pick them off by hand."

"One by one?" Sydney asked.

"There's no other way. And no, there's no way we're going to spray the vines." Kate crossed her arms and stared at Sydney.

"I wasn't going to say that." Sydney looked hurt. "I understand how you feel."

At the moment, Kate couldn't remember what she had or hadn't told Sydney. "Look, beetles aren't the worst problem—more like a menace than a fatal disease—but they have to be dealt with immediately. They could do devastating damage to the leaves. And without the leaves, there would be no growth whatsoever."

"So the plan is to pick them off one by one?" Jerome also asked.

"And we have to kill them as we remove them." The nonchemical way was to put a bit of detergent in water and drop the beetles in as they picked them. Dropped into soapy water, they'd drown. Terrible death, but in this case, it had to be done. "They're actually easy targets. And we'll have to keep them away going forward. I have an idea, but Magda and Amber will be here soon with probably a better one."

As if on cue, Magda and Amber's old Ford pulled in the driveway.

"We have pheromone traps and neem oil," Magda soon explained. "We'll lather every other row with the oil. If there are beetles, or if more come, they'll ingest it and die. We have to get to them before they mate. They feed, they mate, they reproduce. It's not a complicated life."

"You sure know your bugs," Sydney told her.

"Technically they're insects, not bugs," Kate interjected, then caught her tone. "Sorry, just nervous."

Amber sidled up and put one arm around Kate's shoulder. "Buckets and brushes, everyone!" She juggled a bucket in her left hand. Magda held up brushes in one hand and a can of neem oil in the other.

"Are we ready for a fun day of pick and paint?" Magda asked. "Hey, Sydney, welcome back."

"Thanks," Sydney said. "Good to be here. And just in time, eh?"

"Shall we?" Kate asked.

Kate's ever-faithful army started toward the vines as she mentally started her thank-yous.

❖

By noon, Kate's back ached. Picking off the beetles was easy, if a little creepy, according to Sydney. Bending over each plant, painting on the oil, then straightening, that was another story. She looked at the plant she had just painted. Its tiny trunk was smaller than her own wrist. The nature of farming was that plants would always be vulnerable. That was a fact she'd grown up with. But it seemed especially cruel at this point. These plants were just a year old. She couldn't afford to replace them. Kate leaned over the plant, the reality sinking in.

"How's your back?" Sydney asked.

Kate stood upright. She hadn't heard her walk up. "Fine, just checking on this plant. Yours?"

"No complaints," Sydney answered.

During the course of the morning, Kate recalled that Sydney had been through all the back-breaking work when they first put in the baby plants. She was there when they put in all the posts and tied the plants to stakes. And after the beetles were managed, they would need to attach the fruiting wire to all the posts, another tedious but necessary job. Sydney was as upbeat and indispensable today as she had been then.

"I have an idea. But it'll be your decision," Sydney began.

"Go ahead, please."

"I think we should consider getting some kids to help us. They're shorter."

Kate hesitated. Let strangers—tall or short—work in the vineyard? But she should at least hear Sydney out.

"What's your idea?"

"We need more help, Kate. Tomorrow's Saturday. I bet I could get some kids off the beach who could help us. They'd love the bug—uh, insect, part. They'd get sun, a good workout, and I'll make burgers at the end of the day. What do you say?"

"I can't just let anybody work here."

"They won't break anything, Kate. At the rate we're going, it'll take weeks, not days. It's your call, but you don't need a degree to do what we did this morning. I'll go get them first thing tomorrow." Sydney wiped the sweat dripping down her face. She had on a hat, but even that had a sweat-drenched band around the brim.

Kate had grown up in a farming community that supported one another all the time. But kids from the beach? They weren't farm kids. Would they even come? She looked over at all the untouched acres. They didn't have to paint each plant, but they did have to make sure they were all beetle-free and put out the traps.

"Do you have any idea where the beaches are?"

"Long Island is surrounded by water. I'll find them. Magda and Amber can't come back tomorrow. Their shop is open." Sydney winced, straightening up, but didn't say another word.

"Okay, it's worth trying. I'll get more brushes and buckets tonight. Shall we break for lunch?"

"Please." She put her arm through Kate's then withdrew it immediately. "Sorry."

They walked down the row silently, looking for the others. Sydney's affectionate touch had surprised her, yes, but her arm still pleasantly tingled.

❖

Sydney arrived around eleven the next morning with six teenagers and two adults. The men said they were curious about the new vineyard. The teenagers all seemed eager to work, or at least to hang around Sydney. And why not? She was wearing cutoffs that showed her long and supple legs. One would have to be blind not to notice them. And a sleeveless cotton top that showed off her flat stomach and strong, tanned arms.

"Where did you find them?" Kate asked, leaning close.

"The sailing club. Where there's water and wind, there are young boys learning to sail. I promised them lessons once we got all the work done."

"I see."

They worked hard, all of them. They pulled off the critters and lathered the vines with oil. Sydney kept up a constant stream of chatter, which kept them all engaged. They stopped at one for sandwiches and took another break around four. Sydney brought out the hose near the house and suggested watering everyone down. The boys couldn't scramble up fast enough. It was amazing to watch their raging teenage hormones. Sydney knew exactly what she was doing. And never let go of the hose for a second.

They stopped around seven thirty. Fortunately, the beetles were only in the cabernet franc and scattered through the chardonnay near the house, so they were done.

Kate's mother had set up two grills behind the house. She'd also brought out a folding table, and on it, Kate noticed, were plates of hamburger meat, hot dogs, buns, potato salad, and pickles. She'd also brought over a giant ice bucket stocked with cans of soda for the boys and beer for the adults. "I know the drill," she told Kate and smiled. Kate marched over and gave her mother a giant hug.

"Oh, Mom, thank you."

"Take a seat, everyone, have a soda," Sydney told the crew. The adults had left. The young men sat immediately. "Dinner will be ready in fifteen minutes."

As the teenagers sat watching Sydney—totally entranced—Kate could only smile. Two out of the three women they were with were lesbians. They hadn't a clue.

❖

Kate was wiping down the tables when Sydney walked back outside. She'd gone in the house to help wash the dishes.

"Listen, I've been thinking," Sydney said. "This wasn't the way you'd planned to deal with the beetles."

"But it worked out. My back thanks you. We all thank you." Kate tried to gracefully work out a tight muscle. She seriously needed a shower.

"Just checking. I wanted to make sure you felt okay about how it went."

"It worked out great. And it was fun to watch you and your boy harem at work."

Sydney laughed. "Boys. They're all the same. So, tomorrow we start putting the fruiting wires on?"

"Back on schedule."

"Good. Then at some point, I'll need a job."

"A job?" Kate asked.

"In town. I need to earn some money. Groceries, gas. It's no longer an option to live off my father's credit card."

Sydney was way ahead of her. Kate needed a job, too. At the moment, she, also, had only expenses and not a single cent coming in. "Yeah, and a job for me is in order, as well."

❖

A week later, after several interviews, Sydney got a job. The owner of a local graphics shop loved the portfolio of ad copy she put together to show off what she could do. She hired her on the spot. It was a straight nine-to-five job, but they would pay her to do extra projects at home.

Kate cobbled together part-time jobs at two of the first vineyards on the North Fork. They probably felt sorry for her, thinking she was just starting out and needed cash, but Kate wasn't proud. It also gave her a great chance to learn and ask questions. The Hargraves told her to come in at nine and she reported to the Lenz Winery at one in the afternoon. Bless their generous hearts. With these jobs, she worked at least six hours every day. That left her early mornings, evenings, and weekends to work on her own vineyard. Thank goodness Uncle Louie had also gifted her his truck, so there was no problem getting to work. Her relationship with her father was so strained, she would have hated going inside the back door for the key to his truck.

❖

The plants were looking healthy, but the weeds had been growing since April as well. Every morning, she and Sydney both were out by sunrise, weeding until eight, then running in to shower and change for work. Kate often met up with Sydney again in the driveway as she hopped in her BMW and Kate climbed into her truck. Every evening at six, Kate found Sydney waiting for her in the shade by the grader. That first week after work, they put sulfur on the plants to protect them from mildew. They didn't talk a lot as they worked separately, ate separately, and went to their separate living spaces. Perhaps that was odd or maybe even unkind, but at the moment Kate didn't want or need to know more about Sydney and her adventures in France.

One afternoon Kate spotted a young man in an Army uniform walking through the vineyard. Her heart sank in terror, but she went down to see what he wanted. Three minutes later, Sydney showed up by her side.

"Sydney, this is Ryan Carmichael. His parents, Mary and Finn, own the stables and training grounds down the road."

Sydney reached out to shake his hand, surprising Ryan, who stiffened but shook her hand, not saying a word.

"Stables? I'd love to stop by and ride. Are you home on leave?" Sydney asked him, motioning to his uniform.

Ryan was forced to answer. "Yes."

Kate said nothing, waiting to see what he wanted. She hadn't seen Ryan since Lily's funeral.

"My mother said you were home. And started growing grapes." He pulled on his collar.

"Correct," Kate said.

"I, uh, just came over to check things out. I see you have your helper."

"We can always use more, right, Kate?" Sydney rapped him on the arm. "You look strong."

"Yeah, right. I have to go." He backed off slowly, then practically galloped down the hill.

"Who is he?" Sydney asked, "other than the neighborhood bully in uniform?"

Kate was amazed at Sydney's intuition. It was all she could do to breathe.

"Kate, look at me. You're all white."

"It's Ryan—" Kate managed to look over at Sydney. "Do you remember me telling you about Lily, the girl I had my first crush on?" She took a breath. "Well, Ryan is her older brother."

"Let's go over to the shade."

They sat down. Kate put her hands in her lap to hide her trembling. Should she tell Sydney? Why not? Maybe she'd learned how to hunt while in France and would shoot him. Never mind that Ryan was the one trained to kill.

"What's the deal? Can you tell me?"

Perhaps it was the tenderness in Sydney's voice. Kate had forced this memory so far down into her subconscious, she was loath to let it see the light. But if Ryan was home, here to taunt her once again, she'd better deal with it. Kate told Sydney about the night, only a week before Lily died, when she'd stayed over at Lily's. They'd laughed and talked like old times. Lily was so weak she was barely sitting up. Lily had twin beds in her room. That night she'd asked Kate to come into her bed to hold her. *Just hold me*, she'd asked. *I'm afraid.*

"My brave Lily had just admitted that she was afraid of dying, so of course I hopped into her bed. At that very moment Ryan burst into the room, pointing his finger, calling us *lezzies*. Lily told me not to pay him any attention, but how could I not? I waited. Ryan ran off to tell his folks. I heard loud voices from down the hall, but no one came back to the room. I went back to my bed, equally ashamed of leaving Lily in bed alone *and* of Ryan's accusation."

Kate stopped talking, overcome by the memory. When Sydney took her hand, it felt comforting, and so she held on.

"Any repercussions? Other than to your psyche?" Sydney asked gently.

"There was never another mention of that evening." But Kate knew she had felt exposed. And ashamed. "Lily died soon afterward. That was all I could deal with. After losing Lily, Ryan was an afterthought. To tell you the truth, I pushed all thoughts of him away until now. He still gives me the creeps." *And scares the shit out of me.* "Maybe that's why it took me so long to come out." And why she was so scared to come out to her father.

"Very perceptive, my friend. Most people need years of therapy to figure out something like that."

❖

The confession changed things up. After that, she and Sydney began talking for real. Putting in the irrigation system was easy by comparison. The plants had never been watered. They'd been lucky to have had enough rain so far. But a scorching hot July? The vines would shrivel up and die without water.

After a brief discussion, the consensus was drip irrigation—for which they'd need to dig a dedicated well—and they'd need to put in a trellis wire specifically for it, purchase tubing, drip locks, emitters and end caps. Jerome told them it would be an uncomplicated but tedious installation. Kate didn't tell either of them that this would almost use up the last of her inheritance. But if they didn't have healthy plants, the whole thing was moot. And she would have dishonored her uncle and his faith and hope for her future.

Jerome consulted with a plumber to make sure the water pressure design was correct and helped them purchase all the equipment they needed. They worked together each morning and late into the evening. Kate told Sydney everything she'd learned in school about growing grapes and Sydney told her all she'd learned about winemaking in France.

❖

By August, they were ready to begin the last job of the summer, installing the fruiting wire. They were already late to start training the shoots along the trellis. When Kate had come back in March to prune, it had been very hard to cut the vines down to tiny, inches-long *trunks*. This second summer, new shoots were robustly growing, producing a strong canopy. As soon as the wires were in, they would have to choose and train two horizontal shoots off the main vine to grow along the wires.

"That's the theory," Kate explained to Sydney, "but I have no experience dealing with wire. Two workers at Lenz showed me what they'd done."

"Well, I've never done wire installation either, but I understand the principle. And I was born to do this kind of work." Sydney strutted around very Annie Oakley-like, making Kate laugh. "If we're going to use a drill gun," she said, blowing smoke from her imaginary gun, "I'm going to buy myself a tool belt."

Kate rolled her eyes but loved her enthusiasm. "Sydney, this is going to be a lot of work."

"Yeah, so what else is new? What's the plan?"

Kate smiled. She explained how to do the work and figured it would take them several weeks to finish the wiring. Especially since it'd be slow going, at least at first. They'd have to precisely measure and place the first wire three feet from the ground and the second wire at five and a half inches, careful not to step on the baby vines. They'd need to work a row apart so they could help each other do the wire work, like pull the wire out or hold the drill while the other measured. Lots of time to talk.

Kate was finally ready to ask about the château and Sydney's vineyard experience. And especially about the chef she had casually mentioned. Kate thought about her last year in college and her relationship with Abby. For the first time, Kate realized it was good she and Sydney had spent the year apart.

One night, as she sat alone at her tiny table eating a bowl of soup, she realized how much she missed Sydney's company, and thought about what the two of them had talked about that evening and what they were planning to do the next day. The signs couldn't be clearer, nor could she escape their meaning. She was as drawn to Sydney as she had been the day they met, and probably always would be. A grin bubbled its way to her mouth just thinking about working with her again every morning, every evening, and all weekend. It was time to call Abby, whom she hadn't thought about in weeks. She and Abby were never destined to be together since neither had any intention of leaving their farms to be with the other. She would forever be indebted to Abby and grateful for their wonderful college relationship, but she needed to officially end it. She was in love with Sydney and wanted to be available to go wherever that relationship led her.

CHAPTER TWELVE

Late August 1984, Cutchogue

As Sydney often did at the end of a long workday, she took her tea—a Kate influence—upstairs to the bedroom to look out the open window onto the vineyard. She couldn't believe how well everything was going with the vines, beyond her wildest imagination, really. Not so much with her feelings about Kate. Sydney automatically looked toward Kate's cottage. The light was on. Kate was probably reading. Sydney could easily walk the short distance between Louie's house and Kate's cottage. Emotionally, she had zero idea how to close the enormous gap she felt between them. She was stuck. She knew it, she hated it, but she had no idea how to move forward. Better to stay in this holding pattern as friends. At least she hadn't messed anything up yet, and she still got to see Kate every day.

Sydney had come close to revealing her true feelings when Kate asked her about living with Cécile. She'd confessed that she'd only accepted her offer so she could stay long enough to get winemaking experience. That was a hard enough admission.

"Were you at least fond of her?" Kate had asked.

"Of course. She was quite kind and generous. And a fabulous chef. We ate well."

"But you weren't in love with her," Kate clarified.

"No."

"So, if it was all about staying there for the learning experience, why did you leave?"

The question had thrown her for a loop. She was not then—nor was she now—prepared to reveal her true feelings for Kate. "I hoped to experience the real thing one day," she'd told Kate. "Love, that is."

Thankfully, Kate had not pushed the conversation further.

Sydney stepped away from the window. Kate was the courageous one. She'd shared with her that horrible moment years ago when Ryan had walked in on her and Lily in the bedroom. In spite of this, Kate had come out on her own terms, and had her first girlfriend. She seemed quite at ease with her new lesbian self, as long as her father wasn't around. But could Sydney, the supposed confident one, ever tell Kate what she was dealing with? About how she felt unworthy? Not for a million bucks.

The only thing she knew for sure was how much she wanted to touch Kate, make love to her. If anything, her fantasies were getting stronger. Just yesterday she had to turn her head from noticing the curve of Kate's breast as she reached up to hold a wire in place. Last week they were sitting in the shade, taking a break. Sydney followed the line of Kate's calves to her thighs, to the zipper of her shorts. Oh, yeah, she wanted Kate. But until she figured out what to do, her brain had to be in charge of this relationship, not her goddamn pussy, and certainly not her tarnished heart.

❖

A week later, Kate was waiting for her in the driveway when she got home from work. Sydney stepped out of her car, tugging her briefcase from the passenger side. It turned out that her design work was taking off. Her drawings, ads, and invitations were all simple and whimsical—with just enough detail, it seemed. She had no idea there were so many birthdays, anniversaries, garage sales, and retirement parties in Cutchogue and the Southold area. She had more commissions than she could finish at work and had started to bring the work home.

"Nice briefcase," Kate said, pointing to Sydney's leather bag.

"Yeah, ever the professional. Love the special greeting. What's up?"

"The Carmichaels want us to come to dinner. They've invited the two of us and my folks to come over this weekend. I wanted to find out if you were interested in going."

"Really? I've been waiting to meet them."

"Fabulous. Oh, and not to worry, it'll be safe. I doubt my father will come since they invited both you and me. Plus, I haven't seen Ryan for weeks. He must have gone back to wherever he's stationed." Kate's arms were all over the place in her excitement. Kate had told Sydney how much the Carmichaels meant to her.

"Walk me to Uncle Louie's?" Of course she wanted to go to dinner, and as she walked, her nimble brain kicked in an idea. At the steps, Sydney stopped. "Want to come in?"

"Not tonight. I promised I would call Mary back after I talked to you."

Sydney let her disappointment go. "How about we add a little something extra to the evening?"

"What do you have in mind?" Kate asked, with an adorable quizzical look on her face.

"What do you say we do a little wine tasting before or after dinner—with the Carmichaels' permission, of course. I think it's time we start talking about our future business."

Kate's mouth dropped open. She blinked then put her hands on her hips. "You've got to be kidding. This is not a wine drinking crew. I think they drink beer or whiskey."

"So they're not opposed to drinking. We have to start somewhere to introduce people to wine and what we're doing. We need your family and their friends on board. Besides, they'll only be taking sips."

Kate shook her head. "I don't think so—"

"Give me a chance to convince you." Sydney sat down on the top step. Kate sat down beside her.

"Go ahead."

"You remember all those wine tastings we went to in Napa? I was thinking of something along those lines but keeping it simple. Three wines. Four maybe. Two dry reds of different varietals to concentrate on flavor and one dry white—to note the color change. And one sweet wine. Beginners always love sweet wines."

"Sydney, I'm telling you they don't drink wine. For sure my mother doesn't."

"But you said they're not opposed to alcohol."

"No, they're just not, shall I say, adventurous."

"Then they might be open to learning, right? Everyone has to start somewhere."

"Not everyone has to drink our wine."

"Please don't say that outside the liquor store that's carrying our wine." Sydney grinned.

"Tell me again your point?" Kate asked.

"The more people get involved in what we're doing, the better. It spreads goodwill and gets the word out. But for your parents—in this case, your mother and her best friends—we want them to acknowledge our goal to make and sell wine."

"I don't know."

Sydney waited. She knew to let Kate think.

"What the heck." Kate jumped up and faced Sydney. "If Mary and Finn agree, let's give it a shot."

"Good for you, Kate. I'm thrilled."

"Why not, they're good sports. But we'll tell everyone ahead of time exactly what we're going to do, so there won't be any surprises."

"Deal."

❖

The Carmichaels' home was humble. They'd spent all their money on their stables and the fenced-in fields where the horses ran. The evening started off on an uncomfortable note. They walked inside the Carmichael's screened-in back porch, their arms full of glasses and wine, and found Kate's father sitting on the sagging couch talking to Finn. Kate had told her mother that he could come *only* if he planned to be supportive. Kate, bless her heart, flinched only once. At that moment, Mary and Rachel came outside, laughing, Mary holding a giant pot of stew and Rachel a bowl of potatoes and vegetables for Kate.

"We decided it was high time you had your first Irish stew." Mary looked at Sydney and smiled. Mary, tall and robust, wore thick pants. She looked like she could handle a rope and corral a feral horse. Finn was the quintessential Irishman, with striking green eyes and a face that was now reddening as he laughed.

"Yes, indeed," Sydney said. Yet another loving and supportive mother. These two women were leagues away emotionally from her own mother. Sydney was overwhelmed.

Mary put her pot on the table. "And then as soon as the boys heard about the stew, they invited themselves. Is that okay?" Kate nodded, as did Sydney, so Mary bustled on, straightening the tablecloth as she scurried back into the house. Sydney assumed by boys she meant Finn and Zeke.

Mary had strung some lights around the perimeter of the porch to give it a festive look. For a few moments, Sydney and Kate had their backs to the outside door as they set up the wine and glasses for the tasting. Sydney was the first to see Ryan enter. A second later, she heard Kate gasp. Sydney immediately grabbed her arm and whispered, "Don't worry." From that moment on, Sydney never let him out of her sight. At dinner, he quietly filled his plate and walked over to sit by himself. Soon he was on his third beer, staring at Kate for several seconds at a time. So much for learning discipline and respect in the Army.

❖

"So, each of you has the red wine." Sydney held up her glass, inordinately pleased that the tasting was going well. "Look at the color. Tilt your glass a little and hold it up to the light. Now give it a careful swirl like we practiced with the chardonnay."

Sydney looked over her small crowd. Mary and Rachel were sitting together in one corner. Sydney swore they were a bit tipsy, even though they'd had the equivalent of about a half glass of wine each. Ryan had moseyed over to sit with Zeke and Finn on the other side of the room. They all were following her directions, surprisingly, even Kate's father. Sydney glanced over at Kate, sitting two feet away in a chair. Sydney expected her to be thrilled with how it was going, but instead she had this unreadable look on her face. They had planned to taste the merlot and then finish with a white zinfandel, which was too sweet for Sydney's tastes, but fitting for this particular group.

"Is there going to be an intermission?" Ryan suddenly asked. "Perhaps some dancing?" He stood up and did a pretend slow dance in a circle. He was clearly drunk.

Kate jumped up and crossed to Sydney in one stride. "See what I mean?" She stood frozen by Sydney's side, her fingers clenched.

"Come over and sit with us, Ryan," Mary quickly chimed out. "But I must tell you, we don't dance." She giggled and looked around. Ryan sat back down. Kate was staring straight ahead, her face ashen.

"What are you going to call the wine you two make?" Finn asked loudly, probably trying to divert attention back to the wine. Sydney quickly pointed to Kate. "Oh, this is Kate's property. She gets to make those decisions. I'm only doing the wine tasting because I have a little more experience—"

Ryan jumped back up, interrupting Sydney's sentence. "That's what I'm talking about. Experience. What kind of experience are we going to have tonight?" He wobbled a little but balanced himself on the back of the chair. Finn stood and put a hand on his son's shoulder. Ryan brushed it off.

"Lemme ask one question," Ryan slurred.

Kate moved to the back of her chair and gripped the wood with both hands.

"Is it about the wine?" Sydney asked, taking an aggressive step forward.

"I guess you'd say that."

"Ryan—" Mary tried to intercede.

"Mom, I gotta ask." Ryan looked away from his mother and picked up his wine glass, looking directly at Sydney.

"Let's say that old Kate here does turn all her grapes into wine. Are you going to stay here and help?" he asked. "You, personally?" He pointed at her with the glass, splashing some of the wine onto the table. "I think we have the right to this information."

Zeke stood up. Ryan ignored him and spoke directly to his own father. "Don't you think we deserve an answer? I do. It's bad for business, Dad, to have two lezzies so close to our farm and stables."

Mary gasped and Finn put his hand on Ryan's arm. "Let's go." He pulled him toward the door. Ryan took two steps with him but then stopped abruptly, shaking off his father's hand and glaring at Kate.

"You haven't changed, have you, Kate? Lily's gone, so you got yourself a new girlfriend."

Sydney's heart seized. She wanted to slug Ryan. Pulverize him. Zeke grabbed Ryan and pulled his shirt tight against his throat. "How dare you?" he said.

"I'll take care of him," Finn interrupted. "You, come with me." Finn pulled his son away and shoved him toward the door. "Out." They were through the door in seconds. Zeke followed two steps behind. A moment later, Sydney heard the barn door creak open.

Sydney pivoted toward Kate, but Mary had already rushed over. "I'm so sorry about Ryan, Kate," she said, then turned toward Sydney. Mary looked from one to the other.

Sydney experienced the wildest guilt that she'd set up the whole situation. Kate had tried to warn her, but she hadn't listened. "It's okay, Mary." Sydney patted her on the arm. "He didn't get the memo on tasting etiquette." Sydney looked over at Kate, who was concentrating on her breathing, head down. Sydney rotated back to Mary. "Maybe—"

"We should call it a night?" Mary guessed. "Yes. You were wonderful to give us this presentation. We'll do it again another time." She gave a taut smile to the two of them before picking up several dishes and walking purposefully into the house.

Which left Rachel standing with the two of them.

"You don't have to say a word, sweetheart," Rachel said softly to her daughter.

Kate's color was coming back to her face, but Sydney didn't miss the sweat droplets on her forehead.

"About the two of us, you mean?" Kate managed. "Or me?" She stood there, looking befuddled or maybe in shock.

Sydney's protective instincts took over. She wheeled toward Rachel and let slip the first thing that came to mind. "Oh, we're not a couple, Rachel. I'm a lesbian, but Kate…" Christ, what the hell was she saying?

"It's fine, Sydney." Rachel put her hand gently on her arm.

Kate turned to her mother, her eyes softening. "I didn't have a clue, Mom, not for the longest time." She was trembling. "It was quite the revelation. Didn't you ever wonder why I never dated in high school? Or college? I did. The guys were nice but…no sparks, no heart beating overtime. Like how you felt for Dad. Then my senior year at Davis I got involved with this awesome fellow student, Abby."

"Sorry to interrupt," Sydney interjected gently. "I should leave. This is your private moment." Sydney grabbed three bottles from the table and walked to the door. "I'll put these in the car and wait for you out back, Kate." She was out the door before either could say a word.

Hurrying to her car, Sydney kicked a stone and watched it fly down the driveway. She was furious with herself for putting Kate in this situation. The wine tasting was a stupid, foolish idea. But Rachel was being amazing. Sydney put the bottles in the empty case in the back of the car. Hearing someone coming up behind her, she tensed up, suspecting Ryan, but was surprised to find Zeke approaching.

"Hold up," he shouted.

Sydney crossed her arms and waited.

"So tell me, is my daughter..." He was searching for the word.

"Gay, lesbian, homosexual? All these terms are appropriate."

"Don't sass me."

"I mean no disrespect. I was merely helping you with the proper terminology."

"You're a smart one, aren't you?"

"You stop right there, Zeke," Rachel declared, coming up to stand a foot away from him and using a tone Sydney had never heard her use. Kate was two steps behind. "This is our conversation with Kate. Leave Sydney out of it."

Rachel was trying to protect her! The three of them were staring at her. Was she supposed to walk away and leave Kate, who was unused to attacks like this, totally exposed? Zeke had gone berserk. God damn it. She'd never in her life wanted to protect someone so desperately.

"Talk to me, Dad," Kate said boldly. All eyes spun toward her.

Sydney took one last look at Kate, then over at Rachel, who nodded. Sydney continued farther down the driveway, just far enough away that they could ignore her but close enough to hear the conversation. She turned around to hear and watch, already in agony. She was responsible for this happening.

"Well, is it true?" Kate's father barked, his hands flailing.

Rachel took her daughter's hand. "You don't have to answer him. I wouldn't, if I were you."

"Yes, she does." He balled up his fists. "We need to know. She owes us that."

"She owes us nothing. Maybe a little respect, but at the moment, you, Ezekiel Bauer, deserve none." Rachel stared defiantly at her husband. Kate stood there, seemingly stunned. But then, surprisingly, she lifted her head, took a breath, and faced them.

"It's fine, Mom," Kate managed, her voice relatively strong. "I am attracted to women. That is what you were wondering, right?" She looked at her father.

"I told you we shouldn't have let her go off to school." Zeke's face was red, his eyes blazing.

Rachel put her arm out to him. "Take it easy. I'm warning you. Let her talk."

Zeke brushed her hand off. "It was one thing, my brother being a homo, but you? What's going on here? Something in the water? I sure as hell raised you better."

Kate leaned toward her father. "This happened all on its own," she stated matter-of-factly. "But you can be sure I knew how you'd feel about it. You made that loud and clear. But let me ask you one question. Who are you to judge? And where do you get your information about right and wrong?"

"I know how people are supposed to be," he grunted. "You should, too."

"Supposed to be?" Kate questioned, her chest heaving. She didn't budge, nor did she take her eyes off her father. Sydney was extremely impressed. Kate was not backing down. "This is who I am," she stated, "and like it or not, I will be living and working within feet of you, your house, your fields. I suggest we go back to not talking to each other. That seemed to work for both of us." She crossed her arms in a show of defiance.

"What about her?" Zeke sputtered, pointing over his shoulder with his left thumb.

Sydney wanted to pounce, at least verbally. Guilty or not, no one *thumbed* her. But she didn't react, out of respect for Kate, who was doing quite fine on her own.

"Sydney is not my girlfriend, as Ryan implied. She's here to help me grow grapes and make wine. If you have a problem with her, come to me."

"You can't—"

"That's enough, both of you," Rachel interrupted. She rotated toward Kate. "I love you, Kate. You never have to worry about that." She hugged her daughter then grabbed her husband's arm. "It's time you and I go home." She pulled him away, and remarkably, he walked on with her toward their truck.

Sydney was dumbstruck. She wasn't sure who she was more impressed with, Rachel or Kate. She waited for Kate's next move, not budging a muscle. Kate walked past her to the passenger side of the BMW and hopped in. "You coming?"

"Sure." Sydney bolted toward the car.

They were back in a few minutes, their vineyard only up the road. Sydney parked. "I'll go back tomorrow to pick up the rest of our stuff," she told Kate. "I'll walk you back to your cottage."

They walked back in silence, Kate taking the lead. Her hand on the door, Kate turned to Sydney. "I should have told them sooner, but I was afraid of exactly what happened tonight. I knew how he treated Uncle Louie." She paused. She'd taken her hand off the door, but her fists were clenched. "I kept hoping he would react differently. I was wrong." She let her head drop.

"Kate, this whole evening is my fault. I'm so sorry." Words failed her, but she wanted, needed Kate's forgiveness. She knew that much. And she didn't want to go back alone to Uncle Louie's. "Could we sit for a minute?" She motioned to the steps.

Kate nodded and sat down on the small step, pulling her long legs in. She patted the step next to her and Sydney sat. After a second, Kate surprised Sydney for the third time that evening.

"You are sticking around to help me clean up this mess, aren't you?" she asked.

"You mean with your parents? Of course."

"And sticking around to help make wine?"

"You bet."

Kate looked at her. "Good. Just making sure."

Neither of them stirred. Sydney finally did what she'd wanted to do all evening. She scooted over and put her arm around Kate. "You're incredibly brave."

Kate looked up and smiled. Sydney tightened her arm. Kate put her head on Sydney's shoulder. "To hell with my father."

Sydney didn't move, shocked by Kate's response. *She says that now.* But Sydney knew that wouldn't last. Kate would soon come to her senses and be furious at her father, and definitely at her. She'd blown it. She'd officially given Zeke reason to further alienate his daughter. She had known she would screw up eventually. But damn, she hadn't expected it to be tonight. She held on to Kate. There was no coming back from this. Surely Kate would soon see that she was not worth keeping around. Mentally Sydney started packing her bags.

Chapter Thirteen

Kate pulled the covers tightly to her chest. Her heart was pounding. It wasn't until she realized that she'd been having nightmares about Ryan chasing her that she calmed down. She was safe. The worst had happened. She'd been outed and had survived. Even better, she had her mother on her side—*I love you*—and by all appearances, Mary and Finn, too. Okay, she still had to deal with her father's hostility, but she meant what she said to Sydney. He could go to hell. She had her life to live. If he wanted to keep believing that she was *unnatural*, well, that was his choice. And his loss. Unbidden, a flash of memory hit her. Upstairs in her parents' house, on the wall between her old bedroom and her father's office, were all the Polaroid photos her father had tacked up over the years. Shots of her taking her first step, riding the tractor for the first time, her first 4-H exhibit, standing in his fields of corn at every age, with her mother by the Christmas tree. Damn, he'd once loved her very much.

Kate slid out of bed. Ironically, the hardest part of the evening happened at the very end, when Sydney let go of her and stood up to go back to Uncle Louie's house. She could have stayed in the embrace of those arms forever. No doubt Sydney's only intention was to show her sympathy and support. But at least she'd touched her. Kate had been craving that touch all summer. She didn't care about Sydney's apologies. She agonized as she watched her walk away. She had to make Sydney realize that her *business partner* wanted to be her lover as well.

❖

The September mornings were even cooler now. Kate looked down at her boots. She'd been sitting on her stoop for five minutes with the intention of tying her laces. Where had her mind gone? She barely recognized herself these days. Yesterday, as she was doing her daily inspection of the vines, she'd found a tiny grape cluster and actually caressed it before snipping it off. As hard as it had been to cut off all the second-year growth of grapes, they'd done it. But this time next year, if all went well, all the grapes would be shades of red, dark purple, or golden yellow. The sugars would be increasing, and they'd be preparing for their first harvest. Kate beamed. She'd just thought *they, harvest,* and *next year* in the same breath. Kate leaned down, tied her laces, and stood.

❖

Almost every evening, she and Sydney met up at Uncle Louie's after their day jobs. More often than not, Sydney made them a quick bite to eat. She still seemed uncomfortable somehow, ill at ease. Kate couldn't imagine what was causing it, but Sydney never opened up about anything. She always seemed to want to project a positive front. Maybe something was going on at her day job. From all the drawings Sydney showed her, she was a terrific artist. She couldn't imagine what the problem might be. Kate hoped she would design the logo for their vineyard one day. *How was that for positive?*

One particular evening they were working on budgets, trying to figure out how they would pay for everything, especially the expensive winemaking equipment. Out of the blue, Sydney asked if she could put in a phone line at Louie's house and told her that she'd gladly pay for it. Kate assumed it was a precaution for any calls that might come from her family. She'd told Kate her mother was after her to come home. Sydney said twice that evening that she wasn't interested in leaving, that she was happy where she was. Kate said sure to the phone line.

"By the way, I printed out all the paperwork we'll need to get our liquor license," Sydney told her. They were sitting side by side at the table upstairs at her uncle's. As usual, her mind was half on the work and half on trying to figure out how to move closer to Sydney. But at the sound of the word *license,* Kate sat straight up. "I'm going to send it off to Albany," Sydney continued. "It's never too early to apply. They might be sticklers about us since we're, uh, new at this."

Sydney's business acumen and focus on making wine was being put to good use. Kate noticed her subtle softening of a key potential problem. There were probably several reasons not to grant them a license, discrimination against women—and more so, lesbians—being the unwritten one. Without that license, they couldn't make wine, much less sell it.

❖

The day before her birthday Kate stayed at work longer than normal washing out barrels for the Lenz harvest. When she stopped by Uncle Louie's, she found a note from Sydney saying she was at the grader. The old machinery had all been taken away. Sydney was working on the insulation. In a winery, temperature control was extremely important.

Kate ambled down the path toward the grader, stopping to replace several stones that had strayed onto the pathway back under the canopy. Those stones would retain the heat of the sun and keep the soil warm at night. Natural insulation. Kate decided to walk down one of the rows, carefully looking for any signs of mold or mites, or worse still, mildew. The last few days had been surprisingly humid. Reaching the end post, she automatically reached up and pulled off a shirt Sydney had slung there. They were used to dressing in layers out in the field, taking off and putting on extra shirts as the weather and work dictated. But this time as Kate held Sydney's shirt in her hands, her whole body tingled. Before she could stop herself, she imagined Sydney without her shirt on. Without any clothes on at all. Kate stopped in her tracks, her heart racing. Good Lord. She could no longer deny what she wanted.

What if she asked Sydney to start celebrating a bit early? Just the two of them. Would she accept? Before she could stop herself, she rushed toward their future winery. Standing in front of the big barn door, she heard hammering. Sydney was inside. Suddenly Kate couldn't move. The door might as well have been five feet thick with an unbreakable lock on it. She looked down at her feet, expecting to see them caught in cement.

"Shit!" Kate heard from inside. Sydney must have hurt herself. Kate immediately put her hand on the door latch and yanked the door open. She frantically looked around for Sydney, finding her calmly looking down at her, a hammer swinging in one hand, the other, unharmed, holding onto the ladder.

"Hi," Sydney said. "Trying to tack up this old insulation."

Kate walked over. "You okay?"

"Oh, yeah. I hit the wall instead of the nail. I guess I'm a little tired."

Kate took a breath. "Listen, Sydney, do you have a minute?" Maybe she should have planned out what she was going to say.

"Sure. Let me come down." She climbed down the ladder and stood a foot away. "What's up?"

Kate could feel the beads of perspiration forming on her forehead but kept going. "My birthday is tomorrow. Believe it or not, I have a bottle of champagne in my refrigerator. I thought we could toast my birthday and celebrate all the work we've been doing." She paused, working up her nerve. "Want to come over to my cottage and share it? Tomorrow night?"

Sydney's eyebrows shot up. "You're inviting me over?"

"Why not? It's time I showed you my humble abode." She'd once been jealous that Sydney and Cécile had cozied up in a cottage. Now she knew why Cécile wanted Sydney there. She wanted Sydney in her cottage for exactly the same reason.

Sydney stared at Kate but said nothing. Kate thought for a second she would make up some excuse.

"Well, sure, yes. Fantastic idea. How about I make us a few hors d'oeuvres and maybe dinner?"

Kate was thrilled. "That would be great, but only a few things." She had no idea how Sydney felt. She only knew how she felt. She didn't want to push Sydney, if she wasn't ready. Or had no interest or intention of changing the status of their relationship.

Sydney was staring at her, her surprise and puzzlement utterly charming.

"You haven't even seen the place," Kate babbled. Now she was nervous. "How do you know I even have a stove, much less a refrigerator?"

"Because Jerome was bragging about what he put in for you." Sydney set the hammer aside and brushed off her hands.

"You and Jerome were talking about my cottage?"

"Remember the day I sat with him while he worked on the tractor engine?"

"Yes," Kate replied, smiling. "You said you missed out on auto mechanics in high school."

"Not everyone grew up with a Jerome around."

"You came to dinner that night with grease along the side of your neck." Kate remembered.

"He let me help."

They stood there, staring at each other. Neither shifted a muscle until Kate finally stepped back.

"Why don't you come by now and have a quick look. You'll see what you're getting into. It's really small—maybe too small for you to even make hors d'oeuvres."

"Right now?"

"If you can take a break." It was all she could do not to stammer.

Sydney immediately took off her tool belt and threw it in the corner. They headed for the door.

"But I warn you," Kate said, "it's a—"

"Mess, right? Not to worry."

They walked down the worn path together, neither saying a word.

At the entrance of the tiny wood-shingled cottage, Kate stepped back and signaled for Sydney to go in. Sydney looked over at Kate and smiled.

"I can't tell you how many times I've wanted to come over here."

Kate watched her take a breath and open the door. She had no idea how Sydney would see her place. Sydney came from real wealth. But then she had been working all summer doing field labor, saying how much she loved the work. There was certainly nothing fancy about her uncle's farmhouse. She did seem content living there. Sydney stopped at the threshold and didn't move.

"I've tried to imagine for so long what it'd be like inside." Sydney stepped through the door and Kate followed.

All Kate noticed were the covers askew on the bed and her nightshirt lying on the pillow where she'd thrown it. Her nightstand, to the left of the bed where she slept, was piled high with books. Thankfully she had closed the closet and bathroom doors. She tried to see what Sydney saw. The rug that Amber and Magda gave her brought gorgeous red and orange-toned color to the room. But as she stared at it, Kate noticed it could use a sweep or a vacuum.

"The bathroom's inside there." Kate pointed to the door next to the built-in closet. "Jerome did all this," she said, motioning to the sink and the stove and refrigerator to the right. "Not that I cook much." She smiled. "It's home." Kate made one last sweep of her hand around the room.

Sydney hadn't said a word. She had stepped inside and stood on the rug. The whole cottage was about four lengths of her lovely, lithe body. Kate was used to it. She liked the compactness, the ease. No excess. She had one mug, one plate, one glass.

"It's perfect."

Kate let out a breath.

Sydney walked over and took both of Kate's hands. "It's you, Kate." Kate's blood pressure shot up. She knew her face must be bright red. Sydney let go of Kate's hands and headed toward the door. "I'll bring over something easy. Finger foods, something light. If the night is as nice as tonight, we can eat outside."

Had Sydney noticed she had only one small table and chair tucked into the corner by the bed, the table piled high with catalogues? When Kate finished with a project, she'd take it upstairs to the office at Uncle Louie's. There she was meticulous about her filing. Here she had only the nightstand, table, or floor.

"Any chance you have two champagne flutes?" Sydney asked.

"Nope."

"Let's not tell anyone that two future winemakers don't have two champagne glasses between them. I'll pick up two when I go shopping for the food." She opened the screen door and walked out into the night. After two steps, Sydney veered around. "I'm taking the afternoon off. They won't mind at my work." She had the biggest smile on her face. "I want to shop and prepare a few things. Oh, what time?"

"Six?"

"I'll be early."

❖

Kate stayed up past midnight stacking her books and papers, and cleaning. She dusted everything, swept clean every corner and even under the bed, something she'd never done before. The bathroom sparkled; the sink shined. Her cottage had never, ever, been this clean. Finally, she changed the sheets but lay on top. Once she pulled up the comforter, she was asleep in two seconds flat.

❖

They sat outside—sipping champagne—in two rustic chairs Kate had borrowed from Jerome.

"I can't believe the variety of food you've put on these little round pieces of bread," Kate said.

"It's a sliced baguette, Kate."

"Yeah, but look at the different kinds of cheese. And avocado. And peppers, right?" She picked up the *crostini*, as Sydney had called it, and loved the crunch. "Fabulous." She wished she didn't feel so nervous.

"Everyone at work told me to make a spinach dip and put it into a cut-out round of bread. It's all the rage."

"But—?"

"I couldn't do it. This is a little classier, don't you think?" Sydney looked at Kate indulgently. "To go with champagne." She picked up her glass. "Happy birthday."

They leaned toward each other and clinked glasses. Kate smiled. "Thanks." Already her birthday had exceeded her expectations. Sydney served the appetizers from a silver tray. And she'd brought cloth napkins.

Kate took another sip. She'd have to slow down on the champagne. Her brain wobbled and her body was all goosebumps.

"And what are these?" she asked Sydney, in lieu of kissing her, which was what she wanted to do. Had wanted to do for months.

"That's goat cheese and basil. You recognize the zucchini and tomato, I hope." She pointed toward a second plate of finger sandwiches.

"Very funny."

They were using Kate's nightstand for a table. They'd decided it was the easiest to take outside. Their chairs were facing west to capture the last of the setting sun.

"More champagne?" Sydney asked. They had almost finished the bottle, but Kate knew Sydney had brought another.

"No thanks. I need a break." Kate looked down at Sydney's long, tanned legs. Had Sydney worn jeans, Kate might have been better able to concentrate. Their hands had touched often as they—both clearly ravenous—went back for thirds and fourths of Sydney's savory concoctions. She leaned her head back against the chair, suppressing a sexual desire so profound, it shocked her. "I'm not a big drinker. Yes, I know, don't tell that to our customers." Kate let out a feeble laugh. "Oh, dear, let me see if I can even stand up."

"Allow me." Sydney jumped up and faced her, stretching out her hands in front of her. Kate reached for her hands and Sydney pulled her up.

She found herself standing face-to-face with Sydney, who had changed how she was holding Kate's hands so that their fingers were intertwined. They were within inches of each other. She could feel Sydney's breath. She saw only Sydney's eyes staring back into hers.

"You don't have a light out here. Shall we go inside?" Sydney asked.

"Yes," Kate said, to going inside. And yes to whatever else they might do inside. The look of desire in Sydney's eyes reflected her own longing. But Kate wanted no regrets. "Are you sure you're good to come inside? You once said—"

"Yes," Sydney answered immediately. "Definitely." She stepped back, dropping one hand to let Kate pass, gently holding on to the other. "After you."

It was mere steps to the door. The whole ritual was silly, but so perfectly *Sydney* that Kate couldn't help but smile. Sydney opened the door for her. She stepped inside, then waited for Sydney. The screen door hadn't even clicked into place before they reached for each other. When Sydney kissed her, Kate's world settled into place.

Maybe it was the champagne, but Kate felt herself sinking into Sydney's lips. She was surprised by their fullness, the suppleness, the exquisite feel of Sydney's mouth on hers. She was being whisked off to a whole other private, sexy world. Kate could have spent the rest of her life right there had Sydney not run her tongue slowly over her bottom lip. Suddenly her knees went weak. A gush of arousal hit her. Did she cry out? She must have, for Sydney started kissing her mouth again, and then moved on to her neck. Kate tried to hold on but knew she wouldn't last another minute standing.

"Sydney—" was all she could manage.

"You okay?"

"Yes," She pointed and was relieved that Sydney recognized she meant the bed. They backed up and sat on the edge.

"I don't want to stop, Kate, not anymore. I tried to stop. I thought that would be better for us, well, me. But all summer, all I thought about was you and me, like this."

Kate tried to speak. She thought she should say something, but no words came out. Instead, she kissed Sydney. Sydney pulled her gently back up to the pillow where they lay facing each other. Craving Sydney, Kate shifted closer. They held on to each other, their bodies linked breast to breast, belly to belly, leg to leg. Albeit with clothes between them. That had to change. She pulled back, breathing heavily, and gently put one hand on Sydney's shoulder to give herself enough space to start unbuttoning Sydney's blouse, a lovely cotton shirt that Kate wanted to rip off.

"Great idea." Sydney sat up immediately. She stood and gently pulled Kate up with her. "I was trying not to rush." She kicked off her shoes, pulled off her own top, then helped Kate slip off her sneakers, then her shirt and jeans, her eyes savoring every inch of Kate's body. Kate was having difficulty breathing.

"Everything," Kate managed.

Within seconds, they were naked.

"I haven't been able to stop thinking about you, wanting you like this—" Kate said. She hopped back on the bed. "Come here, you." Kate opened her arms and Sydney lay gently against her. She pulled Sydney to her, wanting to run her hands through her hair and over every inch of her luscious body.

"No work tomorrow. I may never leave the cottage again," Kate murmured, kissing Sydney on the sides of her cheek, down her neck. Then because she couldn't wait another second, she maneuvered Sydney onto her back and raised a shaking hand to cup Sydney's breast. She couldn't believe the depth of her desire. Sydney lay still for a minute, but then she slowly began to move her hands up and down Kate's back. Before Kate knew it, she was on her back, and Sydney's eyes were sparkling. Spasms of pleasure shot through her. Sydney continued kissing her until she was a puddle of want. If Sydney didn't release the pressure that was building up, she'd surely die, right then, right there.

"Your tight T-shirts have been driving me up a wall all summer," Sydney whispered.

"Sorry," Kate said. *Please, Sydney.*

Sydney grinned. "Bet you are," she said, leaning over and pulling Kate's nipple taut. Sydney stayed on Kate's left breast, then nibbled her way over to the right.

Kate moaned. And pushed Sydney's head lower. "There is one gift I'd like right now."

Sydney laughed. "Do I have any say about this?"

"None at all. It's my birthday."

Sydney pulled Kate into a long, sensual kiss before she finally, finally kissed her lower, then lower still. Exactly where Kate wanted her to be.

CHAPTER FOURTEEN

Sydney woke at her usual pre-dawn hour, but imperceptibly jumped at the warm body wrapped around her. Kate! Flashbacks of the evening flooded her mind. Her body twitched in response; her heart rate doubled. Keeping her eyes shut, Sydney revisited each moment, starting with Kate's unexpected invitation, their laughter on the steps, through the passion of their lovemaking. Sydney opened one eye to make sure she actually was in Kate's cottage and hadn't imagined all this. Had they both really let go like that? Kate had unquestionably wanted her last night. Sydney gave herself a few more minutes to indulge in this delicious moment. Kate's breathing was soft and even. Sydney knew once Kate awakened, she wouldn't be able to resist touching her incredible body.

Suddenly terrified, Sydney's eyes popped wide open. How could she have forgotten? She promised herself she wouldn't sleep with Kate. How could she have been so foolish? This was risking their entire business deal. Surely Kate would come to her senses when she woke up and regret inviting her over. Sydney felt the slight pressure of Kate's hand holding intimately on to her breast. Sydney had never seen this side of Kate. She glanced once more at Kate's lovely bare shoulder. The Kate she knew was methodical, rational, and adorably scientific. Sydney was in big trouble. Better to slip out before Kate woke up. Sydney slowly lifted the comforter.

"Going somewhere?"

"Ah, you're awake. Happy day-after-your birthday!" Sydney rolled back toward Kate and—despite herself—seeing the smile on

Kate's face, took a deep, contented breath before gently rolling Kate onto her back and proceeding to tell her with her lips that no, she wasn't going anywhere. Not at the moment, anyway.

"I did think I should slip out before anyone caught us here. You and me. Together."

But Kate didn't seem to be listening. She stretched like a lion awakening from sleep. Sydney was immediately aroused and kissed her again.

"Maybe you're right," Kate finally said, staring at Sydney with a contented grin. "A minute more." She pulled Sydney soundly on top of her, holding her tightly. "I like what you do up there."

Oh God. Sydney was beyond smitten. What was she going to do? She loved this new Kate. Sydney found her irresistible. But she also knew Zeke was an early riser and would be out and about soon. For Kate's sake, she didn't want him to see her leaving the cottage.

"You don't care if your parents are aware I slept over?"

"I don't care if the entire universe finds out." She kissed Sydney again hungrily, letting her hands slide down Sydney's body. Sydney couldn't move. "You've released a monster, I'm afraid. I can't seem to get enough of you."

Sydney beamed. "So I see. I'm glad, but your father—"

"Screw him. Hasn't he made our lives miserable enough? He must see how beautiful you are." Kate ran her hand slowly through Sydney's hair, then caressed her cheek. "I've waited so long to kiss these adorable freckles."

Was Kate in love with her? Sydney's brain kicked back in. Wasn't this exactly what she feared might happen, since Sydney knew this moment wouldn't last? Kate would inevitably discover that Sydney wasn't worthy of her love. She looked at Kate, who was staring lovingly back at her, which only frightened her more.

Any minute Kate would realize her new lover was an imposter, not the person she thought she was. Kate was strong, stable, reliable. Sydney was…a flight risk, a coward. That was the real truth. Maybe she should do them both a favor and leave before things got complicated. Unable to decide what to do, she reveled in one last long kiss before trying to get up.

"Not yet," Kate protested.

"I don't want you to regret this."

"How could I?" She pulled Sydney back down.

Sydney knew this might be the biggest mistake of her life, but she was powerless to resist.

An hour later, Sydney managed to get dressed and made it outside to the front stoop. The chairs from last night still faced the western horizon. Sydney shook her head. Damn, she was happy. Kate was phenomenal. What the hell should she do? Her head was telling her one thing, her heart another. For starters, these days she typically helped Rachel bake first thing in the morning. Saturday was one of her busiest days. Should she go over there? Surely Rachel would be able to tell what had happened. What would be her excuse for arriving so late?

The cottage door squeaked. Sydney came to a full stop and looked around.

"I thought you were leaving." Kate was standing in her doorway, wearing a T-shirt that came barely down to her hips. "Shall I make us some coffee?"

Sydney had never seen such a sexy smile. Jesus. "I was trying to figure out if I dare go over to help your mother this morning. I can't get this grin off my face."

"Try her. She's an amazing woman." Kate put one hand on her hip and looked Sydney straight in the eye. "Go on. Bring me back a scone."

❖

Sydney almost dropped a pie taking it out of the oven. She was unable to say a word to anyone. When Rachel's two helpers, Annie Mae and Justine, left to carry the baked goods over to the farm stand, Rachel tapped her on the arm.

"Is everything okay?" she asked. "It's not like you to be so quiet."

"Of course, everything's fine. I feel bad about coming in so late, that's all." She grabbed a tray of blueberry muffins and tried to nonchalantly move toward the door.

Rachel stepped even faster and put her hand soothingly on Sydney's shoulder. "You coming here is a gift no matter when you get here. You must know that. Say, how was your dinner last night?"

"What dinner?"

"You bought bread yesterday afternoon, remember? You insisted on paying for it. You earn it working here, you know." She ruffled Sydney's hair in the same place Kate had her hands hours earlier. Sydney froze.

Sydney wiped her forehead. All the ovens were off, but the room was stifling hot. "Good. Kate and I had a birthday dinner." Sydney looked everywhere but at Rachel's face. She held up the tray of muffins. "I better take these over. They always sell out. Oh, and Kate wanted me to save her a scone."

"Sydney—"

Oh, God.

Rachel took the tray from Sydney's hands and set it onto the counter. "Would you talk to me a minute? Zeke's gone into town."

Sydney followed Rachel to the kitchen table, her legs suddenly leaden. She sat down but couldn't look up. Goddamn, she had nothing to be ashamed of, but was Rachel going to send her packing?

"I love my daughter, a fact you're quite aware of. I'm guessing that something has changed between you two. After the wine tasting declarations, I must admit I did wonder about you and Kate. Look at me, will you? I'm happy for you both."

"You are?"

"Of course. Loving someone is always a good thing. Besides, I've had two months to think about it. I've been watching you both. You look happiest together. It really is okay."

Sydney couldn't help it. She grabbed both of Rachel's hands and pulled her up from the table and into a bear hug. "I'm thrilled, Rachel." She got up to go, not knowing what else to say.

"Ask Kate to stop by, will you?" Rachel smiled.

Emboldened, Sydney had to ask. "Will Zeke feel the same way?"

"Ah, that's another story. He'll need more time," she said. "Sort of like the vines, he needs to grow and gain vigor."

Sydney laughed out loud. "You compared Zeke to the vines?"

"Why not? I'm hanging around future winemakers. Don't think I haven't heard you two use these terms."

Sydney's description of Zeke wouldn't have been as nice. "Maybe I'll take Kate that scone."

"Take as many as you like."

"Will do. I'm suddenly starving." Sydney hugged Rachel again, grabbed two scones, and shot down the path toward the cottage.

❖

As a kid, Sydney could never get her mother's full attention. Her mother was always too busy. Once she discovered sailing, Sydney was relentlessly competitive and won a trophy in her age group at the end of each season. Her mother never once showed up for the award ceremony—presented on the deck of their very own yacht club. Same thing during the winter season with her swim club when she was in high school. Her mother—invited to every meet—was always a no-show. Sydney felt nothing she ever did was of any value. Worse, she grew to feel she could never do anything right. She felt worthless. It was relatively easy to compartmentalize her anxiety in Cutchogue with Kate. They lived happily in their own contained world. But Sydney knew their time together would end, so each evening she grabbed a change of clothes and met Kate back at the cottage. Until that shoe fell, she wanted to spend every minute she could with Kate.

During the light remaining to them after work, they made sure the vines were securely tied to the stakes, they picked off and discarded any last little grapes—so the energy would go to the trunk, as Kate had taught her—and built little mounds of soil around each of the plants to protect them from the winter cold. Sydney loved her day job as well. More and more people were asking specifically for her to create their flyers, make invitations, draw up ads. It was moderately creative work. Most importantly, she was earning her own living for the first time, at a job she'd found on her own. Sydney tucked her father's credit card even farther back in the drawer.

❖

Sydney asked Kate if she wanted to move into Uncle Louie's with her. "It's much bigger."

"But I love it here," she told her. "Jerome made this cottage all for me. It's very womb-like, don't you think? Cozy and safe. Besides, I'm not ready yet to throw it in my father's face that we're a couple."

A couple.

Sydney stood in the driveway watching Blaye's car pull away. She felt ripped in two, and totally humiliated. But life wasn't done with her yet. When she turned to go back inside the house, she saw her mother standing on the steps, watching.

"So, even your harlot Blaye doesn't love you."

Goddamn her. As if she didn't already feel unlovable.

Sydney made a sumptuous Thanksgiving meal for the two of them. After much pleading from Rachel, they agreed to join her and Zeke for dessert. Sydney wasn't surprised that Zeke gave them the cold shoulder, making everyone uncomfortable. If they were playing chess, Sydney would have described it as a stalemate: Zeke wasn't able to accept his daughter's sexual preference, and Kate couldn't accept her father's homophobia.

❖

One evening in late December they went over to Uncle Louie's to use the bigger kitchen when they both spotted the flashing light of the answering machine that Sydney had installed.

"Look, you have a message," Kate exclaimed.

"That's exciting?" Sydney looked tenderly at her girlfriend. She wondered if Kate had ever played Pac-Man or even seen a VCR. There were only books in her small cottage. "It's my mother. No one else has this number. I'll check it later."

"Ah, let's hear what she has to say."

"Kate—"

"Come on. It can't be that bad."

Sydney knew it could be but gave in to Kate's request. She pressed play.

"Sydney, you're not returning my calls. You've spent Thanksgiving with those people. Come home for Christmas. This is where you belong."

Sydney punched the stop button. "See why I didn't pick up?" Sydney said whirling around. "Let's take a drive through town." She hated her mother.

"Those people?"

"Could we just get out of here," Sydney pleaded. "I don't want to talk about my mother." She took Kate's hand and made a feeble attempt at kissing it. "Please?"

Her mother drove her out of her mind. She hated her, yet ever since she could remember—she had to admit the truth, at least to herself—she'd craved her love. She couldn't change herself, wouldn't know how, even if she tried, yet still—still!—she needed her goddamned mother's approval. What was wrong with her? If she couldn't get her own mother to love her, how in the world could she ever expect Kate to?

❖

Mid-January 1985

Rachel knocked on the cottage door. She was wearing her old winter coat and had thrown a wool scarf around her head. "Sydney, your father's on the phone."

"Oh, Rachel, I'm so sorry he bothered you. I'll be right there." Sydney grabbed her coat. "Be right back," she told Kate.

Both Zeke and Rachel were in the living room, listening to the news. She could hear the TV. She grabbed the receiver and put the phone up to her ear.

"Dad, why did you call here? You're bothering the Bauers. Mom has my number." She tried to keep her voice down. "What? Yes, I've missed a few calls—I've been busy." Sydney stretched the phone cord as far as she could into the hallway. "She and I work together." She wasn't about to tell him more about Kate or the vineyard on the phone. "Why did you call? You're not one to chitchat." But Sydney knew exactly why he was calling and who had pushed him to make the call. Her mother's infamous Red Party was all the rage in Manchester. Only the hoity-toity were invited. Her mother had left another message Kate hadn't heard, insisting she come home to be with JT and his new fiancée. She was determined to get her whole tribe together, especially since her future daughter-in-law's parents were flying in from London to meet everyone.

"I have to go home for a party," she told Kate, slinging her coat onto the chair in the corner.

"When is it?"

"February sixteenth."

"A Valentine's Day party? I'll go with you," Kate said excitedly.

Sydney's stomach coiled into a giant knot, the cottage suddenly stifling hot. She could ignore her mother asking her to return to Manchester, but her father? And JT? She hadn't seen her brother in years. She was very curious about whom he'd chosen to marry. Kate was staring at her, waiting for a response. "It's my mother's annual Red Party. Nothing romantic about it." She stumbled to the chair and sat. "My eldest brother, John Thomas, JT, as we call him, is coming home with his fiancée. My father asked me to come back for it."

"So, you're going? I'll drive up with you. I'd love to meet JT and see where you grew up."

"Not this time, okay? This party is just a command performance for my mother to show off her family to the new in-laws. It won't be fun, I assure you."

Kate pulled herself up on the pillow, closing the book she'd been reading, and rotated further toward Sydney. "You okay? You look so sad. I don't really understand about this party. Want to talk about it?" She pulled back the covers, tempting Sydney to bed. "Or I can take away your blues?"

Sydney squeaked out a smile. Part of her was tempted to talk to Kate. They talked about everything else. But no, her feelings about her mother—or rather how her mother made her feel—were off-limits. She got undressed and climbed in next to Kate. Sydney had always understood that her father followed her mother's lead in family business. When her mother called, Sydney did not miss that she'd not invited—nor suggested—that Kate come with her. Her mother's abhorrence of anything and everything she did hurt Sydney to her core. She didn't think Kate could help with that.

❖

During the first week of February, Jerome mentioned that Zeke had said the weather was going to be unseasonably warm the next two weeks. Sydney suspected Zeke knew they had to prune their vines but didn't want to suggest he was helping in any way. "You see, I can't go to that stupid party. We have to prune," Sydney said, wrapping her arms around Kate. They were stealing time in bed.

"Oh, I didn't know you were still deciding." Kate sat up. "We should have the pruning done by the party. The sixteenth, isn't it? I could still drive up with you."

"I keep trying to tell you that it's not a fun party. Frankly, it's better that I go alone. Drive up, show my face, come home."

"Wouldn't it be more fun if I went with you?"

"No. It's better you don't come."

"I don't understand. We need to talk about this, Sydney."

Sydney let out a long breath. Damn, she wasn't going to let it go. "This is something I need to deal with. Alone. Can't you let it go?"

"No. You're keeping something from me. I haven't had a lot of experience, but I'm quite sure it is not good for us to keep secrets." Kate threw the covers off and got up. "I'm going to take a shower."

The temperature rose to nearly forty the next day. Kate and Sydney both took time off from their day jobs to start pruning. This all-important job had to be done while the vines were dormant. The task was simple: choose the strongest branch to pull off to the right and to the left of the main trunk. And cut off all the rest! The idea of making these choices was both scary and exhilarating. On these branches would grow their grapes next summer. Sydney hated to think about the fact that their future depended on how well they did this pruning.

❖

"Sydney! Watch what you're doing."

It was day six. They'd both been working nonstop and were exhausted. Sydney looked up, questioning what was wrong. Kate had her hand gripped like a vise on Sydney's pruner.

"You almost cut off the main cane."

Sydney looked at the two-year-old growth that had been carefully trained up the stake and the buds that would eventually bear the grapes for their first wine, and at the hardened vine that she was about to cut off.

"We want to cut it back," Kate continued softly, "not chop the whole thing off. What were you thinking about?"

"Sorry. Maybe it's time for a break."

"I think you're right," Kate told her. "We've been at it for hours. My back is shot. How about yours?"

Sydney stood. "Was that my spine I heard cracking?" She tried to make a joke. "Want some hot chocolate?"

They started down toward the cottage. If only people knew how much physical work was involved in a vineyard. At least pruning could be done standing up, but even then, they had to bend over to pick up the discarded wood. Vineyards were not for wimps.

Two days later, after finishing the last row, they were putting away the pruners when Sydney saw the postman's truck pull out. Ten minutes later, Rachel approached them and handed a big envelope to Sydney. "Express," she said, and hurried away. Sydney opened it on their walk back to the cottage but didn't say a word.

"Well?" Kate asked.

"It's a plane ticket." Sydney stepped into the cottage and threw the ticket onto the counter. "My father sent it."

"We could still drive up, you and me."

"No thanks. I'll fly and get the damn trip over with. Then maybe they'll leave me alone."

"Why don't you want me to go? At least tell me that? If it's about your mother, I know how she is. I met her at your graduation, remember? You're out to her now, though, right? Don't you want to tell her about us? Or about the vineyard?"

"She doesn't care about us, or the vineyard. You don't get it." Sydney strode toward the refrigerator, opened the door but closed it abruptly. She stood there, her back to Kate. And Sydney—for the life of her—couldn't understand why she cared so much what her mother thought.

"Then what is it? There's got to be more to this," Kate said. "Have I done anything? What are you afraid of? Talk to me."

"I can't. You must accept that."

Kate stood up and shuffled toward Sydney. "Something's going on and it's driving a huge wedge between us. I can't stand it any longer. To use your words—I can't—and I won't."

There was no room in the tiny cottage. Even taking a step back, they were only feet apart. Sydney wanted to run or hide.

Kate continued. "I have no idea what you're thinking, or, frankly, whether if you go, you'll even come back. There, I've said it. That's my worst nightmare. What's yours?"

Sydney turned aside, her head exploding. There was no way she could talk to Kate about this. She didn't know what to do.

"Sydney, are you even listening to me? You might as well be pouring poison on our relationship. It's slowly killing us, at least me. We can't continue like this." Kate eased toward Sydney.

"Don't come closer." Sydney backed up. The chill of the sink hit her back.

Kate waited.

"I'm sorry." This was her cue to run. It was what she did best. Sydney ducked past Kate and grabbed her coat from the closet. "I need to do this alone." She took the ticket and walked to the door but stopped with her hand on the knob. "I'm going over to Louie's house to work," she said, her back to Kate. "I'll sleep over there and drive to the airport tomorrow."

Chapter Fifteen

February 1985, Manchester, MA

Sydney's shuttle skidded on the landing at Logan, then steadied and pulled up safely to the gate. Walking outside, she noticed the uniformed driver holding up a sign with her name on it. She nodded to the driver. He took her bag, and she followed him to the car. They drove out of East Boston and made the thirty-mile trip up the coast in silence. Foolishly, she'd hoped her father might come to pick her up.

Sydney looked at the familiar storefronts as they drove through Manchester's tiny downtown. Not much had changed. It was early afternoon, only a few people were out on the streets, the summer throng long gone. The town looked pretty bleak. Had she really grown up there? But as soon as they reached Shore Road, the memories blasted their way through. It was the water, with its harbors and inlets, that she adored. It was a dream paradise for those who could afford to sail or spend their days on the beach. She hated her life at home, but that first summer, when she stepped into a sailing dinghy, everything changed. From her first Optimist to her final Laser, she'd won many a sailing competition. She'd been fearless, reveling in the challenge and adrenaline of the wind as ally or antagonist. During the winter, the fierce competition and camaraderie of her swim team kept her going. She'd forgotten how water had always been her element.

They were a couple of miles from heading up the hill to her parents' house. Sydney leaned over and tapped the window to get the driver's attention. "Could you give me two minutes at Singing Beach?"

"It's cold out, miss. You sure you want to get out?"

"I'm sure."

Sydney stepped out of the car, the wind slapping her in the face. Isolated patches of snow stuck to some of the seagrass. Sydney breathed in the heady salt air. Her heart raced remembering the sandcastles, the runs up and down the beach, diving into the waves as they crashed onto the shore. She and her brother, Rusty, both redheaded and fair skinned, looked like burnt crisps at the end of each summer. It was a wonder she never had second degree burns. Feeling rejuvenated, she hopped back in the car.

Minutes later, Sydney snuck in the back door that led to the kitchen. Last minute preparations for the party were in full swing. With so much extra staff on hand, Sydney thought about putting on an apron to see if her mother would even notice her. Then she heard her mother's voice in the hallway. Whatever joy she'd taken from the beach evaporated immediately.

"Emma, darling, how wonderful you look," her mother exclaimed.

Emma? Ah, her future sister-in-law. Sydney stood ramrod straight. She had to force herself to remember she hadn't seen her older brother in two years and was very curious about his choice for a bride. Sydney slung her bag over her shoulder and walked through the door.

Surely expecting one of the staff to walk out, her mother's eyes went rapidly from surprise to annoyance. "Well, you've finally arrived. Come meet John Thomas's fiancée." That was it? After the whole campaign to get her home, no hug, not even a peck on the cheek?

Sydney couldn't mask her hurt. Taking a deep breath and letting it out, Sydney stepped toward Emma. She was tall, slim, decked out in a very form-fitting red dress. Obviously, JT had told her that the Red Party meant one had to wear something red, but the layers of Emma's dress, hitting every curve, dazzled Sydney. Emma didn't at all fit the image of the Margaret Thatcher type Sydney had expected. Her shoulder-length blond hair clasped with two simple barrettes showed off her high cheekbones and killer blue eyes.

Sydney held out her hand. Emma surprised her by gently pulling her into a hug.

"Let's talk later, okay?" she whispered into Sydney's ear. Then when she let go, "I've been dying to meet you," she said out loud, in her very appealing English accent.

JT, well done. Sydney was at a loss for words. She simply smiled.

"Let Sydney get settled, darling," her mother said to Emma. She whooshed her future daughter-in-law away, her arm securely around Emma's waist.

Sydney shrugged, picked up her bag again and went upstairs to change. *Good to see you, too, Mom.*

Sydney scanned her closet for something to wear. Yes, it was de rigueur to wear something red, but she wasn't in the mood to flaunt or even impress. She put on a pair of lined black slacks and a red silk blouse. At least the material's sleek softness perked her up. Taking a quick glance in the mirror, Sydney thought about how Kate loved to watch her dress each morning. Kate loved a lot of things about her. She kicked herself for her rude and abrupt departure. At the very least, she owed Kate an apology. She hoped Kate would accept it when she returned.

Sydney scrounged around her closet floor for shoes. She thought about putting on a pair of work boots but rejected the idea. Her mother, the tyrant fashionmonger, would surely criticize whatever she put on, but Sydney didn't want to ruin the evening for JT and Emma. She slipped on an old pair of flats, added a necklace and earrings, and went down to join the others.

Entering the kitchen, Sydney was surprised to see her father rushing in the back door.

"Sydney!" he called out, seeing his daughter. He opened his arms to fold her into a welcoming embrace. She hugged him back.

"You're just getting home?" Sydney asked, incredulously.

"Yes, late meeting. Your mother's going to have my hide." The scarf around his wool coat was red. Sydney was sure that underneath he'd be wearing a red tie and pocketing a matching handkerchief.

"Thanks for being here, champ," he said. "Sorry I couldn't meet you earlier."

His affectionate old nickname charmed Sydney. Her father always championed her athletic achievement. Sydney looked intently at her father, noting his rugged good looks and wiry, nut-brown hair.

"You asked me to come, so I'm here."

Sydney was going to say more, but Hannah, their long-time housekeeper and the one adult—besides her precious grandmother, of course—she'd always thought loved her, was there immediately to take his coat. She winked at Sydney. Sydney smiled back and watched her walk off. Her mother would be at her father's side within seconds.

After talking to both her brothers, Sydney made the rounds, greeting her parents' friends, close neighbors, her father's business acquaintances, and even many of her mother's real estate clients. Sydney suspected that her mother had invited more people than usual to meet Emma and her parents, wanting to make the most of the social occasion. Emma introduced Sydney to her own mother, who seemed very congenial and self-assured, but reticent to talk. Sydney wondered how these two very different mothers would work out the wedding plans.

At eight sharp, her mother called everyone to dinner. Entering the dining room, Sydney noticed her mother smooth out Emma's dress and pat her on the shoulder. No wonder her own outfit received only a cursory inspection. It hadn't mattered. Her father gave a grand toast welcoming the Suttons, saying how glad he was to welcome Emma into their family. Sydney tried to be present and enjoy the evening. Mostly she felt insignificant.

Sometime after eleven, all the guests were gone. Sydney was exhausted. Her chatter meter had reached an all-time high. She'd talked about her stay in France for the most part, and her new love of wine. She was disgusted with herself for not once mentioning the vineyard, nor even the fact that she was living on Long Island. Did just being in the same room as her mother make her that unsure or ashamed of herself? What was happening to her? Was she now an open coward? She passed by her parents' bedroom, almost to the stairs to her room, when her mother called out her name.

"Sydney."

Sydney stopped. Her mother was standing in her robe leaning against her bedroom door.

"Would you come in a minute?" she asked.

Sydney took in a huge breath.

"Please," her mother added.

And let it out.

Her mother proceeded to walk back into her bedroom, tightening her robe as she sat down at her dressing table. Sydney stood inside the doorway. She hadn't been in her parents' room since she was a child. She vaguely remembered blue-striped wallpaper. Looking quickly around, she noticed more chintz than she believed possible. The lighting was so subtle, she had to walk further into the room to see her mother. She'd give her five minutes. No more.

"Where's Dad?"

"He drove the Suttons back to their inn. Emma is staying with them, of course."

Of course. Her brother knew better than to suggest Emma share his old room. "I was on my way to bed." Sydney glanced at her watch and started counting.

"I want to talk to you about Emma."

"What about her?" Looking at her mother, she was surprised to see wrinkles on her mother's face. It was so rare to see her without make-up. If she didn't know better, she'd say she looked almost human.

"Don't you just adore Emma? And her family! I'm so happy for John Thomas and our family, aren't you?"

"Why our family?" She was going to make her mother spell it out.

"They bring such class, of course."

"Unlike my friend Kate's family, right? *Those people* are lowly farmers."

"I was talking about the Suttons, dear. Tell me at least that you liked Emma."

"I prefer brunettes, but yes, I do like her." Sydney waited. There had to be more.

"She appreciates me a lot."

Ah, there it was. "You mean more than just having someone to fuss over your every word?"

"Never mind, Sydney. I don't know why I bother talking to you. If you had a daughter, you might understand." Her mother harrumphed and retreated to her mirror. "Good night."

Ah, you finally have the daughter you always wanted. But Sydney was her daughter. And her mother didn't care for her at all. That she understood quite well.

❖

The next day her mother took Emma and Mrs. Sutton into Boston to shop while her father showed Professor Sutton around town and took him to lunch at the yacht club.

Rusty arrived a bit after noon. For the first time in years, the three siblings were alone together. "If they're all gone, that leaves the three of us…with all the leftovers!" Rusty declared. "Shall we?"

They rushed to the refrigerator and started pulling out the Tupperware.

Sydney let her stress drain away. They assembled huge sandwiches and brought them over to the table.

As soon as they were seated, JT said, "Tell us more about the vineyard and your friend Kate. Or should I say girlfriend? Rusty told me you called him and told him how you were quite smitten. *He* got to meet her at your graduation. I'm sorry she didn't come up with you. I want to meet her. So, how did this whole vineyard idea come about? I want to know everything. Spill, sis."

"Really?" Sydney kicked herself. She thought it was only Rusty with whom she could confide. But it was both her brothers. Worse, she'd lumped JT in with her mother. "You really want to know the whole story?"

"Absolutely. I want to find out what has gotten Mom's panties tied in a wad."

"JT!" But Sydney was elated and told them how she and Kate met, about their trips to Napa and Sonoma and how she suddenly knew she wanted to make wine. And how she'd fallen in love with Kate. As much as their relationship was in a mess right now—her doing—she *had* fallen in love, something she thought she never would. Saying it out loud felt great.

"And you were equally sure about Kate as you were about creating a vineyard?" JT clarified.

Sydney smiled. Should she tell them her insecure version or allow them the fantasy? "Yeah, it was love at first grape."

Her brothers laughed. Sydney told them more about their vineyard plans and the conversation continued amicably back and forth between them about their jobs and daily lives.

The shoppers came home around four thirty carrying dress bags and various retail packages. Her mother wouldn't have had a drink at lunch with Emma and her mother. The stress of shopping always unraveled her. Sydney noticed some of her make-up had cracked. She must have put on extra protection to counter the cold weather. Heaven forbid her skin be exposed to the elements.

"Did you have a nice time, Emma?" JT asked, after embracing both his fiancée and future mother-in-law. "Here, let me take these. I see you did some damage in the stores."

"Oh, yes, we went to all the fashionable boutiques on Newbury Street. I'm not familiar with any of those stores, but Mikki shops at them all."

Her mother's pet name. Turning to Sydney, *Mikki* finally addressed her daughter. "Where's your father?"

"He called to say they'd be back around five. Evidently they're having a good time at the club."

"Well, then, Rusty, get me a drink, will you?" she said, sitting down on the sofa and smiling up at him. She shifted toward JT. Emma had taken a seat by his other side. "So, what did I miss?" She winked at Emma, then leaned over and grabbed JT's hand. Sydney realized her mother hadn't even as much as patted her on the back since she'd gotten home.

"We were talking about Sydney's vineyard, Mom," JT told her. "They'll be making wine by this time next year."

"Oh, God, that subject. I told her," she said to Emma, "that she'd be better off as a distributor or anything with a bit more class."

"Mom!" JT scolded. "Sydney's vineyard is serious entrepreneurial work."

"It's fine." Sydney stood. She needed to get out of there. She suddenly couldn't stand another minute in her mother's company. She headed out of the room.

"Where do you think you're going?" her mother asked.

Sydney stopped walking. Rusty had given their mother a drink and she'd taken her first sip. Sydney waited. She knew the choreography so well. Her mother took a second sip, then twirled the ice cubes around in the glass. Only then did Sydney turn to face her.

"Well?" her mother continued, looking directly at Sydney.

"Not tonight, Mother. I have a headache," Sydney said.

"What?" her mother exclaimed.

Rusty laughed. "Sydney's making a joke, Mom. She told me earlier she had planned to call MJ, uh, Marguerite." He gave Sydney a gentle push toward the door.

"Did you all think that was funny?" her mother asked the others as Sydney left the room.

Sydney stood outside the door and took a deep breath. This was exactly why she didn't want to be here. Or bring Kate. She had zero defenses against her mother. How could she protect Kate if she couldn't even protect herself?

❖

Sometime after midnight, her father knocked on the door, then gently pushed it open. "Sydney, there's a call for you. Want to take it downstairs in the parlor? It's Kate."

Sydney sat up briskly and wiped the hair out of her face. Kate? She jumped out of bed and, without thinking, pulled her coat out of the closet. She ran downstairs and grabbed the phone off the hook. She heard a click. Her father must have been waiting to hang up.

"Hi, Kate. Are you all right?"

"I'm okay. Sorry to be calling so late. It's my father. I'm at the hospital. I have to make this quick."

"What happened?" *Good Lord.* Yet another reason she shouldn't have left Cutchogue.

"He's unconscious. I thought you'd like to know. Maybe not, I don't know—"

"Of course I want to know." She put her hand against the wall for support and mashed the phone against her ear.

"Long story. He fell from the grain silo. Listen, I've got to go."

"Kate, wait. Which hospital?"

Kate gave her the details and they hung up. *I'll be there as soon as I can.*

❖

Sydney had hoped to talk to Emma and JT before leaving, but that wasn't going to happen. She left a note for her parents on the kitchen table. Rusty was due any minute to drive her to the airport. She knew there wouldn't be another air shuttle at that hour, but there were plenty of rental cars. She needed to get into a car and start driving—right away. She could only hope that modern medicine would save Zeke. Given how she'd left Kate, Sydney was unsure of the reception she would receive on her return. But it didn't matter. Kate was hurting and she wanted to be with her. This mess of a visit had taught her one thing for sure: Manchester wasn't her home anymore, and she needed desperately to make amends with Kate.

Chapter Sixteen

Central Suffolk Hospital, Riverhead, NY

Kate's eyes flicked from her father's bruised face back to the heart monitor. She'd positioned her chair so she could see both equally. He had to live, that was all there was to it. The nurses assured her he wasn't in danger of dying, but she wasn't taking any chances. She'd stopped asking questions, not wanting to get kicked out of his ICU room. She was determined to be there when he woke up. The nurses also assured her he was only temporarily unconscious. Unconscious, for God's sake! She had barely coped with Uncle Louie's death. This was her father. There was no way she could deal with him dying. She loved him enormously, and they had unfinished business. Kate stood and put her hand softly on his chest. If he woke up, he'd be angry she was hanging around him and kick her out of the room. Wouldn't that be wonderful? Get angry, Dad. Come back.

The second green line fluctuated and went through some rhythmic pattern. Kate jumped and pulled her hand away when his left—unhurt— shoulder twitched. Good. She'd learned that this line on the monitor recorded his breathing rate, but it also read body movement. Even unconscious, he seemed to be moving. Why hadn't he asked her to go with him when he climbed up that damn ladder? Or asked Jerome? Her mother had told her there was some leak inside the silo he'd been worried about. But to climb a ladder in icy, cold weather? What was he thinking? He had bruises and abrasions on his face and left arm, and the two bones in his right forearm were broken. Did he try to grab hold of something as he fell? Or just land hard? Kate glanced down to the white cast that covered his left leg from his foot all the way up past his knee. At least it wasn't a compound fracture, the doctor said. And he was very lucky not to have broken his hip. He'd been exasperating lately with his pessimism about the economy, and since the summer, with his huge disappointment in her. But this particular streak of stubbornness could have killed him.

Kate sat back down on the hard metal chair. The afternoon of his fall, she'd been working—and still trying to figure out why Sydney hadn't wanted her to go to the Red Party. Not that her father would have asked her to go check out the silo with him, since they still weren't talking. They were in their seventh month of barely grunting acknowledgments to each other. Was the accident partly her fault? Were he not obsessed about her being a lesbian, maybe he would have been in a calmer state of mind. Kate shifted on the chair, her mind a nonstop whirlwind of chatter. Not sleeping all night surely hadn't helped. Thank God her mother had gone looking for him when he didn't come in for dinner. How long had he been on the ground? Goddamn farmers, with their independence, and their inclination for taking calculated risks.

Kate had heard the stories about the guy who got gored by a bull when he went into the pen, the farmer on the combine who forgot about the overhead wires, the kid who had his arm taken off in the corn picker. Overalls being caught, hands being mauled in balers. She'd heard more tractor rollover related stories than she could count. Ask a farmer to stop working in the middle of a harvest and you'd get laughed at. No matter if he's exhausted or it's pouring rain. Farmers are farmers because they love their independence. They think they can handle anything. And most of the time they do. They have to. Their livelihoods depend on it. Kate knew she'd inherited his work ethic, but her father had also taught her to be cautious. To not take unnecessary risks. Why, all of a sudden, had he been so foolish?

A nurse pulled back the curtain. "Still here, I see."

"I won't get in your way," Kate immediately told her, getting up.

"Stay." The nurse put her hand briefly on her shoulder. "You're fine."

Kate watched as the nurse changed the bag of saline and made notes in his chart.

Despite her desire to stay awake, she finally dozed off. She'd just opened her eyes when her mother walked in, carrying coffees in Styrofoam cups. "My turn," she said, attempting a smile. "It's after six. I slept a few hours. Go, take a walk, get some fresh air." She handed Kate a coffee. Kate knew her mother was terrified and trying not to let it show. "I talked to someone at the nurses' station," her mother continued. "The doctor will be back later this morning."

"Mom, I'm not going anywhere." Kate stood and stretched. "I'm sure Dad will be fine. He's very stubborn."

Her mother smiled. "That's an understatement."

Any optimism Kate exuded—in general, or in this case, in particular—she'd inherited from her mother, who was being tested to the max. Their farm revenue, she'd overheard her father say recently, was at its lowest point. No one was buying the local corn. They all wanted the cheapest corn, which they got from the Midwest. The problem was her father loved farming and had never liked doing anything else. So how were they supposed to pay the additional hospital bills? Would they have to sell their farm? Could her mother's bakery business keep the bills paid?

"Who's baking this morning if you're here?" Kate asked.

"Justine and Annie Mae."

"Mom, maybe we should—"

Both jumped when the curtain yanked open. Sydney walked in with a nurse on her heels, trying to grab her by the arm.

"I told her she wasn't allowed in here," the woman told them.

Sydney put up her hand, as if to say *one minute*, and surprisingly, the nurse paused. "I'll be right out," she hushed the nurse. "I need to see what's going on."

Kate let Sydney look at her father, then awkwardly tugged her away from the bed and outside the curtain. "Let's take a walk outside," Kate said, and marched down the hall, Sydney on her heels.

"Is he okay?" Sydney asked, as soon as they left the ICU and were walking through the waiting area.

"He's patched up, breathing, alive," Kate responded. She was grateful to Sydney for coming. More pleased than she wanted to be that she was here. But...who was Sydney, really? She remembered asking herself that same question for the last three days. Kate headed for the front door, desperate for fresh, cold air, presuming Sydney would keep up.

Kate crossed the road where, miraculously, the parking lot was quiet.

Sydney beat her to words. "Thanks for calling. I got here as fast as I could."

Kate exhaled and looked at Sydney as if for the first time. Sydney was wearing her coat, her cheeks rosy. Kate remembered wandering the hallways last night, waiting for doctors, waiting for x-rays, endless waiting and worrying. She'd wanted Sydney by her side. It had been an immediate impulse to call her. But now she wasn't so sure she wanted Sydney there. "I shouldn't have called you last night," she said, realizing at that moment how furious she still was at Sydney for walking out on her.

Sydney looked stunned. "Of course you should have. Who cares how late it was?"

"I'm not talking about the hour. There was no rush for you to return."

"What do you mean? Your father's here in the hospital."

"Yes, he is, but—"

"But what?"

"I'll take care of my father. In fact, he's the only thing that matters right now." Kate wrapped her arms around herself, suddenly freezing. "Do me a favor, will you? Stay at Uncle Louie's. Work in the winery, do whatever you want, but I want to be in the cottage alone."

"Kate, please, let's talk—"

"Now you want to talk? Is that a joke? I begged you to talk to me before you left. You hurt me by all your silence." Kate turned to go back inside. She was getting more upset by the minute. She remembered how her father had shut her out of her uncle's life. But there was no way she could think anything negative about her father right now. How insensitive could she be? She had to let it go. "I need time alone. That's all I can say. Can you understand that?"

"Yes," Sydney answered. "Whatever you need."

Good answer. "We'll talk later." Talk. Damn that word. Both she and her father used to be so good at it. She crossed the street and rushed back inside the building.

❖

Kate woke from another bad dream and slipped on socks and a sweatshirt over her pajamas. Even with the heat on, it seemed cold in the cottage. Kate put on hot water to make herself a cup of tea and immediately began to make a mental list of things to do. She'd not spoken with Sydney for two and a half weeks—not since the confrontation in the hospital. She had spent most of her time working at her jobs and visiting her father. Thank God she was used to working like a maniac. At least that part of her life seemed normal.

Her father had been transferred to a rehab facility in Riverhead. He was coming home in a week. Had the near-death experience softened him? At least at present the two of them could sit in the same room. Kate or her mother visited him every day. They didn't have a lot to say to each other, but Kate didn't care. He was alive. Mostly she listened to him complain about the food, the nurse, the aide, and the lack of a TV in the room. But this Kate understood. He wanted to be home.

Magda and Amber stopped by her cottage one evening. Kate made them tea and they sat quietly for a few minutes as they sipped. Kate wasn't sure why they were there. Finally Magda looked over at Kate and said, "We're worried about you."

"And Sydney," Amber chimed in.

"You're both working so hard," Magda continued, "but neither of you seems happy. We think you're missing each other." Magda gave Kate a direct stare.

"I'm fine. Just tired. And I'm sure Sydney is fine, more than fine, I'm guessing."

"You seem so good together," Amber said. "I'm sure things will work out between you."

"Things always look bleaker in the winter. If you want to talk, we're here for you," Magda added.

Magda's voice was soothing but Kate was running on empty. She couldn't even think how to respond. Instead she finished her tea and, after a few minutes, shooed them on their way. Kate looked out the window over to Uncle Louie's house and thought about Sydney. She watched as her uncle's angels climbed into their truck and drove away. Maybe Magda and Amber were right. Maybe they were her angels, too.

Sydney was still helping her mother bake in the mornings. Since the accident, her mother had added bagels and dinner rolls to her normal load of baked goods. She allowed people to call her at home to place special orders for cakes and other party items. She told Kate she was determined to make ends meet. Kate looked at her watch. Eight thirty. Her mother would be hard at work. She took a sip of her tea and waited. A few minutes later, she heard the crunching of tires on the driveway as Sydney left for work. Kate put on her coat and walked over to speak to her mother. "Need any help? I could carry a tray somewhere." Kate was not very good at joking, and even worse at baking.

"Honey, I'm glad for your company. Haven't seen you much since—"

"Maybe we could have coffee?"

Her mother's eyebrows rose. "Give me ten minutes."

They sat down at the small kitchen table. Kate remembered Sydney rushing back to the cottage, the first morning they woke up together, telling her about the wonderful conversation she'd had with her mother at this very table. Kate shook the thought off. Taking a sip of her coffee, Kate tried to figure out how to ask her delicate questions. "Mom, did Dad have any insurance? You two own the farm, but how are you going to pay the medical bills? What if he can't plant or work this spring?"

Her mother's hands started to tremble. She carefully put down her mug and immediately put her hands to her mouth, her eyes filling with tears. Kate hopped off her chair and wrapped her arms around her mother. "It'll be okay."

"Look at you telling me that," her mother said after a few seconds, her breathing normalizing. "I'm just glad he's alive." She hesitated. Kate had no idea what she was going to say next. "Do you remember the Wiśniewski family from school?" Kate nodded. "They are the latest to sell their farm. Made a bundle on the land. Buyers are lining up. It's all about the economy. Your father is terrified of losing the farm my parents entrusted to us." She stopped and audibly breathed out. "The truth is I wonder if he intentionally went out in such bad weather." Kate squeezed her tighter. "He has a tiny life insurance policy. He was so proud of that. Remember that man who came around every January? Stayed for dinner? That was the insurance guy. Glad I don't have to collect."

Kate was shocked. Was her father that depressed? The idea that he'd do such a thing never crossed her mind. Kate wanted to get back to the financial situation. "You can't live on cakes and pies. The hospital and doctors will want to be paid."

"Your father has a lot of pride, honey, but he is stubborn. You said it yourself. He was so sure he could take care of us." She dropped her head.

"Don't worry, Mom. We won't let anything happen to you or the house. Jerome is here. Sydney and I can help plant, if that's what Dad wants. Or we could rent out the land." Kate swallowed. Here she and Sydney weren't even talking, and she'd just offered her help. "Mom. This is Cutchogue. Everyone will help."

Her mother stood up. "You still have your part-time jobs. I need to get back to my ovens. We'll figure this out." She swiped a tear from her eye. "Thanks."

❖

March brought some warm days, but it was still easier for Kate to stay holed up when she wasn't working. But come warm weather? And what about all the important ordering decisions they needed to make? Should she make them all herself? Kate grabbed hold of the sink and leaned forward, trying to stretch out her spine. Damn it to hell! This was supposed to be *their* year. They'd planted, fertilized, pruned, done everything right. This was the year the vines would be strong enough to support a grape load. This was the year they could finally make wine. Maybe she should just sell the grapes. Kate stood, grabbed her coat, and closed the cottage door behind her. Bedell Cellars was bottling this morning and had asked her to come in. As for Bauer and Barrett Vineyards and Wines, like the ground, that dream seemed frozen solid.

Walking to the truck, Kate couldn't deny her pride looking at the acres of growing vines, attached to the stakes by twine, spread out as far as she could see. The vines looked like sticks that anyone could cut up and use as starter wood. Below were reserves of carbohydrates stored in the roots from the last growth cycle. When the soil warmed, all this energy would make its way up the vines and out the tiny buds, forming shoots that would, in turn, form tiny leaves to begin the process of photosynthesis. As always, nature astounded her. And soothed her. Tears streaming down her face, Kate forced herself to keep thinking about nature. Anything but Sydney. Trees and the sea plants, her mind went on, absorb the carbon dioxide from the air and gift back oxygen for us to breathe. And flowers! Kate couldn't imagine the planet without the colorful palette of yellows, blues, reds, and all the other combinations.

Kate yanked her truck door open and slid onto the seat. Humans are the ones who wreak havoc on a daily basis. Yet no matter all her self-talk, nor how busy she kept, she missed being with Sydney. Something had to give. Spring and warm weather were only a month away. And then budbreak. That would determine the success or failure of their vineyard. Gripping the wheel, Kate stepped on the ignition and headed out the driveway.

❖

Three days later Sydney followed her into the winery and stood inside the door until Kate acknowledged her.

"May I have a word?" she asked.

"Go ahead." Kate put the hammer down.

"I suggested to your mother that I move into their house. She can't lift your father in and out of bed alone. He's being his usual stubborn self. He won't do his exercises. She said I needed to talk to you."

Because Sydney would be sleeping in *her* old bedroom.

"I don't think that's a great idea."

"I can help your father, Kate. He's certainly not listening to you."

"What? Thanks a lot."

"Well, it's the truth, isn't it? He's got a bug up his ass. I've never seen anyone so stubborn in all my life. But I don't give a hoot, and I will make him do his exercises."

"You think he'll listen to you?"

"You bet he will. I will shame him, cajole him, get him out of his goddamn chair, if only to chase me out of the room. I know how to work with bullies."

"My father's not a bully. He's—"

"What? Still in pain, yes, losing his farm fast, you bet. But crawling up within himself and giving up isn't helping. Not to mention his blatant homophobia. He needs to get over himself."

"You're talking about my father. Not to mention there is no longer an *us*, so he should be happy."

"I'm not going to comment on that last statement." Sydney walked over to an empty area by the door. "This is where we're going to put the bottling machine, isn't it?"

Kate noted how cold it was inside the winery. Next year they might have to think about adding heaters if they were going to be inside fermenting the wine. Then she realized she'd just fallen into thinking about the two of them working together next winter.

"Why are you still here, Sydney?"

Sydney didn't seem surprised by the question. "I want to patch things up, but I haven't figured out how to do that yet. And because I want to make wine."

Kate pulled off her gloves. She hadn't expected such bluntness. She looked directly at Sydney. Well, that was a start. She'd said *something*. As for her request, maybe Sydney *was* the one to work with her father. She hadn't been able to get her father to exercise even his good arm. They certainly couldn't afford any other help.

"Give it a try. It can't hurt."

"Great." Sydney turned to leave, then changed her mind. "Listen, Kate, I've been thinking. It was a good thing you didn't come with me to the party. You were here after the accident."

"That's the best you can do? It doesn't explain what was going on between us before you left. To this day you haven't told me what you're so afraid of."

"I know." Sydney bent over to pick up a pair of pliers that were on the ground and put them on the nearby shelf. "I guess I'm trying to make up for that. I don't really know what else to do." Uncharacteristically, Sydney hung her head.

"You've shut me out, Sydney." Kate walked over to the oak barrels they had been purchasing, one by one. "If you can't tell me what you're afraid of, the best we can do, you and me, is work together. But if you can help my father, no matter what happens to us, I'll be forever grateful."

Sydney didn't hesitate. "I'll help him, you'll see." She headed for the door.

Kate waited for the sound of her footsteps to recede before getting back to work.

❖

Kate and her mother stood outside the living room door, listening. Jerome and Sydney had converted the entire living room into her father's new bedroom and workout area. From their experience with Lily, the Carmichaels knew a place that rented beds with adjustable functionality, as they called it.

"Mr. Bauer, if you would kindly roll your wheelchair over to this pile of weights." Kate heard a sound that might have been Sydney hitting one weight against another.

"Stop calling me, Mr. Bauer. I told you to call me Zeke!"

"Yes, sir."

"What the hell? You're like a taskmaster. It's not easy to move this thing with one hand."

Kate heard the creak of the wheelchair. That did get him moving.

"Who do you think you are telling me what to do? I don't need your help," he said.

"What you need is to move your limbs so your muscles don't waste away. Left alone, you'd sit here and mope yourself to death. Besides, we're all too busy around here to deal with your dead body. If you get some strength back, you might be of some use."

"Goddamn you."

Kate heard a rustling sound in the air. By the light plop it made hitting the floor, she guessed it was a magazine.

"Hey, great work with that arm. Think we can get the bum one moving?"

"Who gave you permission to come in here? I certainly didn't."

"Your wife, who for some ridiculous reason loves you." Sydney cleared her throat. "Let's cut the chatter and get going, shall we? You agreed to do this. I only have an hour."

"Yeah, one hour now and one hour tonight. I was told the drill. Why can't my own daughter help me? She got the same lesson at that place you did."

"We've wasted ten minutes, Mr. Bauer. Move over to the weights."

"Zeke!" he shouted. "If you are going to work with me in my pajamas, you better at least call me by my first name."

Kate heard the chair move again.

"Whatever works for you, sir."

Kate looked at her mother and smiled. Sydney's strategy was working.

❖

Two weeks later Kate's mother forced the four of them to sit down to dinner together. Sydney wheeled her father in, then took the seat opposite Kate.

"There, I'm happy," Rachel said. "We're back together. Stay put while I get dinner."

"I'll help," both Kate and Sydney said at the same time.

Her mother looked affectionately first at Kate, then at Sydney. "Sweet. See how nicely this is working out. Kate, you can help bring in dinner. Sydney, since you made the dessert, that'll be your job. We'll figure out how to do the dishes later."

Kate wanted to laugh, though she most certainly didn't. With all that was going on, her mother maintained her sense of humor. She was the one who had to deal with her father's ill temper the majority of the time. She bathed him, brought him his meals. Where did her mother get her patience?

Her mother had made her father's favorite pot roast for the carnivores and a separate bean casserole for her. At one point, she and Sydney reached for the mashed potatoes at the same time. They were forced to look at each other. Sydney smiled. Kate looked away.

"We have good news." Her mother looked at the two of them. "Jerome took Zeke to the doctor today. The X-rays showed his bones are healing properly and he'll most likely be ready for weight-bearing exercises soon."

"Dad, that's great!" Kate exclaimed. She immediately looked over at Sydney who nodded.

"Yeah, well, the trip over there nearly froze me. How'd you like riding in the back of a truck in this kind of weather," her father asked no one in particular.

"Zeke, we talked about that," her mother gently chided. "It was the easiest way to get you there in your chair. Besides, you had on a dozen layers of clothes. And a blanket." She smiled at him but then turned serious. "Haven't you had enough grumbling yet?"

He looked away.

Kate's mother pushed brusquely away from the table. She walked into the kitchen and returned with more peas. She plunked them down onto the table. Maybe her patience was running out.

"I also have some news," Sydney announced after several minutes of silence. "My oldest brother—I have two—is getting married next month. I like his fiancée a lot. I'll drive up next week to have my bridesmaid dress fitted." She turned to Kate. "I'll only be gone three days."

Kate looked at her, without saying a word. How sad to be hearing about the wedding, second-hand, at dinner, with her parents.

"How nice, Sydney," her mother exclaimed. "I'm happy for you and for your family. Tell us about both your brothers. And what's his fiancée's name? Where did they meet?" Her mother had barely eaten her dinner. She sat up, her eyes sparkling. Clearly this was the pleasant kind of conversation she hungered for.

Sydney quickly joined in. Kate took in every word. Sydney a bridesmaid? She tried to imagine her in a dress, and everyone gathered around for the wedding. She was going to miss out on another singular event in Sydney's life. She gripped her fork and stared down at her plate. Her father was healing, but she had no idea how she and Sydney could possibly recover.

CHAPTER SEVENTEEN

April 1985, Manchester, MA

Sydney lay on her bed, staring up at the attic ceiling. She'd unpacked and changed but was reluctant to go downstairs. Tonight was the rehearsal dinner, tomorrow the wedding. She didn't have to wonder why she was so unhappy. Yes, her own mother was a controlling nightmare, but as she hadn't made things right with Kate, Sydney suspected she'd be miserable wherever she was. Sydney sat up. It was beautiful here in April. She regretted once again not giving Kate the chance to see where she grew up and to meet her older brother. Her plan to keep Kate from genuinely getting to know her remained ill-conceived and nothing short of a total disaster.

Sydney stood, vowing to figure out how to change things between them. She noticed the check her grandmother had left for her on the nightstand. The note accompanying it simply said, *For your new business venture. Hope it helps. Love, Gran.* Sydney was shocked by her generosity. This would almost pay for the wine press. From what she'd learned at Berkeley, it would probably take them five years before they could even begin to make any money. Even with all the odds stacked against them, at least she was certain Kate wanted the vineyard to be as successful as she did. Neither would ever back down on that.

Feeling better, Sydney took another look around the bedroom where she'd spent her teenage years, the room she'd begged for in her quest for independence. The room with a porthole overlooking the harbor, and far away from the rest of the family. Her mother had granted her permission, if and only if Sydney allowed her to fix it up a bit—quite a bit. Mikki Barrett was not going to allow her daughter to live in anything but a highly stylized garret. Sydney glanced over at all the sailing trophies atop her chest of drawers. Like the shiny objects they were, she had all the outer trappings of success. She wished her insides felt as accomplished.

Enough. Time to socialize.

❖

Sydney was seated next to her mother at the rehearsal dinner. This particular Newburyport restaurant had once been JT's favorite, and the wedding couple had insisted on giving the party there. Sydney's mother could not argue against this unnecessarily modest evening since her son had made the request and, more importantly, the couple *had* agreed to have the wedding in the US on Mikki's home turf. They had the whole restaurant, including the bar and deck, to themselves.

The two fathers were placed at the ends of the large center table with their wives to their right. Emma chose to sit next to her mother with JT next to her. Her grandmother wanted to sit next to her grandson. That left Sydney sitting next to her mother with Rusty on her right. The rest of the wedding party, along with close relatives and several of JT's and Emma's closest friends, were all scattered around the sizable dining room. Everyone was clearly enjoying themselves. Sydney had just taken a bite of her filet mignon when her mother leaned over.

"Aren't you glad you didn't bring your little farmer friend? I remember from your graduation lunch that she didn't eat meat."

Forced to keep chewing, Sydney couldn't react immediately. Rusty put his hand over hers, the one that held her steak knife. Did he think she would actually stab their mother? She swallowed, then gently extracted her hand from her brother's, put the utensil down, and reached for her napkin. It was only then she looked over at her mother.

"Her name is Katherine, Mom, but as you recall, we call her Kate. And she's used to eating lots of baked potatoes at meals like this. But had you known she was coming, I'm certain you would have requested the chef prepare something special for her."

Her father stood at that very moment, whether coincidental or not, and all eyes turned toward him.

"As proud father of the groom, may I take this moment to welcome everyone and say how happy we are for John Thomas and Emma. Kindly raise your glasses."

Sydney turned away from her mother and looked over at Emma. She looked blissful. Emma's parents were also beaming. Seconds later Sydney was no longer listening to her father speak as her thoughts returned to Kate. Kate would have liked Emma. Emma was holding JT's hand, staring at him, totally enthralled. Would Kate ever again want to look at her that way? Not to mention how unfair it was that JT and Emma's love could be so openly celebrated. No lesbian and gay couple would ever stand before an altar and be married.

Emma's father stood next, congratulated the couple and said how happy he was to have met the extended Barrett family. Sydney missed the rest of his toast, still bristling over the inequality and her own sense of loss. Her mother kept tapping her on the arm in her unconscious approval of all that was being said. Sydney ignored her, a silly act of defiance, but Sydney knew no other course of action to express her anger and frustration.

❖

"For better or for worse, in sickness and in health…"

Sydney was lined up with the other bridesmaids. The First Parish Church with its total white interior—white altar, white pews, white pillars—was now covered with vibrant colorful flowers. Emma's mother had flown in from London two weeks earlier to make sure the floral arrangements were perfect. Sydney inhaled the lovely aroma and looked around, amazed at the church's transformation.

Sydney rubbed her hand along the seam of her dress. Emma had chosen sexy, figure-revealing, off-the-shoulder dresses in a tantalizing purple silk for her bridesmaids. *Go, Em.* Sydney wondered if the dress or the color had rankled her mother. Sydney remembered Kate teasing her about her fancy outfits and wondered what Kate would have said about this dress. For that matter, had Kate ever wanted to be married? Remembering Kate's ultimatum, Sydney shut that thought down. They weren't even a couple anymore. She looked back toward Emma and JT, who were both beaming. Sydney balled her fists, pushed her pain away, and focused on Emma's stunning gown, with intricate beadwork delicately covering the strapless bodice and repeated along the hem of the gown.

❖

"Sydney, you look beautiful."

"Thanks." She squeezed the groomsman's hand—was he Andy, or was this one Dan?—and pulled away from him as soon as the sultry Cher song, "Baby I Love You," ended. She had danced with all six of the groomsmen—as her mother had requested.

Sydney was impressed with her mother's compromise decision to hold the reception at the Manchester Yacht Club. She'd had to invite fewer guests, but in Manchester the Barrett family prestige rested on its participation at this club. All three of the Barrett kids had grown up around the club and knew its boats and the harbor intimately. Their 1980 Islander Peterson was moored in one of the premier slips outside.

When Sydney was told that the bride and groom were arriving at the club by the Islander, she laughed out loud. But after the wedding ceremony, as Emma and JT stepped off of the boat onto the deck, they looked regal. The deck was sprinkled with rose petals. The waiting guests applauded. It was quite the dramatic arrival. Given an April wedding, the plan for inclement weather was anyone's guess, but Sydney was sure her mother had several contingencies. No one second-guessed Mikki's event planning.

Spotting Rusty, smiling at her from the head table, Sydney sat down next to him. "What are you drinking?" she asked her brother.

"Gin and tonic. Want some?" He held it out to her.

Sydney took the glass and emptied its contents. "Oops, sorry." She handed it back. "I'll get you another."

"Never mind." Rusty signaled over to a waiter. "Wedding party privileges."

Hearing their mother laugh a few feet away, the two of them looked over to find her holding court with a gaggle of boisterous, handsome young men.

"She's in her element, isn't she?" Rusty asked.

Sydney looked at her mother vividly gesticulating about something with the man closest to her. This was her arena, out in public, dressed up, everyone admiring her. Sydney couldn't think of one time when she had been the center of her mother's admiring attention. She thought again of all the swim meets her mother never attended. She remembered standing outside this very room, on the deck, as the whole sailing club cheered her winning the championship trophy. She'd invited her mother, but she had declined, saying she had something more important to do.

"Who, Mommy Dearest?"

"Sydney," Rusty gently chided.

"Never mind." She pointed toward the dance floor. "How do you get away with not dancing with all the bridesmaids?" she asked.

"I'm observing."

Sydney snickered. "Yeah, right. I thought we were given strict instructions to dance and be social."

"I did. Now I'm resting."

She cracked up. Rusty could get away with anything. If she didn't adore him so, she'd be bitter about the obvious favoritism shown him by their mother. Instead, she sat back, kicked off her shoes, and looked around.

"Almost time for the couple to cut the cake," Rusty said, nudging his sister.

Sydney put her shoes back on. She thought about all the cakes and pies and muffins she had helped bake in Rachel's tiny hot kitchen. And the time coming back from Napa when Kate fed her the cheese in the car. She had wanted—and had—Kate's sexy fingers crossing her lips way back then. What a fool and an idiot. How could she have so messed things up?

She walked out onto the deck to get some fresh air and be alone. It was a perfect evening weather-wise, warm with a cool breeze coming off the water. She could hear the combo playing as she leaned over the railing and looked up at the stars.

"Sydney!"

She turned and was surprised to see Emma walking toward her, looking flushed but happy.

"I've been trying to track you down. We haven't had two minutes to ourselves," she gently chided.

"Well, my dear sister, you are the bride. You've been a bit busy." Sydney smiled. "You look radiant. This has been quite the wedding."

"Thanks." She took in a deep breath and grinned. "It's been worth getting past your mother's constant demanding requests to marry your brother. You and I have to share secrets, tell each other our tales. Will you visit us in London?"

Sydney looked at her. "What did you just say? Not the visiting part. About my mother. She adores you. You didn't enjoy all the things you did together?"

Emma laughed. "Guess I'm a better actress than I thought. Sydney, this wedding has been the hardest thing I've ever done in my life. All these parties and that shopping spree!"

"Wait. All that affection between the two of you. Her fawning over you, and your acceptance. That wasn't mutual?"

"Sydney, she's going to be my mother-in-law. I want to get along with her, that's all. For my husband's sake." Emma grinned. "That's the first time I've said 'husband.'" She beamed.

"That's wonderful, but..." Sydney rushed to formulate her thoughts. "You're telling me you're not actually fond of my mother?"

"Of course I'm *fond* of her. That's not the point. You know your mother. Well, I assume you do, the way you two are—how shall I say it—always at odds. Forgive me, but she's the biggest snob I've ever met. Your brother warned me, but I had to see for myself. I chose to go along with her rather than fight. And it worked."

"Hold on. JT feels the same way?" Surely her brain was going to explode.

"Where have you been? Of course he does. But that's who she is, he understands that. Tell me, why are appearances so important to her? Is she that insecure? You obviously know her better than I do."

Sydney couldn't believe it. "But you seemed thrilled about everything, including the wedding."

"I did what I needed to do. I don't let her define me, that's all. This wedding was my gift to JT. Your mother got what she wanted. Your brother and I get to live happily ever after back in London. Which reminds me, I want to hear more about this vineyard of yours. What an exciting and daring adventure." Emma grinned and tapped Sydney playfully on the nose.

"Come, let's go back in," she continued. She took Sydney's hand. "We'll talk more when you come over."

Sydney had a hard time getting her feet to work. Even her insides seemed suddenly frozen. The warmth of Emma's hand in hers propelled her forward. She wasn't aware of moving, but there was the door right in front of them.

"You go on ahead. I'll be there in a minute." She gave Emma a big hug.

Sydney watched her go back inside and, still in shock, walked over to the edge of the immense deck where she'd stood so many times in her life. She thought about what Emma had said. All this time, all these years, she'd internalized all of her mother's criticism. Sydney took that to mean her choices—all her choices, how she behaved, the sports she played, and later, the women she dated—were bad ones, and she would suffer the consequences. It was clear her mother meant no one would ever love her. And she'd believed her! More importantly, she didn't realize until this moment that she'd had a choice. Sydney grabbed hold of the deck railing. That changed everything.

Sydney looked out over the water and realized she liked the woman she'd become. She liked her a lot! Why her own mother hadn't accepted and loved her, she didn't know. But it no longer mattered. She didn't have to prove her mother wrong, she only had to prove herself right.

❖

The band called for the last dance. Afterward she, JT, Emma, Rusty and the bridal party went out on the boat for a last drink. Finally, everyone dispersed. Drivers waited to take the immediate family home. She hugged Rusty, JT, and especially Emma.

Back inside her parents' house, Sydney heard their voices in the living room. Their relationship worked for them, and for that, Sydney was grateful. She smiled at the sound of the clinking ice cubes. Her mother's drinking was no longer her problem. Nor was her mother's thinking. Sydney walked into the room.

Her father smiled, surprised to see her standing there.

"Everything okay?" he asked.

"Absolutely. I'll be leaving first thing in the morning, so I wanted to say goodbye. It was a great wedding, Mom. You did a fabulous job."

"Where are you going?" she asked, moving to the edge of her chair and slowly standing to refill her drink.

"Back to Cutchogue." *Back to Kate.* Thank goodness she had driven up this time. She had so much to think about on the ride home.

"But we're having a family brunch tomorrow."

"I have to go." She turned toward her father and hugged him. "I love you, Dad."

"I love you, too, honey. We'll talk soon."

Her mother was staring at her. Sydney started toward her.

"What are you doing?" her mother asked.

Sydney wrapped her arms around her before she could step back. Her body felt small, fragile. "I wanted to say goodbye, Mom."

"I'm sure the others will want to see you tomorrow," her mother stuttered. "Why in the world are you rushing off like this?"

"Early morning is my favorite time of day. Plus, I want to get a head start on the traffic." Sydney paused. "I love you, too, Mom."

Her mother gaped at her, her mouth wide open.

"I hope you'll come see our vineyard one day," Sydney stated. "I'll let you know when we've bottled our first wines." She smiled and was down the hallway before either could reply.

❖

Sydney had a hard time getting to sleep. She decided to take one more look out the porthole to the harbor. The water had always calmed her. The lights at the club were still on, the moon making everything sparkle. And then it hit her. Her mother was just as homophobic as Zeke! All her mother's fears had been there when Sydney was a kid, and her fate was sealed when she openly dated Blaye in high school. Sydney would always embarrass her. She would never marry a man, never give her mother grandchildren. *Well, sorry, Mom. This strong, independent lesbian is quite content as she is.*

She lay back down and thought about all the things she liked about herself: her strength, her assertiveness, her intelligence, her perseverance, and even her artistic talents. She thought about her grandmother, her friends, her brothers—all the people who'd loved and nurtured her. Finally, exhausted but emotionally exalted, Sydney drifted off to sleep. The only water she wanted to see from now on was Long Island Sound. And the only woman she needed to love her was Katherine Bauer.

At dawn, Sydney brought her bag downstairs and tossed it in the car. She couldn't wait to start driving. She had a lot of explaining to do once she returned. She only hoped Kate was open to listening. It seemed like she'd been gone forever. And in many ways, she had.

Chapter Eighteen

April 1985, Cutchogue

Kate decided to walk the vineyard. It was Sunday, so she didn't have to go to either of her part-time jobs. Sydney was at her brother's wedding, another major family occasion to which she had *not* been invited. Frankly she'd given up trying to figure out Sydney's behavior, let alone what she was thinking. Sydney's silence bothered her even more, leaving her sad and exhausted. If anything could cheer her up, the first sighting of budbreak would do it. The good news was that, depending on the temperature, forty to eighty days after budbreak, the process of flowering and pollination would begin on the tiny button-like clusters that would eventually become grapes. But the bad news was that after budbreak, the shoots would be particularly vulnerable to bad weather. And without a proper budbreak, there would be no crop. Detrimental weather—cold, wind, rain—could severely affect the flowering process. Nature had its own drama. She had better make sure every wire was bound securely to the end posts, including the crimp connections that she and Sydney had painstakingly attached last summer. Ironically, the wires were now more secure than their relationship, which had slowly deteriorated to zero. Lost in thought, Kate continued all the way down to the other side of the hill by the pond. Hearing a voice, she looked up and saw Sydney waving excitedly.

"There you are!" Sydney yelled and started jogging toward her. "I've been looking all over for you."

Kate shaded her eyes and stared at the woman rushing her way. She hadn't expected Sydney back until late that night.

"I'm *so* happy to see you," Sydney said, catching her breath, smiling as if she hadn't seen Kate in years. She took a step toward her, but then caught herself and stepped back. "You look dazzling. How are you?"

"Fine." *Dazzling*? Sydney must be pumped up on coffee.

Sydney took her eyes off Kate and looked around. "The vines look strong. And look at these buds. They'll burst any day, right? Well, not burst, but you know what I mean."

Kate knew what Sydney meant but was totally befuddled by her cheery persona. "How was the wedding?"

"Life changing."

"What?" Of all the answers, she certainly didn't expect that one.

"We have a million things to do. I'm very excited, aren't you? This is our year. The grapes that grow this year, we'll make into wine."

Kate could only look at her. The person who left and the one who returned were not the same person. "You do remember I don't know how to make wine."

Sydney laughed, then gave Kate an unusually endearing smile. "Of course. I'll be responsible for the wine making. As promised."

"Those aren't exactly work boots." She pointed to Sydney's fancy loafers.

Sydney looked down. "Oh, for heaven's sake. I parked and rushed right out to find you. Listen, everything's changed. Something happened while I was home. A good something. There's so much I want to tell you." Sydney backed up and put her hands in a prayer-like position. "Have dinner with me tonight. Please, Kate. I need to talk to you."

"About what? I'm right here. Tell me." If Sydney was going to talk, Kate did not want to wait.

"Now? Yikes. Okay." Sydney took a step back, shook out her hands then faced her. "I've been a damn fool, Kate, and I'm really sorry." She took a deep breath. "Oh, dear, I thought I was ready." She took one more breath and exhaled slowly. "Since we became lovers—and even before that, since we met, really—I've intentionally kept you at arm's length. I am so, so sorry. Bottom line? I love you. I want us back. Please, give me another chance."

Kate's mind went blank. Her heart was pounding, but her head won out. She needed clarity. "What the hell are you saying? What's happened to you? Who are you?"

Sydney smiled. She reached toward Kate, but again, withdrew her hand. "I can give you details later, if you want, but in a nutshell, I was sure that if I let you in on the real me—the person I thought I was— you'd find me, well, let's just say unappealing. And kick me not only out of your bed, but off your property. I couldn't let that happen."

"What are you talking about? Did I ever give you any indication of that?"

"You most certainly did not. It was all in my head. You did nothing, I assure you. But things got even more complicated when I realized I could lose both you and my chance to be your vintner."

Kate couldn't believe what Sydney was saying. "Where is all this coming from? As long as I've known you, you've walked around all confident and self-assured."

"I know. My confident exterior was hiding what I felt about myself inside."

Kate couldn't believe what she was hearing. "But—"

"At least meet me at Uncle Louie's later? I know this is a lot to take in. I'll make us dinner and your favorite brownies and we can sit out on the step. What do you say?"

Kate thought for a minute. She had no reason to refuse. "I guess."

"I only figured all this out this past weekend, Kate. I swear."

Kate nodded, touching her forehead. It felt clammy.

"One other thing."

"There's more?"

"I'm going to sell my car."

"What?"

"That was my getaway car. I don't need one anymore. I've been thinking about our finances. Soon our expenses will double, even triple. Next fall we'll need a wine transfer pump. And—"

"But you love your car," Kate interrupted, flabbergasted.

"I did. But like I said, things have changed. See you tonight. Six work for you? Seven?"

"S-six," Kate stuttered.

Sydney turned on her pretty penny loafers and headed back up the hill.

Kate watched Sydney until she was out of sight but found herself unable to move or even remember why she had come outside in the first place.

❖

Kate leaned back and waited until Sydney returned from taking the empty plates into the house. The dinner was good, but the brownies were exceptional, moist and fudgy, just the way she loved them. Now what? They'd only made small talk while eating. Was she supposed to continue the earlier conversation or would Sydney? While Sydney settled back on the steps, Kate scanned the acres of leafless vines, illuminated by a beautiful waxing moon. The weeding would be nonstop, and once the grapes were formed, they'd need to thin the clusters and make sure the foliage didn't block the sun from hitting the grapes. Kate wished she'd worn another shirt with buttons or something to fiddle with.

"I hope I can explain this," Sydney began, breaking the silence and sitting up. "Feel free to interrupt with questions."

Kate held her tongue. She'd already heard more from Sydney than she ever thought possible.

"Here goes." She smiled, leaning toward Kate. "For starters, I regret my silence these past months, especially if you interpreted it as a rejection of you. It was totally defensive on my part. And selfish."

"Sydney, you've got to tell me what happened at that wedding."

"I get it. I feel like I was struck by lightning and suddenly see everything differently. But now that I'm sitting here, I'm not sure I can explain it so you'll understand." Sydney started fidgeting.

At least this was a Sydney she recognized. "Did somebody say something to you?" Kate asked.

"That's exactly what happened. My new sister-in-law was talking about my mother. You met my mother. She's quite the powerhouse. And not always positive."

"To say the least." Sydney's graduation and the whole restaurant scene returned vividly to Kate's mind.

"I realized that I took everything she said one hundred percent personally. I went from thinking I was a lousy daughter to thinking I was a lousy human being. If you think you're worth crap, then you think everyone else will, too." Sydney looked out toward the vines.

They sat in silence. Just as Kate was about to speak, Sydney abruptly stood and hopped down the three steps. She crossed her hands across her chest and continued. "Does this sound bizarre to you? Lots of people have tough mothers. I'm guessing very few have mothers like yours." Sydney looked off in the distance, closing her eyes momentarily. "But then Blaye came along and I went off in a spiral of fear that lasted—wow, till this wedding." She shook her head. "I can't believe it took me so long to figure all this out."

"Keep going," Kate encouraged. The moon had gone behind the clouds. The only light came from her parents' back porch. Her mother had probably left the light on for Sydney. "Tell me more about Blaye."

Sydney returned to the steps. "Blaye was my first girlfriend. I was a senior in high school and ready to be rebellious, so the timing was perfect. My mother had been belittling me all my life. I thought I could prove her wrong by hooking up with the most popular kid in class. Who happened to be female. We carried on publicly all over town and went to bars in Boston—and New York City—on the weekends. My parents were scandalized, and I was thrilled. I was sure that Blaye loved me, and that our grand love would matter more than all the stares and comments." Sydney abruptly stopped talking and turned her head away.

Kate's instincts pushed her to move over and comfort Sydney. She put her hand gently on Sydney's hand. Sydney continued.

"I thought that if Blaye loved me, that would prove I was lovable. I didn't know that I was already lovable. I needed someone else to tell me. But that's jumping ahead. As for Blaye, she was looking for a diversion, a fun way to pass the time. She didn't really love me. Blaye left the very day she was handed her diploma. For years, I blamed her for my feelings of mistrust and insecurity. I mistrusted love. I was afraid of getting hurt again, so I ran from getting involved with anyone. And especially from you. Letting you in was the biggest risk of all, or so I thought. I had no idea that *not* talking to you was the surest way to lose you." Sydney put her hand on top of Kate's. "I want us back, Kate. I love you. I want a real relationship. Out in the open. The works."

Kate noticed the heat in their joined hands. The sounds of Sydney's words faded out. Neither she nor Sydney moved an inch. Kate knew Sydney was waiting for some response. But she was not ready to jump back into her arms. In fact, she was afraid to. *Why?* An image of her father in his hospital bed flashed in her mind. Because Sydney wanted to be totally out? Was her father the reason? Or did she not yet trust this new Sydney? Forcing herself to react, she threw out a few polite words. "Wow, Sydney. I'm impressed. That was a lot to figure out." Kate gently withdrew her hand. "I'm sorry, I need to—"

"Think about it. I know." Sydney took a quick breath before continuing. "Took me long enough to get there, so take your time. Mostly I'm sorry I hurt a lot of people along the way, especially you." Sydney stood.

Kate pushed herself to stand, mere feet away from the woman who was once her heart's desire. This should be their big breakthrough. But something was holding her back. Kate couldn't budge. She felt weighed down by a hundred-pound sack of potatoes. She couldn't move, much less react.

"Thanks for telling me all this." It was all she could manage.

Sydney took the few steps to the ground and turned toward Kate. "Oh, by the way, just for the record, I finally figured out the reason for my mother's behavior. She's homophobic, too. I can't believe I missed that. All along she wanted a sweet, compliant daughter who would bring home a boyfriend. And instead, she got me—a tomboy. But here's the fun thing I learned early on—I prefer women. And how much I love having sex, so I suppose I should be grateful to Blaye for something. I had a lot of time in the car to think. Amazing what comes up." She paused. "Too much?"

Kate stood immobile, stunned into remembering how good Sydney was in bed.

"Maybe." Kate hesitated. "And now what?" Kate asked out loud, though the thought was really meant for herself.

"That's up to you. For starters, I owed you this explanation. I'm trying to make up for all the talking I didn't do. But I want more, much more. Whenever you're ready." Before Kate could respond, Sydney added, "Let me walk you back to the cottage."

Kate joined her and they started off down the familiar path. Sydney put her hand protectively around Kate's back, as if there were some potential danger lurking in the darkness.

"I'm taking on extra jobs at the printer," Sydney said. "Baby announcements, birthday party mock-ups, foreclosures, garage sales, you name it. I'm going to make us a ton of money. Oh, and let's hope my car ad works."

Before they reached Kate's steps, Sydney stopped. "I'll see you tomorrow. I'm going to run back to the house." She gazed intently at Kate, before heading back up the path.

"Sydney—" Kate called.

"Go on in. See you tomorrow."

Kate waited until Sydney was out of sight before going inside her cottage. She made tea and sat, unable to take even a sip. Sydney had been totally honest, candid, up front. All that she had ever wanted. She needed to figure out what was holding her back. And fast.

❖

The next day Sydney was laughing and joking and went off to work as if they'd never spoken. No acknowledgment whatsoever of the revelatory conversation. Kate followed suit. They kept up their routine—she worked in the vineyard, and Sydney in the winery, after they both got home from their respective jobs. Nothing from their conversation came up again. Sydney seemed happier than she'd ever been. The following Tuesday, Magda stopped by and asked if that was Sydney's car that was for sale. She'd seen it on a flyer.

"Great drawing. Made me want to buy it," Magda said, laughing.

"Where did you see it?"

"At Key Foods and King Kullen. Amber says she saw one posted at the hardware store. They're everywhere. I bet there'll be a bidding war."

"Magda, don't be silly. Who has that kind of money?"

"For that car? Somebody will."

In three days, it was gone. That Friday evening, Sydney asked Kate if she would give her a ride to work, simply saying she'd sold her car. "I only need to be dropped off. I can get one of the kids to drive me home. Nothing has to change."

Kate remembered all the time she waited and hoped Sydney would change. What was wrong with her? Maybe it was all too much. Her father was still not talking to her. She thought about what Sydney had said about internalizing all her mother's criticism. Maybe she'd internalized all her father's homophobia. Or maybe she was afraid this was all too good to believe.

❖

Two days later, Kate was sound asleep at dawn when she heard someone pounding on her door.

"Kate, wake up. Come outside. There's a problem." Sydney's voice.

Totally confused, Kate threw her legs over the side of the bed and scrambled to get dressed. She was out the door in seconds. Sydney stood on the steps. "What's going on?" she asked.

"Someone's vandalized the vineyard!"

"What?"

"They spray-painted the side of the winery. Jerome woke me. He was the first one up and out this morning. Let's go."

They bolted down the path and cut across the vineyard, Kate on one side of a row, and Sydney on the other. Looking up at the winery wall, Kate read the huge, sloppily written words spray-painted in bold red: DYKES—FAGGOTS—HOMOS—GET OUT OR DIE.

Kate took in the words on the wall and was shocked at the vulgarity, not to mention the outright threat. Then from the corner of her eye, she saw her father making his way slowly toward them on his crutches. She had a flashback to Ryan standing in the doorway to Lily's bedroom, pointing his finger at them. He had said he was going to tell his parents. Maybe this time, he'd told the whole neighborhood instead.

Sydney looked around. "Are those beer cans?" she asked. "Someone had a party here. We'd better check the vines."

"I'll go," Kate said, running ahead. She looked quickly around to see if there were any tire tracks, but seeing none, ran toward her uncle's house. Someone had to have entered on the unused side of Uncle Louie's house. Sure enough, there were tire tracks headed up the row toward the top of the incline. Following the tracks, Kate spotted where they'd rammed several fruiting wires and tried to pull down the vines. It was nearing full light so she could easily see where the ground was torn up. An end post had been rammed and the grapes in that section mashed to the ground. Kate's stomach tightened. Two more end posts farther up the row had been hacked by an ax, but not enough to break through. Down the hill at the pond, someone had spray-painted the vines, the same red color.

"Kate!"

She turned and saw Sydney sprinting toward her.

"I told your father to call the police," Sydney said, catching her breath. She turned toward the tracks. "Two trucks. I bet they stopped at the pond."

"You didn't hear them come or go last night either?" Kate asked.

"Unfortunately not. Let's meet up at the pond—I'll go to the right," Sydney said.

Kate rushed down the left side of the incline to the pond and indeed, the soil was gutted up, beer cans everywhere, including two floating in the water.

"I think it's only in this section," Sydney said when she joined her. "Nothing was damaged on my side."

"The winery?" Kate asked.

"I'll go check. If they got in—" Sydney didn't finish. She put one hand momentarily on Kate's shoulder, then took off.

Kate checked the perimeter of the vineyard, looking down the rows. She heard the sirens, but by the time she got back to the winery, only the lights of two patrol cars were flashing. She could see two officers talking to Jerome and her father. Kate tried to steady her fear.

Sydney ran up. "Locked up. Nobody got in," she said.

"Thank goodness," Kate said, her voice quivering. "I think we should talk to the police."

Sydney nodded. They turned and walked back toward the police cars.

One of the two police officers, seeing Kate, walked toward her. Kate introduced herself. He nodded. "Your father was telling me you own this property. My son was in school with you. This looks like a prank to me."

"A prank? You're not even calling it vandalism?" Kate asked.

"Well, no real harm done. Nothing was really destroyed. With all these beer cans, I'm guessing local kids. All you need is a little clean up." He swept his hand toward the winery wall.

"Are you kidding me?" Kate said. "This was a cowardly act, coming in the middle of the night, not a harmless prank." Suddenly she was all fury.

"If they had something to say to us, they should have said it to our faces. Who's teaching these kids, as you call them, to say these things? It's rude and crude. Juvenile acts or not, they were at a minimum trespassing. And they did damage a whole section of our vines. I suggest you change your report. Get back to me when you find out more."

"Of course." He folded his notebook and looked a little abashed. "Don't worry," he said, his tone changed. "Kids nowadays are big blabbermouths. They'll want to tell others they did this. We'll find 'em." He gave a little nod and walked away.

"That was awesome." Sydney said, stepping up to join her. "I—"

"Listen, could you and Jerome do one final check? I need to talk to my father." She turned toward him and was surprised to find him standing off by himself, his head bowed. He must be preparing his final tirade against her. Surely he'd say this was all her fault. That if she hadn't come out, if Sydney hadn't come here, and on and on.

Kate took a moment to deeply breathe in the cool morning breeze. Her father trudged slowly forward. Kate waited. She'd let him have the first word.

He stopped and started speaking before positioning himself steadily on his crutches. "How dare someone come sneaking onto your property in the middle of the night. Cowards. They have no right. This is your land. Who do they think they are?" He was shouting.

Kate stepped back.

"I came to talk to you about that wall," he continued, "and this whole mess. That was wrong what they did. I'm glad the police came fast."

"Dad—"

"They were talking about you, you know, all those nasty things they wrote."

"I know—"

"Give me a minute," he interrupted. "I've been thinking about this for a while, but what they did, what they said here today, made me realize how wrong I've been." He paused. "I don't have all the words yet." He shuffled a bit to steady himself and wiped his brow. "Someone wanted to hurt you and hurt your business. That made me mad first, then it made me think." He swallowed. "I've been doing the same thing, in my head. Hell, you've heard me say stuff just as bad. I'm sorry." He held up his hand to ask her to wait. "However you've come to be, all that you are, that's okay. You're my daughter. I love you. Please forgive the stubborn fool that I've been."

"Dad—"

"I'm almost done." He wiped his eyes. "I lost my brother to all this…I don't even know what to call it. Hatred? Cruelty? You asked me back at that wine tasting, 'Who am I to judge?' I'm nobody. Those kids, well, I might as well have been the one writing that stuff on the wall. The police should have arrested me." He dropped his head again.

Kate waited, wanting desperately to hug her father.

"I can't get Louie back." He swiped his dripping nose. "But I won't lose you."

Kate couldn't move.

He held up one crutch in the air. "Now about that friend of yours. I resented Sydney coming into our house and ordering me around. But it worked. She's a firecracker. If it weren't for her, I'd still be holed up somewhere, whining and making your mother's life miserable."

Was he praising Sydney?

"I see you two together. I don't get much of a view, just looking out my window. I see you talking. Standing close together, hanging on to every word the other says."

Kate sighed. That was a while ago, but she, too, remembered.

"If she makes you happy, so be it. I was no prince in shining armor, but your mother took me in."

Kate still didn't know what to say.

"Will you forgive me?"

Kate threw her arms around her father. "You know I do."

"Walk me home, will you? How about we have lunch. All four of us. Ah, there's my drill sergeant walking over. Why don't you ask her?"

They turned and waited for Sydney, Kate's familiar goosebumps returning as she approached.

"Dad's inviting us to lunch," Kate said. "Want to go?"

Sydney's glance shot first to her father, then back to her. "Really?"

"I'm sure Rachel has enough for all of us," he said. "You in?"

Those were the first kind, ordinary words he'd ever said to Sydney. Kate could tell by Sydney's expression she was equally surprised.

"Yes," Sydney answered. "Of course."

They walked back to the house together. Kate would worry about cleaning the wall later. This was going to be a fine meal. She couldn't wait.

CHAPTER NINETEEN

Barely registering how cold it was when she woke up, Kate automatically put on a second layer. Still on a high from lunch the day before, she felt lighter than she'd been in months. She couldn't wait to see Sydney this morning. For heaven's sake, she was even excited about their time alone together in the truck ride to work. When she opened the door to go outside, a blast of cold air hit her in the face. The temperature had dropped precipitously since last night. What was going on?

Rushing over to her parents' house, Kate ducked in the back door and immediately heard the meteorologist's voice on the TV in the living room, and then her father's voice, "We need to tell Kate."

"Tell me what?" she asked, walking into the room. Her mother and Sydney stood huddled next to her father's chair. They all turned toward her. "What's going on?"

"A storm's coming," her father said, his face anxious. He wheeled his chair toward the TV and pointed directly toward the screen. "Listen."

After less than a minute, Kate couldn't believe what she was hearing. "Are they talking about snow?"

"Yes," her father answered, turning to face her. "A Nor'easter. We were so, uh, busy yesterday, I didn't listen to the weather."

Snow in mid-April made no sense. It had been cold when she stepped out of her house, but not *that* cold.

"To be clear, they're talking about snow, not rain," Kate confirmed.

"Yes. Aren't the vines kind of vulnerable at this point? Do you know how to protect them?" he asked.

"I hope so, Dad." He was a farmer first, Kate mused, then took a step back, her pulse ratcheting up. The buds! Any damage to the buds and their entire crop could be lost. She turned to Sydney. "Let's go."

"What are you going to do?" her father called.

Kate stopped and turned. "I'll figure it out. Thanks, Dad. It's wonderful to have you on our team." She put a hand on his shoulder as she passed and walked back outside. Sydney followed.

Kate looked up at the sky. It had darkened in just the short time she'd been inside.

"Something is happening, I can tell by the drop in temperature," she said to Sydney, who was standing by her side, still in her apron from working in the kitchen. "The clouds are getting dark. It smells like snow." Kate could feel her body twitching. Even as she gazed up, a small branch from somewhere blew by. "Wind's picking up," she said. "This is serious."

"Kate—" Sydney started.

"We have to protect the buds from freezing. Let me think. I remember a class at Davis where they told us about all the methods people used in situations like this. I did some follow-up reading, thank goodness."

"While you figure it out, I'm going to change and call work. Be right back." Sydney tore off her apron and charged back inside.

Kate ran back to her cottage to check the thermometer at the door. It had dropped to thirty-six degrees. Inside, Kate grasped the edges of the sink, racking her brain. She couldn't let anything happen. If those buds didn't develop, they had nothing. The inheritance from Uncle Louie, all their hopes and plans—gone. She had to come up with something. But what?

Water, she suddenly realized, staring into the sink. They needed water, lots of it, and fast. As she put on her boots, she remembered they had a whole irrigation system. But damn, that was too slow. What else? There had to be a way. She slammed the door on her way out and ran toward the vineyard.

"Kate, wait up!"

"Follow me to Jerome's," she told Sydney.

Kate kept going. "I'm thinking we could use the old machines Uncle Louie used to irrigate his potato fields," she yelled over her shoulder. When she was a kid, Kate had thought the machines looked like giant flies that squirted water as they crisscrossed the fields. Her father used the same machines on his corn, so naturally Jerome kept them in working condition. They dashed past Uncle Louie's and up the driveway to Jerome's. He was surprised to find them knocking on his door. Kate said hello to Jerome's wife, Annie Mae, then turned to Jerome. "Sorry to barge in—"

"I was just listening to the weather. Come on in."

Kate, followed by Sydney, stepped inside. "Those big irrigation machines work, don't they?" She pointed out his window toward the machines in the driveway, covered by burlap. "We need to wet down the vines."

"Kate, a storm is headed this way. Why would you put water—?"

"I can't take the time to explain in detail," Kate interrupted. "Trust me. It insulates them. How long will it take to crank these machines up and get them out into the vineyard?" Kate looked out another window to the rows and rows of vines. "Oh no, what was I thinking? Those machines can't get through the rows. There's no path wide enough."

"Ah, you wanted to spray down the vines from overhead," Jerome said, understanding.

"Yes, but the water for the corn field's overhead sprinklers comes from the pond," Kate mused out loud. "Our irrigation system takes water from our new well. And at every tenth row there are valves. Jerome, do you think we could use the irrigation system valves to water the vineyard? I know we haven't had to turn the sprinklers on yet."

"The control valves?"

"They should work, right? We put them in all around the perimeter for emergency purposes, like if the drip lines ever got clogged."

"Hoses! You're thinking about attaching hoses," Jerome guessed.

"Exactly, up and down the rows, at every valve." Kate smiled for the first time.

"Brilliant, Kate," Sydney told her.

"Let's go take a look." Jerome grabbed his coat. "We'll need a wrench." He walked to a closet, pulled out a toolbox and grabbed one. She and Sydney waited, then followed him out to the vineyard and over to the nearest valve. He turned the nozzle and water came out. "We'll need to increase the pressure," he said.

"And we'll need hoses, lots of hoses, the longer the better,"

Sydney added. "And people. I'll get the hoses. Okay to take the truck? The hardware store should have lots of them this time of year."

"Keys are under the mat. I'll help Jerome open the valves. Oh, there's Mom."

Her mother waved as Sydney flew by, heading toward the truck. The lights in her parents' house flickered off, then back on. The wind had picked up.

"Mom?"

"What can I do to help? I'm closing the stand today."

"Two things. Have Dad keep an eye on the temperature. Second, could you call Magda, Amber, Mary, and Finn and ask if they could help us for a few hours? And ask everyone to bring a hose with them."

"Sure," she said, "whatever you need."

"Ask everyone to come in about an hour. I hate to be dramatic, but we are going to need everyone's help to save the vineyard. Thanks." She hugged her mom, needing the hug more than her mother did.

Sydney once told her that some of the larger French vineyards lit fires in oil drums, burning them all night to keep the vines warm. That was not an option. Kate had read about some California vineyards that ran giant fans blowing all night to prevent the cold air from settling on their vines. Also not an option. Here, they'd have to use what was available and hope that the temperature didn't keep dropping. As long as the temperature stayed above twenty-eight degrees, the tissues around the buds would release heat and protect them. That was the only thing that mattered.

While waiting for the hoses, Kate went back to her parents to get the updated weather report. As her hand grabbed the doorknob, light snow started to fall. Her father, as expected, was glued to the TV.

"What's the word?"

"Snow heading up the coast, on its way toward New York City," he said, "For us, it all depends on how far out island it gets."

"Thanks." Kate rushed back outside.

❖

Two hours later, they had every available hose attached to the emergency valves up and down the rows. Finn and Mary Carmichael were extending hoses down the rows, as far as they could get them. As soon as the hoses were attached, they took turns watering down the vines.

At four p.m. several young men showed up. One of them approached Kate.

"Billy over at Ace said something about you needing firefighters tonight."

Kate remembered how Sydney had gathered up those young guys from the beach that first summer when the beetles attacked the baby vines. But firefighters?

"Hey, glad you're here!" Sydney said, sidling up next to Kate. "We need you guys to be *like* firefighters tonight, spraying the vines with water. Come with me." Sydney took them all up the hill, heading into the wind.

Seven acres. They started at one end and systematically wet down every vine, paying sharp attention to the direction of the spray or the wind would blow it into the air or into their faces. When one acre was done, they'd move the hoses to the next and repeat the process. Kate was well aware that as soon as it got dark, folks would have to leave. She and Sydney would stay up all night if they had to. Row by row, vine by vine. There was no other option.

Magda told her she had put a pot of soup on her stove in the cottage. Kate rushed down to grab a bowl, grateful for the break and the warmth. After several spoonfuls, the lights blinked again. *No!* It would be dark soon and no one would be able to see how to maneuver between rows, see where to hook up the hoses, not to mention see the spray in the thin, cold air. "Flashlights," she said out loud, putting her bowl into the sink. She looked at her watch. The hardware store didn't close until seven. They had time. She grabbed her coat and ran toward the house. Magda was getting into her side of the truck. Kate rushed over.

"Mags, I need you to go buy flashlights and batteries. Amber," Kate continued, "would you go inside and call the store and have them load up five big flashlights with batteries? Oh, and maybe a couple of big lanterns, if they have them. Put it on my account." She paused. "I owe you again, indispensable friends. Yet another emergency."

"Not to worry." Magda said. "Hopefully we'll be drinking your thanks in wine one day." Amber got out, gave Kate a quick hug and rushed toward the house.

"Bring them up the hill when you get back, okay?" Kate yelled to Amber, then rushed up the hill to join the others. Kate had never participated in any sports in high school or college. But she'd wager her sprint now against the best of the runners.

By nine o'clock, there were only a few stragglers left, but they'd covered the vineyard and were on their second go-around. Kate's hands were numb. She needed heavier gloves or a change of gloves. Several cars had stopped on the road, presumably seeing the flashlights move across the vineyard and no doubt wondering what was going on.

Kate took a hose from a teenager who looked exhausted and concentrated on hitting the vine with the water while he held the flashlight. She could barely see.

"Tommy, hold the light a little higher." He did. The snow was blowing right in their faces. Kate could see he was exhausted. "Time for you to go home." She thanked him and insisted he leave. All these amazing people helping out in such cold weather. She knew farmers—and friends—helped each other. That was what they did. But these were strangers.

Kate couldn't help but think of the teenagers who had vandalized her property. Tommy's kindness and generosity eclipsed all their cruelty and ignorance.

An hour later, struggling to maneuver the flashlight and hose, Kate heard the crunch of what had to be Sydney's boots. She must have followed the movement of Kate's flashlight, flickering among the rows.

"How are you doing?" she asked, putting her arm around Kate's shoulder. "I sent Jerome home. It's just the two of us."

Kate flashed her light on Sydney's face, just for a second. "You're all I need," she said, knowing the truth of the statement as the words flew from her mouth. "Ready to continue?"

"Yes, but in an hour, let's take a break, warm up, and check the temperature," Sydney suggested.

"Good idea. Let's work together. It's tricky holding the hose in one hand, the flashlight in the other." Kate smiled, warmer already. Her mind went directly to the heat of their bodies touching each other. Sydney had said she would wait until Kate was ready. If the vines survived, she would be more than ready.

❖

Kate checked her watch. Almost two a.m. "Time for another break. Let's go to the cottage. I'll make us hot tea."

"Have any brandy to put in it?" Sydney joked.

Kate laughed. They crept down the rows, holding their flashlights ahead, stepping carefully, testing the vines every so often to make sure they were covered in ice. Kate was exhausted. Her arms ached. As usual, Sydney didn't complain. The good news was that the snow had stopped. The better news was the hosing solution seemed to be working. The vines were covered in ice. If the temperature dropped below twenty-eight degrees, the frozen buds could not recover. The damaged vines would put out secondary buds, but not enough for a harvest.

Back at the cottage door, Kate checked the temperature gauge.

"Down to thirty degrees. We can only hope it holds here."

Sydney nodded. They went inside.

Kate put the kettle on for tea. "Why don't you take a hot shower? I have clothes you can throw on."

Sydney shot her a stunned look. "You sure?"

"I'm positive," she said, staring into Sydney's eyes. Kate could feel the heat rushing through her.

"Never mind the brandy, I'm getting warmer already." Sydney inched closer to Kate. "It's awfully close quarters here. I'd forgotten." The desire in her eyes was unmistakable.

Kate took one more look at Sydney before regretfully stepping back. They needed some distance between them. *She* needed the distance. "Showers for now but—"

"Later?" Sydney asked.

"Just so you know," Kate said, enfolding Sydney in her arms, breathing in her warmth, "I've missed you." She pulled Sydney to her, kissing her gently at first, then hungrily. But reminding herself they still had work to do, she stopped. "Go shower. Save me some hot water. Okay?"

"If you insist." Sydney gave her a quick kiss and stepped back. "I can wait."

As soon as Sydney shut the bathroom door, Kate let the tension in her body dissolve. All that she'd been holding on to, she let go. When Sydney stepped out of the shower, wrapped in a towel, Kate had to tear her eyes off her. She handed Sydney jeans and a sweatshirt. "Be right back. Make us some tea?"

Sydney nodded.

Kate gathered some dry clothes, then hopped into the shower, leaning under the spray for a solid minute. When she returned, Sydney was sitting in the corner chair, sipping tea. She handed Kate a cup.

"Think it'll really work, all this watering?" Sydney asked.

Kate appreciated that Sydney was trying to keep her mind on the vines. "It should," she said, looking at Sydney, but imagining each bud encapsulated in its own cocoon of warmth. "Nature is amazing." Kate put her tea on the table. She pulled Sydney up from her chair and led her over to the bed. "Now, don't get any ideas. At least not yet," she said. "I need to talk to you, just for a moment." She sat down and patted the spot next to her. Sydney sat and Kate turned so she could face Sydney. "I really thought I could save the vineyard from any harm if I stayed closeted. Yet we were vandalized anyway."

"Kate, you don't have to go into this."

"I do. I want to clear the air so we can start fresh." Kate took a breath. "I thought I could save my relationship with my father by denying who I was. That was wrong. Then I got angry at him for shutting me out. And then I was mad at you for doing the same thing. I didn't know what to do with all my emotions, so I—"

"Kate," Sydney tried again.

"What I'm trying to say," Kate insisted, "is that I got stuck. I couldn't get past my own fears. But all this time, all I've really done is work and miss you. Bottom line? Without you, the vineyard is not enough. I want you back—"

Sydney's kiss took the last of her words. Her one kiss turned into two, then three, and soon their hunger for each other made the rest of her confession unnecessary.

"We do need to finish our work out there," Kate mumbled, hating to pull herself out of Sydney's arms. They'd ended up in a scramble of arms and legs, stretched out on the bed. "I'm certainly warm enough to go back out. You?"

Sydney exhaled. "Sure." She stood up, pulled her clothes back into shape, and held out her hand to Kate. "Let's go."

❖

Kate estimated only an inch or two of snow on the ground, but it was icy and crunchy underfoot from all the water spray. Around four thirty, Kate returned to the cottage to check the outside temperature. It was holding! She rushed back to tell Sydney. They were standing at the highest rise on their farm, looking out over the vineyard, the ground covered with snow. As the moon peeked between the clouds, the light hit the frozen vines. The vineyard sparkled like diamonds.

"Look how wondrous," Kate exclaimed. "It can't be this beautiful and not work. It just can't."

Sydney took Kate's gloved hands and squeezed them. "Nature's resilient. You taught me that. It's going to work, Kate, but we'll deal with whatever happens."

"I say we go back to the cottage and wait," Kate suggested, feeling optimistic. On their way, they stopped to check the ice on several rows. The buds were well coated. The wind had subsided. The forecast called for the temperature to go back up around midmorning, and to reach the mid-forties by afternoon. If the temperature held, the sun's warmth would melt the ice and snow.

Kate had held it together until then, but as they reached the cottage door, she could feel her panic rising. Slowly, she looked at the thermometer. As long as the temperature wasn't dropping—

"Well?" Sydney asked.

"Thirty-one. It's going up!" Kate whooped. "Only one degree, but I'll take it." Kate threw both arms around Sydney and cried out, "We did it!"

Sydney held her tightly. "And it's only going to get warmer."

"Our work is done," Kate said, trying on one of her own seductive smiles. "I say we go in and finish what we started."

Sydney opened the door so fast, Kate was surprised the handle didn't come off. Barely inside the room, Sydney turned toward her with open arms.

"I've been quite patient, don't you think?" she asked.

"Yes, my love. Let's get these clothes off and warm up." Lucky for her, Sydney was of the same mind. They were in bed and under the covers in seconds, not a molecule of air between them.

Kate could only moan her contentment. It had taken them both a while, but they were—at last—back together. Very close together.

Chapter Twenty

October 1985, Cutchogue

After the scary Nor'easter back in April, they'd had a successful budbreak. The grapes had grown into a plentiful crop. But now so close to the harvest, Sydney had almost forgotten about it. Tonight she was busy watching Kate as she shifted into a comfortable position on the couch. She couldn't believe how at home Kate was. Kate had moved in with her several weeks after the storm. Sydney had brought her things back into Louie's house as soon as Zeke was walking around on his own. Sydney was thrilled to have use of the big farmhouse kitchen. Kate was overjoyed to have a large office upstairs for all their paperwork. Best of all, they were together.

"I just got it," Kate said, sitting up. "As the grapes mature, the amount of sugar rises and the acid falls. I had no idea the difference that acid made in the taste of the wine. It's not all about the sugar."

Sydney grinned. "Correct."

"Every time we went out, you ordered a chardonnay and a riesling so I could taste the difference."

"I only did that twice, but your point?" Sydney asked. Kate's hair had gotten so long, strands were curling down her neck. Sydney remembered Kate tucking strands of her hair behind her ear when they first met in San Francisco. Kate was a fidgety mess that day. This evening Kate sat comfortably in a T-shirt, her arms bronzed from all the work they'd completed in their vineyard.

"It's like why you put lemons in your vinaigrette," Kate continued, nudging Sydney from her reverie. "That acidity is important for the taste. The pizzaz. Even Coke would be flat without the acidity."

"Smart woman," Sydney said.

"I guess I finally understand what winemakers do," Kate told her. "What *you'll* be doing soon. Nature gives us the fruit, but the winemaker creates the flavor and the style. That's how each wine is unique."

"Yup." Sydney thought about all the charts hanging in the office to remind herself of each step and each process she had to follow. She was half pumped, half nervous. So many things could go wrong. She was particularly excited about the merlot and cabernet franc and the fermentation process. She could practically smell the yeast in the air. She was sure they'd need more barrels. The wine had to be properly aged. And they needed to rent a bottling machine.

Kate stretched lazily. "Hey, your face just turned from a smile to worry in ten seconds."

"I was thinking about all we have to do."

Kate looked at her watch. "It's getting late. You need your rest, winemaker. Time for bed." She scooted over to where Sydney was sitting upright in the big leather armchair and ran her hand slowly along the side of her cheek.

"Good idea," Sydney said. "As exciting as thinking about making wine is, I have other thoughts on my mind right now."

"Oh, yeah?" Kate said. "Like what?"

At the top of the stairs, their hands were all over each other. Maybe by the time their barreled wine was aging, they'd slow down a bit. But until then, Sydney was not complaining.

❖

"What's the sugar count?" Kate asked Sydney. For two weeks, she had helped Sydney measure the size of the grapes and check the skin color, but mostly she'd watched Sydney test for the sugar count, using the Brix refractometer Sydney had sent her from France.

"Sugar's at twenty-one Brix," Sydney said. "I'd like to see it get up to twenty-three before we pick. A couple more days."

They were in the winery, going over everything they needed to pick the grapes.

"The sugar is finally perfect, but the weather is iffy," Sydney continued. "Last night's weather forecaster mentioned rain for Saturday and Sunday, possibly thunderstorms. Dare we hold off until Monday? It's a gamble, but we'll have more people if we pick on the weekend. But if it rains on Saturday as we pick, the grapes will take on water, which messes up the sugar-acid balance. Worse," she said, running her hand nervously through her hair, "if the berries start to swell and split, then we'll have to worry about spoilage, mold, and mildew."

"That darn nature," Kate said, trying to lessen the tension.

Sydney walked over to the corner where she stood for a second with her hands across her chest. "I say we pick on Saturday. If we wait till Monday and don't have enough people, it'll take us too long to finish the harvest. We'll start with the chardonnay and riesling. The hardier merlot and cabernet franc can wait."

❖

On Friday it was overcast, but the forecast had changed to a Monday rain. When Kate opened the winery door, the light glinted off the stainless-steel press. The press was their largest piece of equipment. The crusher, already moved outside, seemed tiny in comparison. Kate thought momentarily about the loans she'd taken out for the equipment, but let the thought drop, not wanting to spoil the evening.

Sydney gave the big press a pat. "She's a beauty, don't you think?"

"Yeah, yeah, put your shoulder in there," Kate said. "We have to push Big Mama out to the crush pad. Heave ho!"

Using their combined strength pushing against one end, they rolled it out into the open air.

"Tell me again why you're not worried about us having enough people tomorrow?" Kate asked.

"I leafleted the entire town," Sydney told her. "Your mother's had a sign at the farm stand for days, and the folks at work have spread the word. We'll have enough people." They went over their lists one more time to make sure they hadn't forgotten anything.

The next morning, Kate stood in the driveway looking at her watch.

Rachel walked over holding out a mug of hot chocolate. "It's for the morning break. What do you think?" she asked. "I also have coffee and hot apple cider."

Kate took the warm mug from her mother's hand and sipped it. "Delicious. They'll love it. Thanks, Mom."

Rachel had closed her farm stand to help with the harvest. Sydney had advised her to leave a sign hanging on the door: *Closed for the grape harvest! Come help pick!* It was good advertising. And hopefully several customers would be tempted to stay.

MJ and Rusty had arrived and were staying with her folks. The four of them bonded immediately. MJ was up in her old bedroom and Rusty was on the living room couch.

Kate looked at her watch again. It was time. Sydney had gone to the winery to load up all the plastic containers. They had enough pruners and snippers. Kate didn't want people pulling the clusters off by hand—or even trying to. But now, where was everyone? She saw only MJ, Rusty, her mother, Magda, and Amber. Even Jerome was a no-show.

Kate turned as Magda started waving. She pointed toward her father striding toward them, leading their neighbors, Mary and Finn Carmichael.

"I brought reinforcements," he said proudly. "We'll see if they can keep up with me."

Kate laughed and was about to speak to them when she heard a truck. She looked toward the driveway and recognized Jerome's beat-up Chevy. Behind him were three more cars. When they got out of their cars, Kate recognized Jerome's buddies, the ones who had helped dismantle the grader, and waved.

Another two cars pulled up. Out of one car tumbled a woman she'd never seen before. "I'm a friend of Amber's," the woman told her. Then the town librarian showed up. And four people from the Cornell Cooperative Extension and a woman who worked in the grocery store. They'd all seen the flyer, they said. Sydney's boss pulled in with her husband. Then three more strangers joined them.

"I'm here because Louie can't be," one said.

"I'm a friend of Jerome's," another chimed in.

"I came to see the grapes," a third person said. "Who is the winemaker, anyway? I hear she's from France."

Just as Kate started to answer, everyone turned at the sound of a tractor approaching. It was Sydney, driving the old rusty tractor, pulling a flat trailer on wheels with the yellow containers.

"Here's the winemaker," Kate said proudly.

Sydney stopped the engine a few feet from the group and hopped down. The people who knew her started peppering her with questions. More people arrived. The driveway was soon full of people and cars. Kate counted over twenty-five people. They had enough.

Time to begin. Kate caught Sydney's eye and held up her watch. Sydney walked over to join her.

"Good morning, everyone." The crowd immediately quieted down. "Thank you for coming today. My name is Kate Bauer. I inherited this wonderful property from my uncle Louie. I wish he could be here today." Kate paused to honor his memory. "Sorry it's not a sunnier day, but frankly, we've been very lucky with the weather so far. Today we can only hope the rain holds off."

"It's okay, Kate, we came prepared." An old man showed his layers of clothing. "We're farmers. We know how to dress." Everyone laughed.

"We're picking both the chardonnay and riesling today," Kate continued. "The sugar levels are perfect, according to Sydney Barrett." Kate put her hand soundly on Sydney's shoulder. "Sydney is our winemaker."

Sydney nodded.

Kate continued with a careful explanation of how to pick the grapes. As she looked at the friendly crowd, she relaxed. This was going to be fun.

❖

Most of the local people started leaving around four thirty. They'd had a break at eleven and lunch at two, but still everyone looked exhausted. Kate sent her parents home at five, respecting her father's early dinner hour. Magda, Amber, and Jerome were still there, along with Rusty and MJ.

"We're going to grab a bite to eat, then be right back," Amber told her, pointing to Magda, who was two steps ahead.

"You don't have to," Kate said, "you've done enough. Rusty and MJ will help us finish up." She hurried over to hug them. Kate watched them get into their truck, grateful beyond words for their steadfast loyalty and devoted friendship. They had been there, first for her when Uncle Louie was sick, and then for the two of them through every vineyard crisis.

Sydney, Rusty, and Jerome had worked all afternoon picking up the full containers of grapes and bringing them with the tractor to the winery. They looked tired but not exhausted.

"There are five of us. We have enough light. Let's finish the last few rows," Kate suggested. Fortunately, everyone agreed.

"We're done!" Kate announced, about an hour later.

"Thank goodness," MJ said. "I'm ready to drop."

"Congratulations, vintners!" Rusty yelled.

Sydney rushed over to hug her brother and MJ.

Kate hugged Jerome. "We couldn't have done any of this without you," she said.

"The way Zeke was working today, all smiles and pride," Jerome shot back, "I think you may see him wanting to plant grapes next year instead of corn."

"You think?" Kate asked.

Jerome laughed. "Oh yeah. Without a doubt."

❖

Early Sunday morning, Sydney checked a third time to make sure all the hoses were connected, all the clamps tight. They could not afford any leaks. The grapes would go first into the crusher, then to the press, and then finally to the stainless wine tanks. The plan was to crush and press the chardonnay this morning and then—as soon as the machines were cleaned out—crush the riesling, It was a lot for their first day, but she was psyched to begin.

Kate brought over the last of a dozen containers full of grapes and put it next to the crusher.

"Ready?" Sydney asked Kate.

"Absolutely."

Sydney gave her a kiss for luck, then turned on the aptly named crusher, and the giant auger whirled into action. "Here we go!" Sydney picked up the first container and handed it to Kate. "You grew them and they are perfect. Please do the honors."

Kate tossed them in. Immediately the auger started macerating them.

"Our grapes," Sydney exclaimed. "Making juice for our wine. My turn." She picked up a container and took a second to stare at the grapes. Maybe she'd get used to this one day—meaning all aspects of harvesting, crushing, and pressing the grapes—but not today. How often does a dream come true? Sydney pitched the grapes into the crusher.

They took turns emptying crates into the crusher, watching the stems go flying out the end of the machine. Sydney checked to make sure the must, as it was properly called at this point—with the pulp and skin attached—was flowing evenly into the pump tray below and through the hose to the press. Kate took a pitchfork and started loading the back of the truck with all the stems. They were going to put them in a giant pile until they had time to spread them along the rows. Their very own grape compost pile.

MJ and Rusty arrived within the hour. They all worked as steadily as they could, taking turns, until dozens of containers were emptied. Sydney and Rusty had stacked up another ten, when Rachel and Zeke stepped around the side of the winery and onto the crush pad.

"May we take a turn?" Zeke asked.

"Of course," Sydney said.

"Before I forget, this came for you yesterday," Zeke said. He took out an envelope from his back pocket and handed it to Sydney. "Thought it was important."

Sydney took one look at the return address, then ripped it open. "We got it," she said to everyone, holding up the certificate. "Our liquor license!" She rushed over to embrace Kate. "We're good to go," she whispered, holding on to her.

"Ahem," Rusty interrupted. "What does the crusher do, other than the obvious?"

Sydney broke away from Kate. "The crush gets the juices flowing," Sydney explained. "Unlike the red grapes that will be fermented first, the chardonnay grapes go from the crusher directly into the press." She pointed to Big Mama. "The press will extract every last bit of juice from the grapes."

"Does the press part take minutes or hours?" Rachel asked.

"Hours for sure. There are lots of different cycles. Meanwhile we clean the crusher and prepare for the riesling crush."

"I'll let this crew finish up," Rachel said. "Time for me to make dinner. See you all later."

❖

The crew finished around six. Sydney sent Rusty and MJ back to the Bauers' for dinner. "We'll join you in a bit," she told them. They cleaned out the crusher and the press and swept the crush pad. Sydney was exhausted. Kate looked a bit bleary-eyed as well.

"Look what we've accomplished." Sydney beamed. "The chardonnay and riesling are sitting in their beautiful stainless tanks, settling. Everything is sparkling and clean. Let's spend only an hour or two socializing. We need to pace ourselves. This is just the beginning."

Kate agreed and they went next door for dinner.

❖

The conversation and camaraderie recharged Sydney. Leaving the Bauers', she felt invigorated. She already imagined the chardonnay aging in the barrels, going through its malolactic fermentation, smoothing the acidity, giving it a buttery taste on the palate. Unless they wanted a crisper, cleaner taste—truer to the grape's nature. She couldn't believe she was going to be making this decision.

"What are you smiling about?" Kate asked.

"The whole winemaking process. Our red grapes will be ready in about a week. I can't wait to begin fermenting them," she said. "Punching them down. Remember how they did it in Napa?"

"I remember Samantha," Kate said, grinning.

"You would." Sydney laughed. Then turned serious. More serious than she meant to. "I love you, Kate Bauer. You've made me the happiest woman in the world."

"Oh, I think the vineyard and our grapes had a lot to do with that. But I know what you mean." Her eyes sparkled. "I love you, too, Sydney Barrett."

Holding hands, they walked the short distance home. Upstairs in the bedroom, Sydney walked to the window. The moon lit up the partially harvested vineyard and the winery. The juice from the grapes was resting in the tanks. They were making wine! Excitement charged through her body.

Entering the room, Kate switched on the light and slid into bed. "I know you're thinking about our wine."

Sydney laughed. "Our dream has come true." She stepped over to Kate and kissed her, positive their lives and these vines would forever be entwined.

About the Author

As a lifelong feminist, Jacqueline Fein-Zachary is proud of her women's rights activism in Connecticut. A love of languages and diverse cultures inspired her world travels and professional career as a French and Spanish teacher. When she met the love of her life, Valerie, they worked to help secure same-sex marriage rights in Massachusetts. A retired marathoner, Jackie is now obsessed with getting her 10,000 steps a day. A Virginia native, Jackie lives in Boston and Truro with Valerie and more books than she has time to read. Jackie persists as a vegan foodie and advocate, helping to save the planet and promote a kinder world. This is her debut novel. Visit jackiefeinzachary.com.

Books Available From Bold Strokes Books

Curse of the Gorgon by Tanai Walker. Cass will do anything to ensure Elle's safety, but is she willing to embrace the curse of the Gorgon? (978-1-63679-395-5)

Dance with Me by Georgia Beers. Scottie Templeton mixes it up on and off the dance floor with sexy salsa instructor Marisa Reyes. But can Scottie get past Marisa's connection to her ex? (978-1-63679-359-7)

Gin and Bear It by Joy Argento. Opposites really can attract, and as Kelly and Logan work together to create a loving home for rescue cat Bear, they just might find one for themselves as well. (978-1-63679-351-1)

Harvest Dreams by Jacqueline Fein-Zachary. Planting the vineyard of their dreams, Kate Bauer and Sydney Barrett must resist their attraction while battling nature and their families, who oppose both the venture and their relationship. (978-1-63679-380-1)

The No Kiss Contract by Nan Campbell. Workaholic Davy believes she can get the top spot at her firm if the senior partners think she's settling down and about to start a family, but she needs the delightful yet dubious Anna to help by pretending to be her fiancée. (978-1-63679-372-6)

Outside the Lines by Melissa Sky. If you had the chance to live forever, would you take it? Amara Rodriguez did, and it sets her on a journey to find her missing mother and unravel the mystery of her own heart. (978-1-63679-403-7)

The Value of Sylver and Gold by Michelle Larkin. When word gets out that former Boston homicide detective Reid Sylver can talk to the dead, the FBI solicits her help on a serial murder case, prompting Reid to assemble forces once again with Detective London Gold. (978-1-63679-093-0)

When It Feels Right by Tagan Shepard. Freshly out of the closet Marlene hasn't been lucky in love, but when it comes to her quirky new roommate Abby, everything just feels right. (978-1-63679-367-2)

Lucky in Lace by Melissa Brayden. Straitlaced stationery store owner Juliette Jennings's predictable life unravels when a sexy lingerie shop and its alluring owner move in next door. (978-1-63679-434-1)

Made for Her by Carsen Taite. Neal Walsh is a newly made member of the Mancuso crime family, but will her undeniable attraction to Anastasia Petrov, the wife of her boss's sworn enemy, be the ultimate test of her loyalty? (978-1-63679-265-1)

Off the Menu by Alaina Erdell. Reality TV sensation Restaurant Redo and its gorgeous host Erin Rasmussen will arrive to film in chef Taylor Mobley's kitchen. As the cameras roll, will they make the jump from enemies to lovers? (978-1-63679-295-8)

Pack of Her Own by Elena Abbott. When things heat up in a small town, steamy secrets are revealed between Alpha werewolf Wren Carne and her human mate, Natalie Donovan. (978-1-63679-370-2)

Return to McCall by Patricia Evans. Lily isn't looking for romance—not until she meets Alex, the gorgeous Cuban dance instructor at La Haven, a newly opened lesbian retreat. (978-1-63679-386-3)

So It Went Like This by C. Spencer. A candid and deeply personal exploration of fate, chosen family, and the vulnerability intrinsic in life's uncertainties. (978-1-63555-971-2)

Stolen Kiss by Spencer Greene. Anna and Louise share a stolen kiss, only to discover that Louise is dating Anna's brother. Surely, one kiss can't change everything...Can it? (978-1-63679-364-1)

The Fall Line by Kelly Wacker. When Jordan Burroughs arrives in the Deep South to paint a local endangered aquatic flower, she doesn't expect to become friends with a mischievous gin-drinking ghost who complicates her budding romance and leads her to an awful discovery and danger. (978-1-63679-205-7)

To Meet Again by Kadyan. When the stark reality of WW II separates cabaret singer Evelyn and Australian doctor Joan in Singapore, they must overcome all odds to find one another again. (978-1-63679-398-6)

BOLDSTROKESBOOKS.COM

Looking for your next great read?

Visit BOLDSTROKESBOOKS.COM
to browse our entire catalog of paperbacks, ebooks,
and audiobooks.

Want the first word on what's new?
Visit our website for event info,
author interviews, and blogs.

Subscribe to our free newsletter for sneak peeks,
new releases, plus first notice of promos
and daily bargains.

SIGN UP AT
BOLDSTROKESBOOKS.COM/signup

Quality and Diversity in LGBTQ Literature

*Bold Strokes Books is an award-winning publisher
committed to quality and diversity in LGBTQ fiction.*